6-
3rd
3/18

THE GOLEM OF SOLOMON'S WAY

A Magic & Machinery Novel

JON MESSENGER

THE GOLEM OF SOLOMON S WAY

ISBN: 978-1-63422-144-3
Copyright ©2015 Jon Messenger
All rights reserved.
Cover Design by:Whit & Ware Design
Typography by: Courtney Nuckels
Editing by: Cynthia Shepp

"It is much easier to be a hero than a gentleman."

-Luigi Pirandello

CHAPTER

One

ABIGAIL TRAUNT WALKED DOWN THE COBBLESTONE
street, her heeled shoes clicking incessantly on the damp stones.
The streets were mainly empty, most of the civilized world having
already gone to sleep long before such an obscene hour. For a woman like
Abigail, however, the night was her life and, though she loathed to admit
it to anyone with whom she held a personal relationship, her livelihood
as well.

The electric street lamps glowed overhead, their light pulsing and
waning with the unsteady flow of electricity. The unsteady pools cast dark
shadows between them, though the darkness hardly bothered her. She
pulled her fur-lined coat tighter around her, blocking out the night's chill
and the breeze blowing off the river nearby.

As a surprisingly strong gust of wind blew down the street, carrying
with it crumpled bits of discarded paper and the strong smell of offal,
Abigail ducked into a recessed storefront and waited for the wind to die.

She flexed her hand as she reached into the inner pocket of her jacket
and removed a metal cigarette tin. With a practiced flick of her wrist,
she opened it, revealing the neatly packed row of hand-rolled cigarettes
within. She forewent the long, black holder resting at the end of the open

case and retrieved a cigarette, holding it between yellow-stained fingers. Reaching back within her coat, she found the matches. With a gentle shake, she heard the rattle of the half-filled matchbox.

The red-tipped match ignited as she struck it against the coarse exterior. The flare from the tip illuminated her soft features. Her narrow face was framed with blonde curls, meticulously held in place by a small army of bobby pins. A similar collection of clips held her wide-brimmed hat in place, slightly askew on her head. The match glowed only for a second before she pressed it against the cigarette and drew in a deep breath, stealing the flame even as it lit the dry tobacco.

The wind died down as quickly as it had come, a brief gust carried downstream even as it passed through the heart of Callifax. She took a second draw from the cigarette before stepping out of the alcove and continuing down the street.

The cobblestones quickly gave way to large concrete pavers, marking the beginning of Unushire Bridge, her last physical obstacle between the end of her shift and her mediocre flat in Solomon's Way, on the far side of the river.

Abigail wrinkled her nose at the pungent aroma coming from the waterfront. Refuse gathered in the eddied current along the river, gathering in engorged flotillas beneath the bridge's pylons. The smell of rotted food and human excrement turned her stomach, but it was a smell to which she had grown far too accustomed. Glancing over her shoulder, she could see the brilliant glow from atop the aptly named Castle Hill. The crown and its politicians would never know the squalor into which the rest of the city had fallen. Their lives were far too opulent to concern themselves over the well-being of a woman of the night like Abigail. People of her station had little choice but to grow to endure the open sewer that was their part of the capital.

Electric lights glowed evenly along the bridge, illuminating her path. The far side of the river was hidden behind the steep rise of the bridge, which rose high enough to allow barges to pass underneath. Her legs, already exhausted from a long night's work, ached as she climbed the steep incline. She took another drag from her cigarette before discarding the rest, rolling the cigarette between her fingers and letting the packed tobacco tumble onto the sidewalk beside her. She doubted anyone would notice the added trash to an already filthy town.

As she reached the apex of the bridge, she could see Solomon's Way laid out before her. The narrowly packed apartment buildings clung to one another as though for support. Ropes and cords stretched between open windows, spanning across the street like the canopy of a forest. Clothes were pinned to them, wafting back and forth in the night breeze, growing both dry and cold simultaneously. She smiled to herself, her painted lips parting to reveal straight but slightly yellowed teeth. It wasn't much to look at, but Solomon's Way was home.

Her bemused reverie was interrupted by the sound of footsteps behind her. She quickly glanced over her shoulder, surprised that anyone else would be about at such an hour. A man walked a methodical pace toward the bridge, approaching from the same direction from which she had just come. A hat was worn low over his brow, concealing his features from view even as he took his first step onto the bridge.

Abigail shivered against the cold and turned away from the man. Reaching into her jacket once more, her fingers closed over the snub-nosed pistol within. It had only a single shot, but it was often enough to deter an attacker. Encountering strange men in the dead of night was more or less a hazard of her occupation, but she was far from stupid. It was wiser to be safe and apologize than to be dead.

She hurried toward the far side of the river, her heeled boots clicking louder as she began descending the steep slope. Glancing briefly over her shoulder again, she saw the man crest the hill, approaching her far quicker than she was retreating. His pace was still measured and deliberate, but his long strides covered far more ground with each step. Her hand clenched on the pistol concealed within her jacket.

His footfalls echoed louder as he, too, began the more expedited descent down the far side of the bridge. She looked again as the man raised his head, his strong features and bright red hair illuminated by the nearest street lamp. As their eyes met, his widened in surprise. He reached out toward her, his actions striking her more as a warning than a threat.

As she turned back toward her home, she found herself facing a disfigured creature standing no more than two paces away. A hood was pulled over his head, but wispy, black hair still escaped its confines. A hooked nose, set just below of pair of bloodshot red eyes, protruded from the monster's face. Its lips were pulled back in a mixture of a smile and sneer. Most alarming was the creature's green skin, which glowed sickly

3

beneath the streetlamps.

Abigail opened her mouth to yell, her grasp on the pistol temporarily forgotten in her surprise. Before a sound could escape her lips, the green-skinned creature raised a hand to its mouth and exhaled. A cloud of acrid air floated over her and, as she drew in a breath to yell her surprise, the fumes were pulled into her lungs. Her scream quickly became a choke as she doubled over in anguish. Her body screamed for oxygen, but every breath seemed to reignite the smoke within her lungs.

As her chest burned and her muscles tightened, her vision began to swim. She couldn't quite feel her fingers anymore, nor would her arms move even as she willed them to rise. She knew she should run, but she couldn't find the strength.

Her knees buckled and she slumped to the ground, first sitting on her heels before canting to her right and crashing to the stone bridge. As darkness crept into the corners of her vision, she saw the monster stoop over her. It roughly grasped her hands, pulling them over her head as it began to drag her away. Though her mind screamed in protest, her body slumped willingly even as her consciousness fled.

The green-skinned creature barely looked at its prey as it quickly pulled her toward the bridge's railing. The water sloshed below against one of the pylons and the discarded garbage that had collected in the tide. It placed a bare foot against the top of the stone railing as it sought purchase with which to pull his latest prey over the edge.

"Get away from her!" the man yelled from the bridge's pinnacle as he watched the scene unfold.

The creature glanced up at the unexpected witness and hissed, giving the man pause even as he started to rush toward the assault. It glanced down nervously toward the blonde woman before returning its gaze to the tall man. As though sensing its indecision, the man rushed forward once more, his bravery reignited.

With a disapproving snarl, the monster released Abigail's arms before leaping over the side of the bridge.

By the time the man arrived at her side and peered over the stone railing, there was no sign of the monster. The water was no more disturbed than it was before his arrival, nor did he recall hearing the telltale splash of the monster striking the water's surface. The green-skinned creature had vanished.

4

CHAPTER

Two

"**R**EMIND ME AGAIN WHY A ROYAL INQUISITOR HAS been assigned to this case," Simon Whitlock said as they reached the foot of the bridge.

He tilted his top hat forward slightly, blocking the glare of the sun reflecting off the river. The day was quickly becoming warm as the sun reached its peak, and he could feel the first droplets of sweat forming underneath his suit. Absently, Simon ran a hand across his thin moustache, smoothing it down as he and his entourage approached the busy scene.

Luthor Strong opened a notebook and read his nearly illegible scrawl, a series of chicken-scratch markings and shorthand notes from their meeting with the Grand Inquisitor.

"Inquisitors, plural," the apothecary corrected, gesturing toward Thaddeus Poole and the three other Inquisitors following behind them. The dark-skinned Inquisitor nodded at his attention. Luthor adjusted his wire-framed glasses as he continued. "There were reports of a monster attack, sir. An eyewitness claims it was…" He cleared his throat and looked up from his notes. "He claims it was a troll living beneath the bridge."

Simon frowned. "I'm assuming the creature was fresh out of billy goats to harass?"

"Do try to take this assignment seriously, sir," Luthor pleaded. "You did volunteer for it, after all, against my better judgment. You should still be resting after your ordeal in Whitten Hall."

"It's been nearly a month," Simon replied flatly. "I need work to keep my mind sharp."

Wooden barricades ahead had cordoned off the area. Constables stood impassively near the barriers, their dark uniforms and tall, rounded hats unmistakable even from a distance. A few detectives milled about within the area, but none disturbed the crime scene near the bridge's stone railing.

Simon approached the nearest constable, who stepped impolitely in his way.

"Be off with you," the constable demanded. "Can't you see a crime has been committed?"

"Indeed I can," Simon said, "which is why nearly a half-dozen Royal Inquisitors stand before you, feeling cantankerous and rather put out. So if you could please stand aside, it would be greatly appreciated."

The constable looked him over before his gaze drifted to the other Inquisitors. "You don't look like Inquisitors."

Simon sighed and turned toward the apothecary. "How many times have I told you that we need badges? No one ever seems to know who we are."

"That'll be all, Constable," one of the detectives said as he approached the standoff. "Forgive the zealousness of our constabulary. Their hard work within the walls of Callifax is so often overshadowed by your organization's work beyond our borders."

Simon extended his hand. "Royal Inquisitor Simon Whitlock. We've been told there was a supernatural attack last night."

The detective shook his hand. "Detective Sugden. Charles Sugden, at your service, gentlemen. Indeed, there was an attack of sorts, though to be honest, it's a bit out of our realm of expertise, which is why I had your order contacted."

"Describe to me, in great detail, the events of last night."

The detective retrieved a notebook from within his jacket pocket and opened it to a marked page. "A Miss Abigail Traunt, aged twenty-three, was returning home from a—" He flipped closed his notebook and looked up apologetically. "Forgive me, sir, but does her occupation matter? It seems a bit embarrassing for the lady for me to continue."

Simon arched an eyebrow. "Detective Sugden, I can guarantee you will not offend my delicate sensibilities by continuing. However, it's a wasted effort. I've already gleaned what I need from your report. A young woman, attractive, I would imagine, returning home at an ungodly hour to Solomon's Way? She's clearly a prostitute."

The detective flushed but concealed a smile behind his hand. "Of course, sir. Are you intimately familiar with Solomon's Way, then? Every man has a vice, even a Royal Inquisitor, I would imagine."

Simon narrowed his gaze dangerously. "My fiancée happens to reside in Solomon's Way, though I would warn you not to draw too many conclusions about a residence and an occupation. I have many vices, but if you're asking if I partake in ladies of the night, then my answer is a resounding no."

"Forgive me, sir," Sugden said, coughing in his awkwardness. "I meant no offense."

"Yes, you did, Detective, I just didn't happen to take any. Now please, do continue with the report."

Detective Sugden was glad to return to the notebook. He opened back to his marked page and continued reading. "Miss Traunt was returning home at approximately four in the morning when she was assaulted by a green-skinned creature that appeared as though by magic before her. She remembers little after his appearance, other than her limbs went numb immediately before she lost consciousness. A passerby, a doctor, witnessed the attack and interceded before the… shall I call it a troll, sir?"

"It seems a fitting description until I can prove otherwise," Simon replied.

"The troll, then, was scared away, where it leapt over the side of the bridge to a most certain death."

"That is a presumption, Detective, and one that I will most certainly disprove. If you please, my men will now examine the crime scene."

"Of course, sir."

Simon glanced over his shoulder, to where the other Inquisitors waited patiently. He motioned toward the bridge. "Take the others and search the scene, if you please, Mister Poole. Report anything out of the ordinary to either myself or Mister Strong."

The dark-skinned Inquisitor nodded before leading the rest past Detective Sugden. They immediately set to work, examining the stonework for footprints as well as any physical evidence left behind. Simon, Luthor, and the detective watched them work for a few quiet moments.

"You're lucky to have such a group of professionals at your disposal," the detective remarked.

Simon shrugged. "Under normal circumstances, you'd be lucky to have even a single Inquisitor respond to your request. It just so happened that there were a number of us within the Grand Hall when your request arrived. With the accusation of a supernatural being within Callifax itself, everyone was more than overjoyed to help."

"Do you think it could possibly be a troll, sir?"

"Everything's possible until it's been proven impossible."

The detective chewed on his lower lip before turning toward the Inquisitor and apothecary. "Forgive me if this sounds abnormally callous, but there's a part of me that truly hopes this is a troll, or at least some other beast from the Rift."

Luthor furrowed his brow. "That does sound callous. Why would you want this to be a creature of magic?"

Detective Sugden removed his hat and ran the back of his sleeve across his brow. "Ever since the Rift was discovered, crime within the capital has been on the rise. A decade ago, the worst the constabulary had to worry itself with was petty theft and spots of vandalism. Now, the city is full of murderers, arsonists, and downright evil men. Perhaps it's a side effect of magic seeping into our world, but I'm tired of fighting against men. I'd rather something horrible, like the attempted murder of a woman, be relegated to a crime of the supernatural."

Simon watched the man's face as he talked. "You seem personally affected by the increase in crime. You lost someone, didn't you?"

Sugden sighed and nodded. "My son, two years ago now. He was a good lad, smart and polite. For no reason whatsoever, he was stabbed twelve times on the way home one evening, a night not too unlike last night."

"My condolences. For your sake, if not for our own, I'll hope this troll is real as well."

"Thank you, sir," the detective said, though his heart was clearly no longer in the conversation. "If you'll excuse me, gentlemen, I'll go check on my men."

"Of course," Luthor replied. When the detective had gone, the apothecary turned toward his mentor. "That poor man."

Simon no longer seemed to exude the compassion he had shown just moments before. Behind his blue eyes, Luthor could already see his mind at work, considering all the possibilities.

"Are you sure you're doing well?" Luthor asked. "There's no need to rush back into investigations so soon after Whitten Hall."

"I'm fine, Luthor," Simon said dismissively.

"You went through quite an ordeal."

Simon turned abruptly toward his friend. "I said I was fine. This is not the first time you've brought it up, nor is it the first time I've explained I don't wish to discuss it further."

Luthor sighed, but he didn't press the issue.

"What do we know about trolls, Luthor?" Simon asked, changing the subject.

Luthor shrugged. He hadn't had much time to research their mythology before they departed. "I believe they're traditionally green skinned, consistent with the eye-witness accounts, and have the ability to heal at an exorbitant rate."

"Do they have a weakness to sunlight?" Simon asked.

"Possibly, sir, though that's more in line with vampires."

"Moonlight, then, perhaps?"

Luthor looked incredulously toward his friend. "I'm pretty sure nothing has a weakness to moonlight. Then again, I guess there are myths that say that werewolves can only change shape during a full moon, but we've already thoroughly disproven that one."

"Silver?"

"Again, werewolves and, apparently, some demons."

"Holy water, then."

"Vampires and demons, sir. We're retreading similar ground."

"Fire?"

Luthor sighed. "You're grasping at straws, sir, but I'm sure fire is fairly effective against practically everything."

Simon turned toward the apothecary and smiled. "Good, then we have a plan."

"Fire is your plan?" Luthor asked dryly.

Simon gestured emphatically with his hands. "More along the lines of setting things *on* fire, but yes, more or less."

Luthor shook his head. "Some days, I don't think you even try."

Simon concealed a sly smile as they observed the other Inquisitors continuing their investigations. Luthor wrinkled his nose at the odd scents assaulting his nostrils. The smell of human filth was mixed with a faint sickly sweetness in the air. Although, for the life of him, he couldn't identify the source.

"Sir?" one of the Inquisitors shouted. "I believe I've found something."

Simon and Luthor exchanged glances before approaching him. The man stood beside the crime scene, the marks of Abigail's heels dragging through the soot on the cobblestones still visible. Rather than focusing on the ground, however, the Inquisitor examined an oily liquid on the stone railing. He dabbed it with his bare fingers before lifting his hand and rubbing his fingers together.

"It's thick," the Inquisitor said, "almost like syrup."

As Simon reached the man's side, the Inquisitor shook his head quickly, as though dissuading a persistent fly from landing on his face. He blinked as he peered down at his dark-stained fingers.

"Sir, I don't feel so well," the man said as his knees buckled.

Simon and Luthor caught him as he slumped toward the ground. The man's arms fell limply to his side and his breathing grew shallow.

"What's wrong with him?" Simon asked.

Luthor lifted the man's hand, careful to avoid the viscous liquid staining his fingers. The apothecary adjusted his glasses and leaned forward until his face was mere inches from the Inquisitor's hand. As he turned the man's hand, Luthor nodded knowingly.

"He has a small abrasion on the back of his knuckle."

"What happened?" Detective Sugden asked as he rushed to the scene.

"He's been paralyzed," Luthor explained, even as the weak Inquisitor's eyes darted in panic from side to side. "He has an abrasion on the back of his hand, which has been coated with the syrupy droplets."

"A paralytic of some sort?" Simon asked.

"It appears so, sir."

Simon patted the side of the man's face, certainly drawing the man's ire, though the incapacitated Inquisitor was able to move little more than his eyes.

"What would be capable of causing such an abrupt reaction?"

Luthor rotated the man's hand once more. "It would have to be a toxin of some sort. With this consistency, I would guess Curare?"

Simon glanced toward the apothecary. "Is that phrased as a question, as though I should know the answer?"

Luthor set the man's hand by his side and adjusted his glasses once more. "Forgive me, sir, that was just an educated guess. Curare is an exotic toxin that's poisonous in its most natural form, but it can be refined into a viscous, syrup-like fluid that can be used as an anesthetic, a syrup like the one on this Inquisitor's hand and on the railing."

Simon glanced toward the detective. "I would presume that Curare is not easily purchased. Could your constables determine if any had been stolen or purchased from local apothecaries?"

"We're glad to help however we can, sir." Sugden said, nodding.

Luthor furrowed his brow as he turned toward the detective. "Before you depart, Detective, can you refresh my memory on the specifics of the attack?"

The detective looked skyward as he recalled the information. "Miss Traunt was attacked by the troll, went limp and fell unconscious, and then was being dragged away."

Luthor nodded. "Thank you, Detective. Sorry for delaying your work."

The detective nodded before departing, returning to his awaiting constables.

Luthor sniffed the air. "Can you smell that, sir?"

Simon sniffed but immediately frowned. "Someone is suffering from digestive distress."

"Beneath that overpowering smell," Luthor chided. "There's a faint sweetness in the air. I noticed it when we were standing near the cordon, but it's stronger here."

Simon remained silent, awaiting Luthor's continuation.

"The victim went limp and then fell unconscious," Luthor said, as though the truth were evident. He smiled to himself as Simon continued to stare. "Forgive me, sir, but I'm savoring this moment as I realize I know more about the investigation than you."

Simon was still quiet, though his lips pulled into a bloodless line.

Luthor cleared his throat. "The Inquisitor merely went limp, paralyzed by the Curare. He's still conscious, just unable to move."

"There was something else mixed with the Curare, then?" Simon surmised.

Luthor nodded. "Ether. It leaves a sweet aroma after its use, one that's only lingering in the air because it's been deposited on the stonework all around us, as though sprayed."

"Aerosolized?" Simon asked. "Like the chemicals we used in Haversham?"

"Indeed, sir. It would explain why the Curare is formed in a series of droplets rather than an even spread like I would expect to see if it had been poured or dripped from a rag. The pressurized spray created uneven droplets as a result of the Curare mixing with the ether."

"Is it safe to assume that trolls don't, by mythology, spit or spray ether?"

"Not that I'm aware."

Simon frowned. "It casts a doubt on the more monstrous aspects of this case and forces me to take an active role in this investigation."

Simon stood, allowing the paralyzed Inquisitor to slide to the cobblestone bridge. He approached the edge, careful to avoid touching the paralyzing toxins staining the railing. Leaning as far forward as he dared, Simon glanced over toward the filth-filled waters below. He had no doubt that once upon a time those very waters were clear and beautiful, a refreshing source of drinking water against which the city had been built. That had clearly been generations past. The waters were now dark, even during the day, and filled with floating islands of debris.

He shifted his gaze away from the foul waters and closer to the stonework of the bridge's exterior. As close as they were to the far shore, the final pylon was exceptionally thicker than the others, grounding it into the soft riverbed. Dangling near the base of the bridge, an iron-mooring ring was affixed to the pylon.

"Detective Sugden," Simon called.

The detective huffed as he hurried over once more. "Forgive me, sir, we haven't had enough time to query the nearest apothecaries about the missing chemicals."

Simon waved his hand dismissively even as he continued glancing over the edge of the bridge. "I'm no longer concerned about the chemicals."

The detective stared at him for a moment, as though determining if

Simon were merely jesting. When he determined that the Inquisitor was quite serious, Sugden sighed heavily. "Sir?"

"Am I to believe that this bridge has been fitted with netting beneath, to keep birds and bats from nesting in its undercarriage?"

The detective shrugged. "It would be a safe assumption, sir."

"Excellent," Simon replied as he leapt over the railing.

CHAPTER
Three

"**T**HERE WAS NO WAY YOU COULD HAVE BEEN SURE that the iron ring would hold your weight," Luthor chided as they waded through the knee-deep muck that passed as a shoreline.

"Nonsense, Luthor," Simon replied. "How else could the troll have disappeared beneath the bridge without a trace? He leapt from the bridge at the intervention of our eyewitness, grasped ahold of the ring, and climbed onto the netting beneath. From there, it was a simple matter to follow the netting to where it finally deposited him here, at the mouth of the sewer tunnels."

"He could have had a boat waiting, which would explain why the witness heard no splash," Luthor countered.

Simon paused before furrowing his brow. "I hadn't considered that. I guess I'm damn lucky that ring held my weight."

Simon gestured toward the metal cage that had once covered a rounded sewer entrance. The bars of the grill had been bent aside as though with superhuman strength. Simon stared for some time at the metal bars, though he couldn't determine if a man had forced them aside or if it had been the result of a rather violent storm passing through this area.

Beyond the twisted, wrought-iron bars, the round tunnel was barely taller than a man. The darkness past the entryway was nearly impenetrable. Even during midday, the shadow of the bridge overhead blocked any light from reaching the sewer.

"Our culprit went this way," Simon said. "We'll need torches."

Once lanterns and torches were procured, he claimed one before pushing forward. Simon stepped into the debris that gathered beneath the Unushire Bridge, scowling as the filth filled his shoes and soaked through his socks. He could hear the sloshing footfalls of those that followed him through the eddying muck, runoff into the otherwise-majestic Oreck River.

He paused before the torn manhole cover, a steel latticework cage that once blocked the entrance to the sewers below the city. The metal was yanked free from its moorings, steel bent backward until its ends pointed toward the Inquisitor like spears.

Simon raised the lantern in his hand, pointing its light toward the impenetrable darkness beyond the sewer's opening. Water glistened like crystals within the rounded tunnel as it reflected his meager light. He raised his silver-plated revolver, pointing it down the tunnel as he stepped toward the opening.

"Are you all right, sir?" Luthor asked from his position behind the Inquisitor.

Simon paused and frowned. "Yes, Luthor, I am."

The Inquisitor started forward again when Luthor spoke once more.

"Would you like to talk about what happened in Whitten Hall, sir? You haven't really mentioned it since our return."

Simon sneered and lowered both lantern and revolver. Perturbed, he turned toward the apothecary. "No, I wouldn't."

Luthor shrugged apologetically. "I only ask because you haven't really discussed it at all, with either Mattie or me. We just figured you accepted this assignment so quickly upon our return because you were trying to avoid discussing the situation."

Simon set his jaw in irritation and glared at his companion. "No, Luthor. I took this assignment so quickly upon our return because I figured hunting a troll through the sewers of Callifax might keep you from asking me if I was all right for the four hundredth time. Forgive me for my miscalculation."

The Inquisitor behind Luthor cleared his throat unapologetically and motioned toward the other men standing unhappily in the filth.

Simon gestured toward the men with his hand holding the revolver. "See, now you've irritated the rest of the Inquisitors with your incessant nagging."

The Inquisitors moved briskly aside as Simon pointed the barrel of his pistol toward them. Simon glanced at the weapon in his hand and sighed.

"For God's sake, do grow up. I wasn't going to shoot you."

Disgusted, Simon turned away from his colleagues and approached the sewer entrance. Even with the pointed lantern light, the darkness beyond the mouth of the tunnel seemed to absorb the meager attempts to illuminate its interior. With a sickening squelch, Simon pulled his foot free of the muck and stepped into the curved tunnel.

The smell of feces was even stronger within the sewer than it had been emanating from the river. Simon was glad Matilda had foregone joining them on their city adventure. Her keen werewolf senses would have left her dismally nauseated had she been within the close confines of the sewer.

For his part, Simon refused to look down as he waded through the shallow water. The lantern threw light out a dozen feet before him, catching the occasional reflection of red eyes glowing just beyond his range of vision. He could hear the rats scurrying quickly away at his approach.

"There are footprints, sir," Luthor whispered. Even hushed, his voice carried well.

Begrudgingly, Simon glanced down. There, in the thick muck beside the floating offal, clear boot prints were visible. The footprints, obviously from the same source, indicated that someone had walked in both directions, in and out of the sewer.

"Our troll wears shoes, apparently," Simon remarked. He cringed as he heard his own hushed voice echoing from the myriad of twists and turns within the sewer tunnel.

Simon raised his gaze and pushed deeper into the tunnel. He reached out with his pistol as he walked until the barrel struck the nearest wall. There wasn't much space between his shoulders and the widest part of the curved surface, leaving little room to maneuver should they encounter the monster.

Ahead, just beyond the range of his lantern, where the light died to shades of barely visible gray, the wall seemed disfigured. Simon took a few steps forward until he could see the protruding stonework and the gaping hole in the side. As he stepped again, his foot struck a large chunk of stone that had clearly been blasted free from the otherwise smooth sewer wall.

Simon raised his hand, bringing the rest of the group to a halt. Alone, he walked forward until he reached the edge of the hole. The gap was wider than Simon was tall and appeared as though it had shattered into the tunnel. Stonework and mortar, much of which was a thick paste as it mixed with the murky water, littered the floor. Human refuse floated around the debris as best as possible, but the stones had created a make-shift dam. The smell was atrocious. Even with his quick glance at the stone barrier, Simon realized that crawling over all the stones would be difficult in such a confined space.

There were splashes behind him as someone approached, but Simon didn't need to turn to know it was Luthor.

"Could our troll have done this?" Luthor asked breathlessly.

Simon reached out and touched the edges of the protruding stone-work. The closest edges were charred and blackened. He shook his head. "It's possible, but I doubt it. I think these stones were blasted apart."

"Not very troll-like."

"Perhaps our myths about trolls are so very wrong." Simon smiled. He glanced past Luthor before motioning for Poole and the rest of the Inquisitors to join him.

The dark-skinned Inquisitor ran a hand over his bald head with one hand while adjusting the grip on his shotgun with the other. The long-barreled weapon seemed ill suited for the close confines of the sew-ers, but Simon knew that if he could bring the weapon to bear, there was nowhere for the troll to go that could escape its wide blast.

"Inquisitor Poole, if you'd be so kind as to lead the way," Simon said. "My pistol feels rather impotent compared to your much-larger rifle."

Thaddeus Poole smiled. "Of course."

He stepped into the mouth of the blasted hole, the light from Si-mon's lantern following him through the gap. The room beyond was surprisingly well kept, considering its proximity to the foulness of the sewer, as though the shattered wall had led into an ill-maintained but dry basement of a nearby dwelling. The barren stone walls, unadorned with basic human amenities, radiated a coolness that was a stark contrast to the sour humidity of the tunnel. A wooden table, empty as well, was set against the wall. A few books rested on a bookshelf next to the table, their leather spines worn from use. Otherwise, only a narrow stairwell leading to an upper floor was visible.

The area was small, more the size of a wide corridor than a proper room. Beside the narrow staircase, the broad hallway—for that was what it was—bent to the right at a sharp angle. A faint scent of cooked meat filled the air. The flickering of a campfire reflected off the passage's back wall and illuminated the stairwell in dancing shades of red and gold.

Simon held the lantern aloft as the other Inquisitors passed him, entering the room one at a time with the benefit of his source of light. When they had fully entered, Simon and Luthor stepped over the threshold.

Inquisitor Poole glanced over his shoulder, his expression questioning whether to climb the stairs or explore the bend in the room. Simon motioned toward the flickering firelight, and Poole nodded in response.

As Poole stepped forward, he stumbled, tripping over something unseen. He tried lifting his foot, but the nearly invisible fishing wire had thoroughly snagged on his muddy shoes. The wire pulled taut and the clicking of gears was immediately audible. He looked backward pleadingly as a mist sprayed from small holes in the walls.

Luthor tackled Simon, knocking the mustachioed man to the floor. Simon could feel droplets of the chemicals settling on his skin, though he avoided the vast majority of the blast. Where the syrupy oil touched exposed flesh, he could feel a tingling numbness spreading. His vision swam and his body felt weak, even as he struggled to remain coherent.

Through his blurry vision, he watched the other Inquisitors drop heavily to the ground, their weapons falling forgotten beside them. Wordlessly, they collapsed into a heap where they lay.

"Luthor?" Simon slurred, his cheek and lips feeling detached from the rest of his body.

The apothecary forced himself into a seated position, though his arms were heavy and hung limply by his side. His jacket was smeared with black droplets, where he had taken the majority of the blast while protecting Simon.

"Luthor?" Simon repeated.

Luthor turned his head slowly toward him, his muttonchops soaked with the spray. He moved his lips and blinked heavily as though trying to focus, but his eyes were red and aggravated from the gas and tears ran freely from the corners.

Simon cursed internally, not risking the preposterousness of using profanity with numbed lips. He propped himself up on his elbow as he examined the room. Simon knew he had to move, since they were all helpless as they were, exposed in the center of the room.

On the far side of the room, a shadow fell onto the wall as a figure passed in front of the campfire. It stretched to inhuman proportions as the figure moved, arms growing abnormally long while the head stretched unbelievably wide.

Simon looked for his pistol and was surprised when his gaze fell upon it, still clutched in his hand. He wiggled his fingers, but they lacked any sensation. His fingers may well have been blocks of ice for all the use they were to him. Simon placed his other hand on the cool ground and was pleasantly surprised by the small amount of pain he felt as a stone dug into his palm. Glancing back toward the shadow, he hurriedly switched the silver-plated revolver from his right to his left hand. He lacked the accuracy or finesse with his offhand, but it would have to do under the circumstances.

The dark figure stepped into the causeway between their room and the makeshift kitchen around the corner. The flickering campfire left the man silhouetted. Though his features no longer looked quite as elongated and distended, he hardly looked human.

The lantern was lying on the ground beside him. With numbed fingers, he knocked the lantern aside until the light angled roughly toward the troll. When it was no longer merely a silhouette, Simon withdrew from the monster's appearance.

A hood that normally concealed its features was thrown back, revealing green skin and wispy tendrils of black hair. Large, bald patches were visible between the clumps of hair, the skin scabbed and disgusting. The eyes were red, though they appeared far more bloodshot than supernatural. As the troll snarled at Simon, it revealed blackened teeth that were rotting in the creature's skull.

Simon's eyes watered as he raised the pistol. Sensing the danger, the troll rushed toward him. He couldn't trust his aim, knowing that his bleary vision smeared the details. Instead, Simon squeezed the trigger, hoping for luck rather than skill.

Sparks flew against the far right wall as the bullet went far wide. Despite the poor aim, the report from the gunshot caused the troll to pause. Simon quickly covered his right eye, opting for a lack of depth perception over double vision as his eyes refused to focus as one any longer.

The troll howled, its cry reverberating in the narrow room. It rushed forward again, barely acknowledging the Inquisitors it stepped on as it hurried toward Simon.

The Inquisitor focused as best as possible through his one eye and squeezed the trigger once more. The revolver fired. For a moment, the troll seemed unfazed, but then its momentum died and it stood disbelievingly atop the pile of unconscious Inquisitors.

Simon didn't wait for another opening, firing again instead. He didn't know if the round struck the troll, but it stumbled backward just the same. The Inquisitor's vision grew worse and he had trouble focusing on the creature as it retreated, resting its hands against the wall for support as it stumbled away.

His supportive hand began feeling weak as well and Simon slumped to the ground, resting his head on the unmoving leg of one of the other Inquisitors. He turned his unfocused gaze toward Luthor, but the apothecary was already prone as well, his shape blurring with the others in the middle of the room.

He had no idea how long it would take before the paralysis wore off, but Simon passed the time praying to a god he didn't believe in that there was only one troll in the room.

<hr />

Simon dusted off his pants as he stood. Luthor grasped his hand, helping him to his feet. Despite the amount of gas to which Luthor was exposed, he recovered far quicker than the others had, Simon included. The others were only just beginning to stir.

With the apothecary in tow, Simon stepped over the others and approached the bend in the room, around which the campfire still burned and the scent of roasted meat wafted. He clenched his revolver tightly back in his right hand, glad the sensation had once again returned to the limb.

He peered slowly around the corner. A small hallway connected the two rooms, and a fire smoldered in the center of the far room. Most importantly to Simon, a body lay sprawled before the flames, unmoving.

The Inquisitor approached cautiously until he was at the foot of the troll. Its green skin glowed sickly in the light, accentuating the red pool of blood that had spread beneath the creature. Rather than tapping the monster's foot with his own, Simon raised his pistol and fired twice into the troll's exposed back. The body lurched with each gunshot but offered no other reaction.

Simon glanced over his shoulder and shrugged. "I think it's dead."

"Good riddance," Luthor replied.

The apothecary walked the perimeter of the larger room, checking the assorted butchering supplies and racks of cooked and dried meat. He picked up a small piece of cooked meat and sniffed it. The meat was greasy but well marbled, a clearly fine cut.

"What sort of meat do you suppose this is, sir?" he asked. "Beef? Lamb?"

Simon knelt beside the troll. "I have my suspicions."

As Luthor continued perusing the room, Simon examined the body. The troll's eyes were still open, though they were unseeing. Blood seeped from between its open lips, mixing with the blood from the bullet wounds. Reaching forward, Simon touched its cheek but quickly withdrew his fingers. The skin was tacky and, as he examined his fingers, he saw green paint staining his fingertips.

Slipping his hands beneath the corpse, Simon rolled the troll over. It flopped onto its back, the gunshot wounds now more visible. Grasping the beast's shirt, he pulled it open, popping the buttons as he did so. The skin beneath the shirt, covered from prying eyes, was pale and pink.

"This is no troll." Simon sighed. "It's just a man."

Luthor paused at the far side of the room, where the tables blocked the light. There, barely visible in the deep shadows, the apothecary saw an eyeless human skull staring up at him. He dropped the piece of meat in disgust and suppressed the urge to vomit.

"This isn't beef or lamb, either," he choked.

"As I suspected," Simon replied. "He is… *was* a cannibal."

Luthor raised a hand to his mouth, suddenly glad he hadn't tasted the meat. With his fingers so close to his nose, he could smell the scent of the cooked human flesh staining his fingers. "I think I'm going to be sick, sir,"

Simon gestured toward the sewer tunnel. "Do me a favor and purge out of this room. I don't want you destroying evidence."

Luthor took a deep breath and forced down the bile that seemed to be billowing about in his throat. "I'll be fine."

"Good, then I can use your assistance sorting through the monster's belongings."

Luthor approached the deceased green-painted man and looked down disapprovingly. "I guess we should correct ourselves and call it a man rather than a monster."

Simon stared at the corpse at his feet. "Make no mistake, Luthor, we killed a monster today. You seem to forget that before the Rift, humans really were the worst types of monsters on the planet. I would classify this man, and believe me, I use that term loosely, an abomination far quicker than I would Miss Hawke and her ilk."

A sparkle of light reflecting off metal caught Simon's attention. He pulled up the man's sleeve, exposing a long, metal rod, capped on either end. A thin tube protruded from one end.

"I believe we found how our troll sprayed its noxious fumes."

Luthor arched an eyebrow in surprise. "He appears as little more than a transient, but he uses a remarkably advanced bit of technology."

Simon stood, feeling the stiffness in his body. "Looks are often deceiving, though we'll never know this man's story. Three bullets apparently ended any chance of interrogation."

Luthor shrugged. "I find no fault, sir. What shall we do now?"

Simon glanced down at the body once more before shaking his head. "This man may be a horrible example of a human being, but he's just that. Inquisitors investigate the supernatural. Let's ensure the others are awake and coherent, and then go retrieve the constabulary. This man is their problem now."

"I guess I was wrong, sir," Luthor remarked as they walked into the other room, catching the surprised gazes of the awakening Inquisitors. "I see that you truly have recovered well from your episode in Whitten Hall."

Simon shook his head as he offered Poole a hand. "Don't be preposterous, Luthor. I'm still quite off my rocker."

CHAPTER

Four

"**S**O HE WAS A CANNIBAL?" MATTIE ASKED, LEANING
forward as far across the sitting room's table as her corset would
allow.

Luthor nodded as he pushed his wire-frame glasses back up his
nose. "Rather mundane, all things considered. A part of me was actually
thrilled about the prospect of encountering an actual troll. After a few
days to absorb the events of that night, it seems incredibly anticlimactic."

She laughed as Luthor retrieved the teapot. He held it up inquisitively. She nodded, and he refilled her porcelain cup.

"Sugar?" Luthor asked, the small tongs hovering in his hands above
the tray of sugar cubes.

"Please," Mattie replied.

"How many?"

Mattie laced her fingers together and laid them in her lap. "Let's
make it three today."

"So many?" Luthor asked as he dropped the cubes into her cup.

"I guess I'm feeling rather excitable. We barely had a chance to enjoy
Callifax before being dragged away to Whitten Hall. There are so many
things that you take for granted that seem the epitome of opulence to me."

Luthor arched his eyebrow. "Like sugar cubes?"

"Exactly like sugar cubes," she answered breathlessly. "For instance, how do they form them into such perfect shapes?"

Luthor lifted a cube from the tray and shrugged as he examined it. "You know, I haven't the foggiest."

"In Haversham, few people enjoyed such frivolities as sugar with their tea. It was so dreadfully expensive that those living within the city barely enjoyed the commodity. Let's not even discuss our limitations in the tribes beyond the city walls." She poured cream into her tea until the light brown swirled to the top. Lifting her delicate teaspoon, she swirled her drink. "To be honest, only the excessively rich enjoyed sugar with their tea."

"Men like the governor or Gideon Dosett?" Luthor asked with a sly smile.

Mattie frowned and brushed her wild, red hair from her face before taking a sip of her drink. "I'd rather not discuss that lecherous man," she said curtly.

"Only the very rich and those who, quite literally, sold their souls could afford it?" the apothecary continued. "Did the demon lord enjoy a spot of sugar with his tea?"

Mattie frowned, but she was saved from replying by a thump at the front door. The smile returning to her face, she stood and walked briskly to the townhouse's door. Pulling it open, she let the morning sunlight pour into the foyer as she collected the rolled newspaper that had been deposited on their doorstep. She waved as she retrieved it, though the youths delivering the papers paid her no mind.

She closed the door and walked back into the sitting room, joining Luthor once more. She unfurled the newspaper, and he set a cucumber sandwich on her plate.

"Speaking of our beloved Inquisitor, is Simon not joining us this morning?" she asked, glancing back toward the front door.

Luthor shook his head as he chewed his bite of sandwich. "He's otherwise occupied today. Miss Dawn has him working on a list of wedding preparations."

"Is he excited about the wedding?"

He smirked as he looked at the redheaded woman. "I believe he'd much rather be hunting another den of vampires. Not that he's not excited about marrying Veronica, mind you; it's just that his skills are better suited for hunting the undead rather than choosing flavors of cake."

"Speaking of which, how are you recovering from your last mission?"

Luthor frowned. "I believe my fragile male ego is far more damaged than my—"

"Fragile male body?" Mattie interrupted, teasing.

His frown deepened. "My body," he concluded brusquely. "I'm embarrassed that a psychopath was able to so readily trick me into walking into his trap. Had it not been for Simon, we would have all been killed."

"The irony," she said, taking another sip of tea. "You've survived assaults by demons, werewolves, and vampires, only to be nearly killed by a mortal man."

Luthor laughed heartily. "In our defense, we've been nearly killed by everything on that list at least once."

They sat in silence, enjoying their light breakfast and one another's company. Mattie flipped quickly through the pages, reading as she absently sipped at her tea. As she finished an article on the front page of the crime section, she quickly turned to the middle of the paper, continuing the story. The apothecary glanced up as she read, watching her forehead furrow in concentration.

"What have you found?" he asked.

"Have you heard about the string of murders here within the city?"

"I hadn't, but we've been gone from Callifax so much recently. I presume the newspaper tells more?"

"Barely," she replied with a sigh. "The victims are women of, well, looser morale character, if you get my drift."

"I do," Luthor said, thinking about the woman of the night they just saved from the supposed troll. He waved a hand dismissively. "I can't say that I spend much time reading the newspaper anymore. I've been so preoccupied hunting down creatures of sorcery that I hardly have the time to concern myself with humans killing other humans. Does that make me callous?"

She shrugged. "A bit."

"Well, that's exactly why I stopped reading the paper. It's dreadfully depressing business. I'd much rather drown myself in a good work of fiction than hear about how terrible the real world can be."

Mattie laughed softly. "Your world is a work of fiction, the likes

every great author of history would love to experience. Write
r Inquisitor missions and I guarantee your rendition of real life
would be the muse for all the next great works of literature."

He set his teacup back down on its saucer. "This is a dismal topic so
early in the morning. What would you like to do with the rest of our day?"

Mattie folded the paper and set it down on the edge of the table. Her
enthusiastic smile had quickly returned. "I'm sure I can think of something to keep us entertained."

Simon was not entertained. He sat impatiently near the window of
the bakery, watching the pedestrians wandering past, wishing he could
disappear within their numbers. Veronica stood at the wooden counter, a
fork in hand, as slices of cake were laid out in front of her.

"This one is raspberry, madam," the baker said, holding out a red
cake for her to try. Veronica took a bite and slowly closed her eyes.

"Simon, you must try this," she said. "It's simply divine."

The Inquisitor sighed. "I couldn't possibly eat another bite," he lied.

Veronica laughed as she walked over to Simon. "Forgive me, my love.
I know there are a hundred things you'd rather be doing than tasting
cakes, but this is important to me. Please bear with me."

"This is important to you," he said, taking her hands, "along with
sampling catering options, trying on an assortment of dresses, research-
ing venues, and—"

She slipped a hand free and placed a finger on his lips, silencing him.
"There's no need to continue."

He took her hand once more and lowered it from his face. "I love
you with all my heart, Veronica, but I'm far better suited to examining
a crime scene or conducting an autopsy. These hands are designed for
sword fighting and pistols at dawn, rather than picking floral arrangements."

She smiled as she slipped her other hand from his. Adjusting the veil
draped from her top hat, which hung over her eyes and nose, ending just
before her painted red lips, she gave Simon a wink before turning back
toward the baker. She glanced over her shoulder as she continued their
conversation.

"It may not be your cup of tea, but we still have so much left to do
before the wedding, and not nearly enough time in which to do it. We

need to select a caterer today and, lest you forget, tomorrow we have the Pre-Cana at the Callifax Abbey."

Simon shook his head, but he didn't protest. The wedding counseling was important to her faith, even if he found the entire ordeal rather droll. "How could I possibly forget?"

She smiled as she took a bite of a lemon cake. "Promise me you'll be nice to the bishop."

Simon sighed as he ran a hand over his thin moustache. "For you, my dear, I will try."

Veronica set down the fork and leaned on the counter, her bustle swelling against the wooden table. "I'm under the impression that's the closest I'll get to a commitment on the subject. Come and try cake, Simon."

"I trust your judgment," he said dryly. He turned his attention back out the window. Cars rumbled by, clouds of smoke spewing from their exhausts and filling the air like a dark fog. Men lowered their head against the pollution and ladies delicately waved lacy fans before their face.

"How do you feel about the red velvet cake?" Veronica asked.

The Inquisitor realized she was talking to him and glanced over his shoulder. "Whatever you want. I won't deny you."

"It's... it's not cheap," she said hesitantly.

Simon turned slowly until he was resting his back against the large glass window. "Money is no object. I haven't spent the past few years of my life dedicated to the Royal Inquisitors, not to mention so many times deployed to distal lands, just to become miserly for our wedding. If you desire the red velvet, then you shall have the red velvet."

He gestured to the baker, who nodded appreciatively. "Your cake will be ready for your wedding, sir and madam," he said to the couple.

Simon, glad to be finished with the baker, turned away from the window and lifted his top hat from the hook on the wall. He angled it on his head as he opened the door for Veronica. A bell above it jingled as they walked out into the warm air. He offered his arm, which she took gladly as they started the long walk to the caterer.

"You could at least act like you're interested in our wedding," Veronica reprimanded as they walked.

Simon furrowed his brow as he turned toward his fiancée. "My love, if I have ever given you the impression that I wasn't excited about marrying you, then I apologize profusely. There's nothing I want more than to have you as my wife."

"However?" she asked.

"However, the preparations for our wedding are dreadfully boring. Isn't there someone we could hire that could do all this for us?" He smiled as he took her gloved hands in his. "Imagine, if you will, we could be in bed, sleeping away the morning, while some poor soul slaved away from sunup to sundown just to ensure we have the perfect wedding. Tell me that isn't a dream come true."

Veronica laughed, pulled a hand away, and shoved him playfully. "I happen to enjoy planning our wedding. There are very few people I trust in this world to get it right, and I most certainly am not entrusting our wedding to a complete stranger. You knew when we first met I was not a woman of considerable wealth. This may come as a surprise to you, but poor little girls have very little to do with their time other than to imagine their fanciful weddings."

"And thus you chose someone with money to marry, so that your dreams could be fulfilled?" Simon chided with a smile.

"I did no such thing. Your wealth is an added benefit to our love." She leaned forward on her tiptoes and kissed him gently on the lips.

"I work tonight," she said as she pulled away. "Will you come and see me?"

"I'm sorry, but I promised Luthor and Matilda that I would pay them a visit."

She smiled. "You don't seem as excited as you should be."

"Luthor has been an incessant nag since our return. It's like having a second mother."

Veronica reached up and brushed his cheek softly. "Spend time with your friends. Perhaps you can visit me tomorrow night, then?"

Simon slipped an arm around her waist, not caring about the men and women who were inconvenienced by the couple stopped in the middle of the sidewalk. "I will be there tomorrow, that I promise you."

"I'm glad to hear it. We must go or we're going to be late for our next appointment."

"We certainly wouldn't want that," he said dryly.

CHAPTER

Five

SIMON TOOK OFF HIS COAT, HANDING IT TO LUTHOR as he entered the townhouse. Once his jacket was hung, the apothecary led him into the sitting room. Mattie stood and he hugged her lightly, kissing her on the cheek.

"It's so good to see you again, Simon," she said.

"You as well, Matilda. I've been so engaged since we returned, I've hardly found the time for you and Luthor."

"Well, I'm glad you found time for us this evening," she replied.

Luthor gestured toward the armchair, and Simon sat. The couple took seats next to one another on the couch.

"How have the wedding plans progressed?" Luthor asked.

Simon tapped his chin as he considered the best way to respond without using profanity. "Veronica forbade me from carrying my pistol, which is the only reason so many businessmen and women in the city still live and breathe."

The apothecary chuckled softly while Mattie smirked.

"Gideon Dosett was a demon, using mind control to steal the lands from the indigenous peoples," he continued, glancing toward Mattie, "and yet, I don't think he was half as deceitful or vile as the people I've encountered today."

"Surely you jest, sir," Luthor said.

"Only just!"

Luthor stood and gestured toward the kitchen. "Can I offer you a drink, sir? I could put on a pot of tea if you feel so inclined."

Simon shook his head. "After the day I've had, I'll need something a bit more potent. Scotch, if you have it."

Luthor turned away from the kitchen door and angled toward the liquor cabinet. Opening the glass doors, he pulled out a tumbler and a carafe of brown liquid. "On the rocks?"

"Of course."

Luthor lifted the lid to the ice chest but saw only a few half-melted cubes within. Glancing cautiously over his shoulder, he noted Simon in deep conversation with Mattie. Turning back to the ice chest, Luthor traced the loops and swirls of a rune into the air above the puddle of water. The rune flashed a stark blue white before snow crystals fell onto the melted cubes. The water coalesced, forming perfect cubes of ice. Grasping the tongs, Luthor retrieved a few cubes and dropped them into the tumbler, followed quickly by the scotch.

Turning, he offered the glass to the Inquisitor.

"Thank you," he said absently, continuing his conversation with the woman.

"Have you heard word from the Grand Inquisitor?" Mattie asked as Luthor stepped away to make drinks for her and himself.

"Unfortunately, no," Simon replied, resting his tumbler on the arm of the chair. "Aside from turning in my report from Whitten Hall, I've barely had a moment alone with the man. It's almost as though he were intentionally avoiding me."

"I can't imagine why he would," she replied.

Simon sighed. "I understand your difficult predicament, Miss Hawke, but in this instance, you'll just have to be patient."

"Do you realize you only call her Miss Hawke when you're delivering news you know she won't like?" Luthor asked as he took his seat and offered a drink to Mattie.

"I do not," Simon replied.

Mattie took a drink and nodded. "You do, actually."

"Well then, *Matilda*," he said with unnecessary emphasis, "I'm sure the Grand Inquisitor will make a determination soon."

"You make it sound so simplistic, as though he were deciding upon which tie to wear to dinner. This is my life and the lives of my tribe."

"Forgive me," Simon said, quickly serious. "I meant no disrespect. I know how important this is to you. I just feel rather powerless to force the man's hand, and I fear that forcing a decision will result in the wrong one being made. However, I promise I shall broach the subject with him again when next I see him."

"Have you heard anything about our next assignment?" Luthor asked in an attempt to defuse the tension in the room.

Simon took a sip of his scotch but shook his head. "No, nothing. I feel that our assignment to Whitten Hall was a fluke, one assigned to us solely because the Grand Inquisitor wanted time in private to examine Miss… Matilda's situation. Now, with no other pressing issues, we've been placed at the bottom of the queue. If all goes well, it should be a month or two before we're dispatched once more."

"Months in Callifax, you say, sir?" Luthor asked with an approving nod. He raised his glass. "A man could get used to that."

Simon raised his glass as well. "I will gladly drink to the idea."

As the men drank, Mattie swirled her liquor around in her glass and smiled. "I hardly know what to do with myself. I've never before explored a city as large as Callifax, save for the abrupt few weeks we spent here before the nasty business with the vampires. It's genuinely pleasant spending this time here, with no pressing concerns. We truly could do anything we desire without worries about being called away on assignment. We are just three friends spending the evening together, like normal men and women."

"Here, here," Luthor said as he leaned back into the couch.

Simon nodded slyly and took another drink of his scotch.

They stared at one another in silence, nodding politely and taking sips of their drinks, but saying nothing.

Luthor finally exhaled loudly. "Well, this is certainly awkward."

"Thank God someone else said it," Simon replied with a sigh. "I fear we're not suited for domestic tranquility."

"I don't know who I was kidding," Mattie added. "I haven't the foggiest what a normal man and woman does in Callifax. It seems absolutely dreadful."

Simon winked mischievously. "We could find trouble, then."

Mattie smiled. "What did you have in mind?"

"We could pay Veronica a visit at work," he said, shrugging.

Luthor glanced back and forth between Simon and Mattie. "Sir, I'm not quite sure the Ace of Spades is quite the right establishment for Mattie."

Mattie frowned as she turned toward the apothecary. "Not quite the right establishment for me? You have this odd illusion that I'm a lady of proper upbringing, yet I find myself once more needing to remind you I most certainly am not."

Her eyes flashed a threatening yellow, mimicking that of a wolf. A guttural growl rolled from her throat. Luthor set down his drink and raised his hands defensively.

"Forgive me for defending your womanly virtues," the apothecary said. "If you wish to visit a club of ill repute, who am I to stop you?"

"Don't let Luthor fool you," Simon explained. "He's never actually been inside himself."

She turned toward him, her eyes returning to their natural color as she smiled. "Never? Then it seems our evening plans have been settled."

CHAPTER

THE TRIO CROSSED THE BRIDGE INTO SOLOMON'S WAY, passing the unremarkable stretch where the young woman had been attacked a few nights before. Compared to the opulence of the Upper Reaches, where Simon and Luthor called home, Solomon's Way had a filthier feel. Dirt and soot were caked along the windowsills they passed. Refuse lined the street, blowing gently across their path in the evening's breeze. The streets were busier, however. At night, the Upper Reaches were quiet as politicians and members of the royal court rested for busy days ahead. For those who rebuked sleep in lieu of nightly entertainment, they found their way across the bridge, where the dirty streets hid concealed brothels and nightclubs galore.

The Ace of Spades glowed like a torch in the night, shining brightly against the backdrop of the city. Brightly colored paint on the building's exterior glowed under the sea of harsh fluorescent lights, reflecting a rainbow of patterns in the puddles lining the street before it. A line stretched along the front of the building, an odd assortment of men and women dressed in finery, intermingled with denizens of the Lower Reaches, wearing patched jackets and frayed hats.

A large man stood at the door, a veritable mountain of flesh and muscle. He stopped the throng of eager patrons from entering; no one rebuffed him as he decisively held up a hand, ordering couples and individuals alike to stop short of the door. A pair of scantily dressed women stood on either side of the padded double doors, awaiting an opportunity to open them for patrons coming or going.

Mattie and Luthor angled toward the back of the long line, though Simon could see their disapproval at having to wait most of the night just to enter. Simon shook his head as he grabbed them by their arms.

"We don't wait in line," he explained.

The bouncer, dressed in fine livery, glanced up at Simon's approach. He warily glanced back and forth to Simon's companions, but the Inquisitor slipped a gold coin into the man's hand as they paused before the towering brute.

"Welcome back to the Ace of Spades, sir," the bouncer said, ignoring the expressed indignation of those still standing in line. Simon smiled as the bouncer turned back to those waiting, yelling profanity and expressing his severe lack of concern at their sense of favoritism.

The two ladies at the door grasped the heavy, wrought-iron handles and pulled the doors open. A wave of noise and sweetly scented smoke rolled from the club's interior. Leading the way, Simon stepped within. They entered onto a raised arc of seats, overlooking the sunken main floor below. Patrons, their eyes affixed on the stage, took all the seats around the curved bar. A woman danced slowly on the main stage, unlatching bone clasps on her corset in perfect rhythm with the pounding drums.

Simon descended the few stairs onto the main floor and headed directly toward an empty booth near the left wall. Curtains were hung beside the booth, offering privacy if so desired, but they were currently opened, revealing a small plaque sitting on the table marked "reserved". Simon slid into the booth, moving the sign aside as he did so. Luthor and Mattie joined him, even as Simon signaled toward a server.

A well-endowed woman clad in lingerie approached the booth. A small cap rested on her head, held in its odd angle by a number of pins. A leather sash hung around her neck, attached to a tray held at her waist. Atop the tray was an assortment of goods: cigars, cigarettes, and a few other unmentionables that made Luthor blush at the sight.

"A cigarette, if you please," Simon said, loud enough to be heard over the music.

"Of course, Inquisitor," the woman replied.

Handing Simon a cigarette, she pulled a lighter from the tray and ignited a steady flame. Leaning over the table, revealing more of herself than Luthor would have believed possible, she lit Simon's cigarette. The Inquisitor took a long drag before pulling it from his mouth and exhaling.

"Thank you, Juliette," Simon said with a grin on his face.

"I didn't think you were coming in today," Juliette said, her dark curls bouncing as she spoke. "Veronica said you were otherwise occupied."

Simon gestured toward the other two in the booth. Juliette nodded to them both as though she hadn't noticed them before that moment.

"We decided our evening plans should include the Ace of Spades," he explained. "Juliette, I'd like to introduce you to some very close friends of mine, Mister Luthor Strong and Miss Matilda Hawke."

"A pleasure. Shall I tell Veronica you're here?" the waitress asked.

Simon shook his head. "Not at all. I'd rather surprise her, if it's all the same."

Juliette smiled, though Luthor noted wistfulness in her expression. He glanced knowingly toward the Inquisitor, though the mustached man seemed oblivious to her subtle advances.

"Absolutely, sir," she replied. "Be quick, though, if you intend to see her. She goes on in a few minutes. I hope you all have a wonderful evening."

Juliette turned away and disappeared into the crowd, hawking her wares as she went. Luthor turned toward his friend and gestured toward the door beside the stage.

"Shall we let you out, sir?"

Simon stroked his chin thoughtfully. "I considered watching her perform, first, but I ought to let her know we're here. The last thing we need is to catch her off guard halfway through her performance."

Luthor glanced nervously toward Mattie. "Should we avert our eyes when she comes on stage?" His eyes drifted to the nearly naked woman gracing the main stage. "I'm not entirely sure I could properly look her in the eyes were I to see her naked."

"You've lived such a sheltered life," Mattie replied. "You've both seen me naked during my transformations and, if anything, it's only strengthened our bond."

"I believe that's Luthor's point," Simon offered. "The bond that you

35

mention happens to involve quite a bit of lust on Luthor's part."

If it were possible for Luthor to turn even more scarlet, he did. He fiddled with his glasses as though they suddenly required his utmost attention.

"I don't think he'd feel quite right lusting after my fiancée," Simon concluded.

Mattie arched her eyebrow. "Forgive me if I'm not capturing the subtle nuances of the club, but isn't that quite the point of this establishment?"

"Quite right you are." Simon patted Luthor on the arm and forced the apothecary from the booth. "You didn't miss a thing, Matilda. If you'll both excuse me, I have a gorgeous brunette to seduce before her moment in the limelight."

Mattie laughed heartily, but Luthor seemed to have lost his voice. The apothecary collapsed back into the booth without as much as a farewell. Simon walked briskly to the stage entrance and slipped past the bouncer. The room beyond was a flurry of activity. Women in various stages of undress scurried about the room, applying makeup or borrowing pieces of jewelry, most of which Simon immediately recognized as fake. Despite the amount of exposed flesh around him, the Inquisitor mostly ignored their curious stares as he moved toward a closed dressing room in the back.

He was nearly there when a blonde woman stepped in his way. Unlike those around her, she was completely dressed, a tight corset around her waist and long skirt adorning her hips. A shawl was draped over her shoulders, and she carried a closed parasol in her hands.

"We've missed you, Simon," she said as she leaned forward and kissed him on the cheek.

"Gloria, my dear, I have missed you as well." Simon gestured toward the closed dressing room. "Is your roommate in? I thought I might surprise her."

She glanced up and nodded. "Veronica's changing for her show, but I have no doubt she'll be glad to see you. Will I see you at the apartment later this evening?"

"I suppose," he replied with a knowing smirk, "if all goes well. Where are you off to at this not-at-all-obscene hour?"

"My shift is done," she explained. "For once, I thought I might enjoy the peace and quiet that comes only from having my roommate and her incessant fiancé out of my life for a few hours."

Simon smiled at her backhanded insult. "Enjoy your peace and quiet while it lasts. I'll be sure to wake you when we get home."

"Do, Inquisitor, and it may be the last thing you do in this life," she warned. Despite her being nearly a head shorter than Simon, the Inquisitor took her threat quite seriously.

Smirking, Simon walked to the dressing room door and knocked. A voice called from within. "Who is it?"

"Nobody important," Simon replied.

The door opened and Veronica, covered in a robe and clearly in a state of half dress, smiled broadly. "I thought you were too busy with Mister Strong and Miss Hawke tonight to come see me?"

Simon shrugged. "We're terrible company, unless we're in the midst of a sword fight or chasing monsters through the countryside." He lowered his voice, as though sharing a secret. "Truth be told, they're dreadfully boring people. All they want to talk about is the fascinating things they've done on the last assignment and, frankly, I was there for most of it. We all agreed that you seemed like far more interesting company."

"Did you now?" she asked slyly. "I presume you had no influence at all on that decision?"

"I may have swayed the conversation in that direction, but I assure you, they heartily agreed."

"Heartily?"

"Well, they agreed, nonetheless."

Veronica turned and walked back into the dressing room. "I have to finish preparations. Why don't you join them, so they don't feel quite so awkward watching me perform?"

Simon leaned against the doorframe. "Trust me, my dear, it's far too late for that."

She laughed and playfully pushed him out of the doorway. "Go. I'll come and see you all once my song is done."

She closed the door in his face and, with the corners of his mouth still upturned, he walked back to Luthor and Mattie at the table.

Gloria heard the catcalls as she left the Ace of Spades. She barely acknowledged the whistles or inappropriate suggestions; she had grown so accustomed to them during the past couple of years. She walked hurriedly away, her tight curls bouncing with each step.

Though her night was finished, the night itself was still young. People crowded the streets, entering or leaving the bars that lined the road. As the rest of Callifax settled in for the night, the main thoroughfares of Solomon's Way came alive. She pulled the fedora lower over her face as she tried her best to ignore the prying eyes.

Despite her chosen profession, Gloria wasn't interested in engaging the drunken strangers on the street. Some she recognized; the politician, drunk as he might be, was still surrounded by very large and very sober bodyguards. His propositions, however, fell on the same deaf ears as everyone else's.

After a few blocks of walking, she turned off the main avenue and onto one of the residential roads. The crowds disappeared instantaneously. She could still hear the revelry—the music, yells, and laughter—but it was muted as though heard through a closed window. The street lamps were sparse between the terraces of townhouses, the pools of lights splashing onto the dark street.

Gloria pulled her coat tighter around her, not to ward off a chill, but merely for a sense of protection. The stillness of the night air felt surreally detached from the boisterous road from which she had just left. It left her feeling awkwardly alone and vulnerable.

She was startled by the sound of a shoe scraping on the pavement behind her. Turning abruptly, she saw a tall, lanky man walking nearly a block behind. His head was lowered and his hands shoved deeply into his pockets. Part of her wanted to call out to him, but before she could find her voice, he turned and ascended some stairs leading into a townhouse. With a sigh of relief and a stifled, nervous laugh, Gloria turned around and continued her way down the road.

As she passed the last of the townhouses, her apartment building came into view. She approached the building from the side, the main entrance being on a cross street ahead. Cars rumbled along, though none turned down the darkened road on which she walked.

She lengthened her stride, eager to be home, where she could change into something far more comfortable and fall asleep, hopefully before Veronica and Simon returned.

As she raised her head toward the brightly lit street ahead, hands came out of the alley and closed around her, one covering her mouth while the other dragged her into the darkness. She screamed, but it was lost in the gloved hand over her face.

Gloria kicked backward, catching her assailant in the shin with the long heel of her shoe. The man grunted and his grip weakened around her waist. She struggled free, lashing out with her elbows against her attacker. She had nearly slid free from his grasp when much larger and much stronger hands closed over her. She was wrenched from her feet and tossed handily into the alley.

Landing awkwardly, she groaned on impact. The air was knocked from her lungs, stifling any chance she had of screaming for help. She looked up at the massive hulk of a man silhouetted above her just as she felt something thin and sharp pierce her neck.

Gloria's head spun and her vision grew blurry. She struggled to sit upright, but her arms refused to respond. Her legs, likewise, were numb and limp, flaccid against the cold asphalt. The thinner of the two men knelt above her, his face lost in the tears welling in her eyes. She tried to speak, but her tongue felt three sizes too large for her mouth and merely flopped limply against her teeth.

Tears streamed down her face, and her heart pounded in her chest. The thin man held up a long blade for her to see, its metal glinting in the weak light bleeding into the alley.

It was far too early in the morning when Veronica finished her shift. Luthor and Mattie had retired nearly an hour earlier, begging off remaining until the club closed for the night. Their sense of adventure only extended to reasonable hours of the night. Simon, on the other hand, enjoyed another glass of scotch as Veronica changed back into regular attire.

The street beyond the front door of the Ace of Spades was surprisingly quiet. A few drunkards wandered the street, either too inebriated to find their way home or homeless to begin with; Solomon's Way had more than its fair share of both. The partygoers of the earlier evening had returned to their more respectable districts of Callifax, leaving the Way to its lowly natives.

Simon offered his arm, which she gladly took, as they walked toward her apartment. They watched bars close and lock their doors for the evening. Many of the fluorescent lights that lit up the street like a second sunrise were extinguished for the remainder of the night, leaving the street far darker than it had been in hours.

They turned off the main road and onto a residential street. Rows of townhouses stretched ahead, ending blocks away on another main street through the district. A few cars rumbled across the road, mostly taxis returning people to their homes after work or nights of excess. They walked calmly and slowly, not in a hurry to get home but rather enjoying one another's company.

"You were magnificent tonight," Simon remarked.

"You say that every night," she replied.

"That's only because it's been true every night thus far. Have no fear, the one night you give a subpar performance, I will be sure to let you know."

She laughed lightly and leaned into his arm. They walked arm in arm past the townhouses until the terrace gave way to the taller apartment buildings. The one she shared with Gloria was on the corner. Walking brusquely to the corner, they turned and caught sight of the evening doorman.

"Good evening, Miss Hawke. Sir," the doorman said with a tip of his hat.

He held the door for them and they entered, angling immediately toward the elevator on the far end of the lobby. They rode it upward, stopping at her floor, and walked down the hallway to her apartment. The door was locked, though that wasn't unusual. Veronica unlocked it and stepped into the dark interior.

She turned on the electric lights, which glowed dimly before the coils heated. As the room was bathed in light, Veronica frowned slightly. Gloria's bedroom door was ajar and, through the narrow opening, she could see that her roommate's bed was empty and unused.

"I thought Gloria was coming home," Simon remarked, following her gaze.

Veronica shrugged. "She said she was, though it wouldn't be entirely unlike her to have found a gentlemen caller. For all I know, she had a date all along, which is why she requested an earlier shift." She turned and slipped her hands around his waist. "Nevertheless, what it truly means is that we have the apartment to ourselves, for whatever debauchery we so desire."

Simon smiled as he brushed a strand of dark hair out of her face.

"Are you sure that's wise, since we're visiting the Abbey tomorrow?"

"I'll say a few extra prayers for all the sinning I intend to do tonight," she replied.

Smiling broader, he pushed the front door closed.

CHAPTER

Seven

T HE NEXT MORNING, SIMON FROWNED AS HE AND VE-
ronica walked down the street. He wasn't unhappy being with his
fiancée, quite the opposite. It was their destination that had him
on edge. The Callifax Abbey loomed in the distance, its pointed spires
towering over the buildings nearby. Amidst the sweeping splendor of the
city, the Abbey was an archaic structure of sharp angles and jutting pro-
trusions that reminded Simon of spears and swords. To add to the coarse
exterior, horrific gargoyles perched atop the towers, staring damningly
down on the passersby.

Simon had never been religious, nor had he ever concealed his dis-
taste for organized faith. The devoted who attended church every week
were indoctrinated, mindless masses who blindly followed a belief structure completely unsupported by science. Placing one's faith in a creature
that rose from the dead was, as far as Simon was concerned, little better
than praying to the mystical abominations he hunted as a Royal Inquisitor. They might as well place their faith at the feet of Chancellor Whitten,
the vampiric brute the Inquisitors recently dispatched.

"Relax," Veronica demanded, squeezing his arm for emphasis. "You're
as stiff as a board."

"I am relaxed," Simon lied, smiling toward the dark-haired woman.

"You are not, and you know it. You look ready to pounce, like a tiger in the woods stalking prey. These people aren't prey, you know?"

He remained silent, which garnered a jab to his ribs.

"You do know that, don't you?" she asked again.

"These people—" he began.

"My people," she corrected. "Need I remind you that I attend services at this very church?"

Simon frowned but shook his head. "I meant no disrespect."

"Of course you did. Luckily, I had the foresight to stop you before you said something too inflammatory. However, that's exactly my point. When meeting with the bishop today, please do try not to say anything too upsetting."

"I will try my best," Simon said, knowing that his tolerance for religion was far lower than it should be.

They approached the church, and even Simon was daunted by its size. The building stretched the length of the city block, its edges broken only by the small groves of trees planted between it and the buildings on either side. A round, stained glass window towered overhead, reflecting the sunlight like a second burning sun. In such a position, dwarfed by the enormous structure and feeling the burning eyes of gargoyles staring down upon him, he understood why patrons felt intimidated, like the eyes of their god were upon them as they walked through the door.

The doors themselves were closed as they approached. Carved motifs lined the middle of the doors, images depicting the trials and tribulations of their faith. Simon paid them little heed as he stepped in front of Veronica and grasped the wrought-iron handle. He pulled the doors open, which creaked loudly from the effort.

Simon removed his top hat as they stepped into the cooler building. The interior of the church was well lit, if not mostly abandoned at such an odd hour. There were no services offered. The church was open solely for the use of its parishioners, for those seeking spiritual guidance. Tea candles were lit in glass bowls against the left wall, but Simon hardly noticed. His breath caught in his throat as he stared upon the vaulted room before him.

The cathedral ceiling stretched dozens of feet over his head, rising and falling between the massive marble pillars throughout the room.

Rows of wooden pews stretched toward the altar on the dais on the far end of the room, but the middle was what caught Simon's attention far more than the gilded golden altar or the statues flanking the dais. Where the sun had poured through the stained glass window, a rainbow of colors filled the church's interior. Colors danced with one another, sparkling against the tiled floor and filling the air with a sense of magic and wonder.

Simon frowned as the logical part of his mind assumed control. It was a charade, as much as any charlatan he had investigated. The light, the size of the chamber in which they stood, the stark contrast between the harsh exterior and the mystical interior, and the general opulence, all fed the sense of wonderment and a belief that anything, even their religion, was possible.

His analytical mind had taken hold, and he tensed again. He viewed the few patrons distributed quietly amidst the pews with a clinical eye, wondering for what, if anything, they had come here, seeking absolution.

A robed man approached them, a broad smile cast upon his face. His face was smooth, freshly shaven. Deep wrinkles creased the corners of his eyes and mouth and most of his well-coifed hair was silver from age.

"Miss Dawn," the bishop said while taking her hands. "I'm so glad you were able to attend today."

"I wouldn't have missed it, Bishop," she said, her demeanor much more forward and relaxed than Simon had seen in some time. "I don't say that solely because you wouldn't marry us without it," she added with a wink.

The bishop laughed. "I find extortion is the most effective means to bring people into the church." He turned toward Simon and bowed his head slightly. "You must be Mister Whitlock. I have heard a great deal about you, sir." He offered his hand. "I am Bishop Hartford, assistant to the Abbot of Callifax. Welcome to the Abbey."

Simon shook the man's hand and forced a smile. "A pleasure to meet you, too, sir."

"I don't think that's entirely true," replied the bishop, touching the side of his nose knowingly, "but I hope to change your mind before this is done."

The bishop gestured toward a closed door to the right of the chamber. "Perhaps you would both care to join me in my chambers so that we might discuss your wedding preparations without disturbing our fellow parishioners?"

"Of course, sir," Veronica replied. "Please lead the way."

As the bishop turned, she shot Simon a warning glance. He shrugged his shoulders unapologetically, knowing he hadn't said anything inciting. They followed the priest to the chambers and entered the much more humble abode.

The office in which they found themselves was nothing like the lavishness of the main cathedral. The ceilings were low, only a few feet over Simon's head. He felt obliged to duck as they entered, though he wasn't in any true risk of bumping his head. Were he wearing his top hat, rather than carrying it in his hands, however, he was sure it would have been knocked from his head as they entered through the doorway.

The walls were lined with bookshelves, on which sat ancient tomes and even older scrolls. The air smelled musky from their scent, a mixture of ancient parchment mixed with the reek of mildew and mold. Though the shelves were free from dust, it hung permeably in the air, like a thin blanket coating his mouth with each breath.

The bishop offered them chairs, high-backed, red leather beasts that were recently oiled to keep from cracking. Simon gingerly touched the leather before sitting, ensuring the sheen of the oily treatment was dry before taking the offered seat. The bishop walked around his desk and sat in his own throne-like chair, the only truly opulent item in the entire chamber. Absently, he cleared away a few stacks of papers that lined his desk, organizing what had previously been a garbled mixture of notes, scrolls, and books splayed open upon the table.

"Forgive me, I've been busy with my many other responsibilities," the bishop apologized as he finished hastily organizing his desk.

"Think nothing of it, Bishop," Veronica replied for them both. "We're just glad you were able to make time for us today."

"So you wish to be wed in the eyes of God?"

Simon nodded, knowing that Veronica's gaze would fall upon him soon enough.

"Do you both understand the obligations of a couple, married in the church? To love one another unconditionally, placing only God above their devotion to one another? To remain eternally loyal to your spouse, through their youth and eventual age, through their inevitable sicknesses and tribulations?"

Veronica nodded. "We do, Your Holiness."

The bishop gazed at Simon, who kept his focus locked on the robed man, offering neither confirmation nor contempt for the bishop's beliefs. While Simon had little consternation about lying to a man, it seemed in poor taste to lie to a man of the cloth within his own church, especially with Veronica's piercing gaze upon him.

"Why do you think that holy matrimony is right for the two of you?" the bishop asked.

"Because we love one another," Veronica quickly replied. She turned toward Simon, but the Inquisitor was chewing on his lip. "Simon?"

The bishop arched an eyebrow before folding his hands in his lap. "Inquisitor Whitlock, how would you respond to that question?"

Simon glanced to Veronica and smiled sheepishly. He was glad to finally be presented with a question for which he so readily knew the answer, one that wouldn't, in any way, require lying to the bishop. "I want to marry Veronica because, to be perfectly blunt, I trust her with my life."

The bishop nodded. "Trust is a good foundation on which a healthy marriage can be built. Certainly there's more to your love for one another, though."

Simon shook his head. "For me, trust is enough."

He cleared his throat when both the bishop and Veronica stared at him expectantly. "Forgive me. As a Royal Inquisitor, it becomes very difficult to trust someone. Our line of work is predicated on the idea that anyone could be a threat; that anyone could, at any given moment, present magical maladies. When you spend your life under such an auspice, you tend to categorize people into one of two categories. They are either assets or threats. Those closest to you are assets. I generally see them solely based off the skills they possess and the ways I can best utilize them to eliminate threats. Threats, of course, are dealt with accordingly."

The bishop rubbed his chin thoughtfully, but he looked puzzled. "I'm not sure I understand."

Simon reached out and took Veronica's hand. "There are those who say that a Royal Inquisitor should be marrying a noblewoman at the very least, not a commoner like Miss Dawn. Yet, when I met her, she was only the second person I had ever met who I saw not as a conglomeration of their individual skills, but as a friend. She was the first person to truly touch my soul. It was at that moment that I knew I loved her and, furthermore, that we would be together forever."

Veronica slipped her hand free from Simon, only so that she could open her clutch and retrieve a handkerchief. She dapped at the corners of her eyes, ensuring she didn't smear her makeup in the process.

"That was a beautiful sentiment," the bishop replied breathlessly. "You're a God-fearing man, I presume, Mister Whitlock?"

Simon shook his head again. "I've never put much faith in God, nor he in me."

"Simon," Veronica said harshly, the beauty of his previous statement immediately evaporating into glaring disapproval.

The bishop raised his hand. "No, Miss Dawn, there's no reason to reprimand the Inquisitor. He's speaking honestly and from the heart, of which I would expect nothing less during this discussion. Tell me, Simon—if I may call you Simon—what is it that makes you so hesitant to embrace your faith?"

Simon cleared his throat and glanced at Veronica, meeting her warning stare. He knew she wanted nothing less than for him to immediately be struck mute. If ever there was a moment for divine intervention, Simon realized, this was probably it. When nothing happened, when the bishop still stared at him expectantly, he realized the truth. He had been in for a penny, now he was committed to being in for a pound as well.

"God is supposed to be omnipresent, yet I have seen the dark corners of this kingdom in which God no longer resides. I have faced the horror of a demon, raised from the depths of the hell you so fear. I have struck down a vampire with my own hand, whose very existence predates your most religious texts. If ever I had my belief in a just God, my faith was crushed by the very existence of the Rift. Its presence, and the monstrous abominations that dwell within its depths, prove that either God doesn't exist, or He has turned a blind eye on the suffering of His people."

The room fell into silence. Though he had been honest, Simon wanted nothing more than to suddenly vanish, to dissipate into the air or, more sensibly, to stand from his chair and walk from the Abbey, never to return. He stole a glance sideways and saw Veronica's immense disapproval. Her lack of condemnation was solely a result of her inability to find her tongue.

"Forgive me, Bishop," she finally stammered. "I didn't—"

The bishop raised his hand, interrupting her apology. "You have no need to apologize, Miss Dawn. To be perfectly honest, Mister Whitlock and his experiences fascinate me. I would love to hear more, at a more appropriate time."

When Veronica looked surprised and, Simon noted, relieved, the bishop explained. "A core belief in God doesn't come by surrounding one's self with those of similar faith. Those of similar faith merely reinforce our own ideology. A true test of faith comes when confronting someone who so strongly disagrees with our very dogma. An atheist, one who believes there is no God, or an agnostic, like Simon, who believes there might be a God but he is not as omniscient as we would believe, tests our resolve and further proves that our belief in God is based in a solid foundation."

Simon swallowed hard, relieved, and found that he liked the bishop more and more. "I had feared you'd have me thrown from the Abbey."

"The thought crossed my mind," the bishop replied with a smile. "We have much more to discuss today, but a lack of faith in God's true might does not disqualify a couple from being married in the church. Quite the opposite. It strengthens my resolve to convince you of God's absolute right."

The conversation continued for hours, a heated debate at times, other times settling into a friendly dialogue about experiences and generalized beliefs. When it was done, Veronica no longer glared at Simon with unabashed anger, her frown becoming a warm smile. Near the end of their Pre-Cana lesson, she took Simon's hand once more, a sign to him that he would not be sleeping alone for the rest of their relationship.

The bishop stood, and Simon and Veronica quickly followed suit. "Mister Whitlock and Miss Dawn, while I have my concerns about your shared faith, I have no doubts at all about your commitment to one another. This will, as I'm sure you're more than aware, not be our last meeting, though I can say that I eagerly look forward to our next discussion."

"I am glad that at least some of my preconceived notions on organized religion have been quelled," Simon said.

The bishop arched his eyebrow. "Which preconceived notions would those be?"

"You're not a close-minded bigot, so there's that."

The bishop laughed even as Veronica's frown returned. "Yes, Simon,

I very much look forward to our next meeting."

They all shook hands, and the bishop escorted the couple to the massive front doors. As he pushed them open, warm sunlight flooded the church. "We shall see one another again soon. Miss Dawn, I encourage you to convince Mister Whitlock to join you for services one of these days."

She glanced toward the Inquisitor and slowly shook her head. "I think it might take the full might of God to make that happen, Your Holiness, but I will see what I can do."

"God bless you both," the bishop said as they stepped out of the Abbey and into the warm air.

They walked in silence to the sidewalk running in front of the walled-off Abbey property and turned back toward Simon's townhouse. From his periphery, he could see her stealing glances in his direction.

"I'm sleeping alone tonight, aren't I?" he asked bluntly.

"Oh, yes, you're very much sleeping alone tonight," she replied, her voice level and calm.

He quickly found that a strangely calm woman, when clearly battling a raging torrent of anger within her, scared him far worse than any monster he'd faced.

CHAPTER

Eight

S IMON SIGHED AS HE DRESSED IN HIS NIGHTGOWN
that night. He wished to say that he hadn't foreseen the day going
so poorly, but he knew better. Religion had been the only point of
contention in their otherwise wonderful relationship, one that was mostly ignored for the sake of both their sanity. It had been sadly unavoidable
when he had been marched directly into the proverbial lion's den.

He poured himself a stiff drink from the carafe and wet his lips,
letting the warmth from the scotch roll down his throat and settle in
his stomach. He didn't need the drink to sleep, although it helped. The
warmth from the drink would have to be a poor alternative for the
warmth of Veronica's body, but sacrifices had to be made.

After he turned off his bedside lamp and laid the tumbler on his
nightstand, he climbed into bed and settled underneath the down-filled
blanket. His eyes were starting to flutter closed, even though his mind
was still a jumble of activity, when he heard a faint knock on the front
door.

Curious, he sat up in bed and listened intently. Moments later, the
knock sounded again, a little more insistent than the first. He swung his
legs out of bed and found his house shoes. Slipping them onto his feet,

he walked toward the bedroom doorway, pausing only as he passed the armoire. He opened the wardrobe door and pulled from within his silver-plated revolver. Thusly armed, he left his room and quickly descended the stairs, even as the persistent knock came again.

Upon reaching the foyer, he glanced out the front door's narrow window. To his surprise, he saw a harried-looking Veronica standing on his doorstep. She caught his eye and gestured for him to open the door. Without pause, he threw the lock and opened it wide.

"I didn't think I'd have the pleasure of your company tonight, my dear," he said.

"Gloria didn't come home tonight," she stated matter-of-factly.

Simon furrowed his brow. "It's only been two nights. Is it truly that unusual for her?"

"It's not unheard of," she admitted, "but normally, she at least returns briefly for changes of clothing. I'm far more concerned that she didn't show to work tonight, either, which is highly unlike her."

"That is a bit more disconcerting. Shouldn't you still be at work, my dear?"

Veronica shook her head. "When she didn't show, I grew concerned and begged off for the night."

"I'm sure there's a perfectly viable explanation as to her absence. There's an equally good chance that when you awake tomorrow morning, she'll be sleeping soundly in her bed, none the worse for wear."

Veronica frowned and placed her hands on her hips. "You're not giving this the seriousness that the situation demands."

"Forgive me," he said, rubbing his eyes. "You've caught me at a time when I'm hardly awake. What would you like me to do?"

"We could look for her," she said, forcing her way past him and into the townhouse's foyer.

"At..." He paused and glanced at the grandfather clock standing against the wall. "At eleven o'clock at night? I wouldn't have the faintest idea of where to begin our search."

She started to object, but he took her hands and held them tightly. "If she has simply met a gentleman caller, then she'll be in his home. We couldn't very well go searching door to door, knocking on every house and apartment in Callifax to search for her. Stay here with me tonight and first thing in the morning, I'll accompany you back to your apartment. If she still hasn't shown and there's no sign she's been back to the apartment during the night, we'll go straight to the constabulary and file a report."

She frowned again, though she wasn't as committed to the gesture as she'd been earlier. "I told you quite clearly I had no intention of spending the night with you tonight."

Simon shrugged. "The decision has been taken from us. You can't very well go wandering the streets of the Upper Reaches alone at such an ungodly hour. There's no other recourse but to spend the night here, with me."

He smiled slyly. Begrudgingly, she smiled as well. He closed the door, locked it, and led her upstairs, hiding the pistol behind his back as they walked.

The next morning found Gloria's bedroom as it had been the night before: unsullied, the bed still made and all her clothing hanging untouched in her closet. Veronica passed through the room three times, searching for clues of Gloria's whereabouts, even entering the bathroom to look for loose strands of blonde hair that might have fallen about the room. When she found nothing, she returned to Simon in the living room.

"She hasn't been home," Veronica said, the concern evident in her voice. "This is highly unlike her. Gloria's an eternal optimist and prone to flights of fancy, but she's dependable. She wouldn't miss work and she wouldn't leave for an extended time, even with a man she adored, without letting me know."

Simon took her shoulders and pulled her close, feeling her body shake as he held her. "If you're truly concerned, then let's go to the constabulary. We'll file a report with them. Perhaps they've heard from her or, if not, at least they'll have the manpower to properly search the city."

She nodded gratefully and he took her hand, leading her from the apartment.

The Solomon's Way police station wasn't far from her apartment. It stood on the same side of the road as her apartment building, detached from the debauchery of the main thoroughfare but close enough to respond to trouble, should it arise. Its brick exterior was weathered but looked in fine condition compared to much of the rest of the Way.

They climbed the front steps and entered the building. A desk sergeant stood at the front desk, flanked by rows of desks and individual offices. His tall, curved hat was set upon the desk before him, and the sergeant was busy smoothing his unruly moustache. He looked up as Simon and Veronica approached.

"Can I help you?" the sergeant asked.

Simon glanced at Veronica, but she clearly deferred to the Inquisitor. "My name is Inquisitor Simon Whitlock. This is my fiancée, Miss Veronica Dawn. We would like to report a missing person."

The desk sergeant straightened at the mention of Simon's title, though it didn't seem to be out of respect for the position. The Inquisitors and constabulary hadn't always seen eye to eye, each organization often overstepping their bounds and into the realm of the other group in the process of investigating their respective crimes.

"Is the missing person an acquaintance of yours, then?"

"My roommate," Veronica said.

The sergeant relaxed slightly when Veronica spoke. He turned his attention toward the dark-haired woman. "I'm sorry, madam... Miss Dawn, was it?"

She nodded, and the sergeant wrote her name on a sheet of paper in front of him. "And who is it that's currently missing?"

"Her name is Gloria Cloverfield," Veronica said, the words spilling quickly from her. "She's approximately my height, though a more slender build. She has long, blonde hair, usually in tight curls. Her eyes are—"

The desk sergeant's expression sank, and his eyes softened. Veronica might not have noticed the subtle change, but it didn't go at all unnoticed by Simon. The Inquisitor arched his brow as the sergeant turned away, ignoring the rest of Veronica's explanation.

"Find me the detective," the sergeant yelled to one of the other bobbies. "I need him at the front desk, if you please."

Veronica's voice faded away, not so much stopping as each word came slower and slower until her sentence died on her lips. "What's the matter?"

"Sorry, madam," the sergeant stammered. "I'm not at liberty to say. You'll have to wait for the detective."

Veronica turned toward Simon, who could only shrug in equal confusion. They didn't have to wait long before a slightly heavyset man in a long, brown trench coat hurried to the front desk. Simon recognized the detective at once; they had so recently met on the bridge during Simon's last investigation.

"Detective Sugden," the Inquisitor said.

The detective paused, eyeing Simon warily, before his mind made the connection. "Inquisitor. I'm rather surprised to see you here. What can the constabulary do for you?"

The desk sergeant leaned in to the detective and whispered a quick explanation. The detective blanched slightly as he nodded. "Gloria Cloverfield was an acquaintance of yours?"

The use of the past tense of the verb wasn't lost on Simon.

"She's my roommate," Veronica said, her nervousness rising as well. "We share an apartment. Do you know where she is? Is she all right?"

"I think you should both come with me," Sugden said dryly, leading them away from the front desk.

The trio walked to a stairwell. Detective Sugden descended the stairs, leading them into the cool basement of the police station. Simon could feel the chill emanating from the walls and could hear the distant hum of machinery. The further they walked, the colder the air grew until he was forced to drape his arm over Veronica's shoulders to keep her warm.

"I don't understand," she said. "Where are you taking us?"

Simon looked up and saw the steel doors ahead. He frowned, knowing only too well where they were going. "The morgue," he said softly.

The detective's steps faltered momentarily, but he regained his pace and led them to the frigid metal doors. Wordlessly, he pushed them open. Simon followed the man inside, Veronica already shaking, though not as much from the cold any more. The Inquisitor's gaze fell on a thin man standing over a raised, metal table. The man was dressed in a blue gown as he worked, and Simon immediately shielded Veronica's eyes from the sight of the autopsy being performed.

"Doctor," the detective said, "would you be so kind as to cease your work momentarily?"

The thin man paused and glanced over his shoulder, noting the detective, flanked by Simon and Veronica. Coughing apologetically, he pulled a sheet over the corpse before him and stripped off his blood-soaked gloves.

"She's dead, isn't she?" Veronica asked.

"I'm afraid so, madam," Sugden replied. "Miss Cloverfield was found by passersby yesterday afternoon. She had identification on her but no address, so we had no way of contacting anyone." The detective glanced toward the thin man. "This is Doctor Youke Casan. He will assist in identifying your friend's remains."

Doctor Casan walked forward. He was gangly as he moved, as though his limbs were slightly too long for the rest of his body. He was thin but still healthy. His blond hair was cropped close to his scalp, revealing the beginnings of a receding hairline at his temples, despite his otherwise youthful appearance.

The doctor extended his hand, which Simon shook. "I'm sorry that we have to meet under such circumstances."

"Thank you for your concern," Simon replied. He glanced toward Veronica, who seemed to have fallen mute from shock. "How did she die, if I might ask?"

Casan glanced cautiously toward the detective.

"Unfortunately, that's part of an ongoing investigation," Sugden replied. "My apologies, but I will share whatever information I can once the investigation has concluded."

Simon frowned. Natural deaths didn't require the ambiguity that Sugden was offering.

Doctor Casan stepped to Veronica's side, though he towered over her. Simon realized the doctor was actually a few inches taller than he was. The Inquisitor wasn't used to looking up to people, and he found the effect disconcerting.

"I'm sorry to ask this of you, madam," the doctor said politely, "but if you could come with me, I need you to identify Miss Cloverfield. It's entirely procedural, you understand."

Veronica nodded. The detective placed a warning hand on the doctor's arm. "I believe she's the one in 2D," he said. "The one from yesterday."

Simon watched the conversation transpire, frowning deeper. The doctor led the group to a row of small, metal doors, no more than three feet tall by three feet across. Casan ran his hand across the metal plaques lining the front of the doors until his fingers paused atop 2D. He pulled the lever on the door and opened the cooler. Cold air poured from the open doorway as the doctor grasped a protruding handle and pulled. A drawer slid out with a smooth hiss. When the drawer had been pulled only halfway out, the doctor paused, letting it rest where it stood.

Atop the metal slab, a sheet had been draped. Where it had settled, it conformed to the general shape of a person: the rounded shape of a head, drooping to sloped shoulders.

"I apologize if this is somewhat disconcerting," Casan said as he pulled back the top of the sheet.

Lying on the slab, her blonde curls splayed out around her like a golden halo, lay Gloria. Her eyes were closed and her skin a pallor of death, no longer pink but turning a dull gray. Her lips were bloodless and dark. She looked remarkably peaceful.

Veronica screamed and collapsed into Simon's arms. She buried her face in his chest as she sobbed uncontrollably. Simon reached down, stroked her hair, and kissed the back of her head gently, soothing her as best he could as she moaned softly.

"I presume this is your friend?" the detective asked quietly.

Simon nodded. "Unfortunately, yes."

Veronica's sobs began anew with Simon's confirmation. She shook even as Simon cradled her tightly to him. The detective reached out his hands and motioned toward Veronica.

"Perhaps it would be better if we took her from this room," Sugden offered. "I could help you if you like."

Simon nodded but when Sugden came near, the Inquisitor detached Veronica from him and handed her fully to the detective. "If you could, please escort her outside. I want to ask Doctor Casan a few questions about her death, if you don't mind."

Sugden frowned but had little choice, as he was already supporting Veronica. "This isn't an Inquisitor matter," the detective warned. "The constabulary is more than capable of conducting our own investigation."

"I mean no disrespect, nor do I have any intention of interfering," Simon said calmly, though his frustration boiled just beneath the surface. "That being said, the woman on this table was a friend and I want to know why she is dead."

Detective Sugden watched him for a second longer before the weight of the sobbing Veronica became too much to bear. He nodded, as much to Casan as Simon, and then led the brunette from the room. Simon watched them leave before turning back to Gloria. She looked calm and at ease, but Simon didn't believe that was true. He reached out and ran a hand along her forehead, watching the still-faint lines and creases between her brows.

"Sir, I would ask you not to touch the body," Doctor Casan said.

"Her brow is still furrowed, as it was at the time of her death, annotating that she was either in severe shock or incredible pain," Simon said, his hand not leaving her clammy skin. "No matter your hesitation at admitting the truth, Gloria didn't die of natural causes. She died horribly, if I had to wager a guess, one that you aren't keen to share." He looked up at the nervous doctor. "Am I close?"

"I'm sorry," Casan stammered. "I'm not at liberty to discuss."

Simon shook his head and pointed toward the half-exposed metal slab. "There's no need. I knew there was more to her death when you refused to fully expose her body, even covered beneath the sheet. I would presume a rather significant lower extremity wound?" Before the flushed doctor could reply, Simon continued. "I wouldn't expect you to answer, though your pause gives me all the proof I require."

Simon touched Gloria's cheek, feeling his heart ache at the sight of the deceased woman. It wasn't just Veronica's anguish that gave Simon pause; he genuinely cared for the feisty, petite woman who had once shared his fiancée's apartment. Eventually, he removed his hand and turned, walking toward the exit of the morgue and the woman he loved. He didn't trust the detective to properly console the mortified woman. He paused at the door, however, and glanced over his shoulder.

"There was more than just Gloria, wasn't there, Doctor?" Simon asked. "The detective was very clear that you were only to reveal the body from last night's murder, telling me there were more before her."

Doctor Casan didn't reply, but Simon merely shook his head. "I know you won't tell me, but trust me, I will find the person responsible for her death. Good day, Doctor."

CHAPTER

Nine

SIMON DIDN'T WANT TO TAKE VERONICA HOME. HE knew her apartment would be full of constant reminders of her former roommate and would only exacerbate her anguish. Hailing a taxi outside the police station, they rode in silence across the bridge and into the Upper Reaches. Pulling his handkerchief from his jacket pocket, he offered it to Veronica. She dabbed her swollen eyes as well as possible, though her face was splotchy and red. He looked at her sadly, wishing there was a way to take away her pain. Unlike her, Simon didn't feel overwhelmed by the morose sensation, though he could feel his sadness whispering in the back of his mind and settling in his chest. He was an Inquisitor and in times of darkness, he swallowed his emotions and focused on the investigation at hand.

The dark car rumbled as it turned onto his street and rolled to a stop outside his townhouse. The driver opened the door. Simon slid out before reaching back inside and helping Veronica to her feet. She cradled her head in the crook of his neck as he supported her. As the taxi pulled away from the curb, they walked up the steps to the townhouse door.

Simon took her immediately upstairs and settled her into his bed. He wasn't sure she'd sleep, but he knew she'd be safe within his home. She brought her knees to her chest as she lay on her side. He pulled up the blanket, ignoring the fact that she was fully clothed, and covered her, save her head. Brushing her hair out of her face, he leaned forward and kissed her gently on the forehead. As he started to stand, her hand emerged from the blanket and grabbed him tightly on the arm.

"Please don't leave me," she said hoarsely.

Simon shook his head. "I will never leave you. I'm only going to get you a drink."

She held him tightly a moment longer before he slipped free of her grip and left the room. He hurried downstairs, sure that she wouldn't want to be alone for long. In the kitchen, he put a pot of tea on the stove before retrieving a teacup from the cabinet. He poured honey and sugar into the cup. Walking into the study, he found a bottle of whiskey. Veronica needed more than a cup of tea. She needed a hot toddy—a stiff drink to help her sleep.

As he poured a splash of whiskey into the teacup, the pot began to whistle gently. He started back into the kitchen before pausing and pouring in a second shot of the liquor. Adding the tea, he hurried back upstairs, delicately balancing the full cup.

Veronica was curled beneath the blankets, still sobbing silently into the pillow. He sat on the edge of the bed.

"Drink this," he offered. "It'll help."

She shook her head, but he was insistent. He helped her sit upright before handing her the teacup. She took a sip and immediately coughed.

"This is awful."

"It's strong, to be sure," Simon replied. "Drink it nonetheless. What you need right now is sleep and, trust me, this will do just that."

She cringed as she took another drink, this one more solid than the last. Suppressing the cough that threatened, she tipped the teacup backward and drank the remainder of the hot toddy, all at once. Grimacing, she handed him back the teacup and lay back down in bed. Simon covered her once more and caressed her hair. He sat beside her, stroking her face until her tears dried and she fell asleep.

When he was certain she wouldn't awaken, he stood and quietly walked from the bedroom. He walked downstairs, avoiding the steps he knew creaked, and paused when he reached the foyer. Simon glanced over his shoulder, listening intently for any sound of her awakening or moving. When he heard nothing, he opened the front door and walked back into the warm daylight.

Closing the door behind him, ensuring it didn't slam, he hurried down the steps and to the sidewalk. A short walk later, the Inquisitor was climbing the steps to Luthor and Mattie's shared townhouse. He knocked loudly, pausing only when he saw a shadow fall though the door's window.

Luthor opened the door and stared at his friend. "Sir? Forgive my surprise; I just wasn't expecting you today."

Simon raised his chin and took a deep breath. "I need your assistance, Luthor."

"Is anything the matter?" the apothecary asked. "You seem rather distraught."

Mattie stepped into the foyer, curious about the exchange. She smiled at Simon, but her smile quickly faded. She wrinkled her nose as she sniffed the air, and her brow furrowed in concern.

"You reek of death," she said in concern.

Luthor glanced quickly between the two. "Who has died, sir?"

"If you would be so kind as to invite me inside, I'll gladly tell you everything."

Luthor stepped aside, and the Inquisitor hurried within.

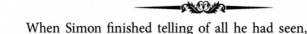

When Simon finished telling of all he had seen, Luthor and Mattie sat in stunned silence. Simon nodded, expecting nothing less, and walked calmly to the liquor rack. He poured himself a scotch and took a long draw, sighing as the liquid burned down his throat.

"Are you sure it was murder?" Luthor asked.

"Nothing that I can confirm," Simon replied as he took another drink. "Mere speculation, but speculation supported by observation. Doctor Casan was nervous when I was querying about her death."

"I can't imagine how Veronica must feel," Luthor said solemnly.

"It's a brutal feeling," Mattie said quietly. "It's a feeling that you have been impaled through your chest. There is no way to lie that doesn't cause your body to hurt in some way or another."

The two men turned toward her. She looked up at them, not with sadness but with brazen determination. "Losing those you know and love, as my tribe did so often while in the thrall of Gideon Dosett, is pain, but pain eventually fades and life returns to a semblance of normality."

Luthor nodded. "You just don't think murder will happen to those you know, not in the heart of Callifax."

Mattie furrowed her brow. "This is hardly the first murder in your city. Your newspapers reported a string of murders recently."

"How many?" Simon asked, intrigued.

Mattie shrugged. "I couldn't say. The newspaper was painfully vague, only reporting that a lady of the night had been murdered three nights ago, that the victims had all been ladies of questionable morals."

"Gloria was not a woman of loose morals," Simon sternly replied.

"Nor was I insinuating she was," Mattie countered, "but she went missing while returning home late at night, was she not?"

The Inquisitor and the fiery-haired woman stared sternly at one another. Luthor cleared his throat, hoping to cut through the tension in the air. "What can we do to help, sir?"

Simon turned toward the apothecary. "I need the Solomon's Way mortician's—a Dr. Casan's—death reports." Simon paused and stroked his chin. "On second thought, if there have been multiple murders, I'll need everything the constabulary may have on their deaths. Clearly, they think they're connected, but they're perusing the facts without the discerning eye of a Royal Inquisitor."

"I can go by the Solomon's Way station tomorrow in the afternoon," Luthor said. "If you have the official request sent over tonight or even in the morning, so that the reports will be waiting, it shouldn't be too much out of my time or way."

Simon frowned. He stared at Luthor, all the while biting the inside of his lip. Luthor noted the Inquisitor's hesitation and frowned as well.

"There won't be an official request from the Royal Inquisitors, will there, sir?"

"It's not entirely an official Inquisitor investigation," Simon hedged.

"And the constabulary has no prior knowledge that you want these reports?"

"I may not have vocalized my needs as such, no."

"Then what, exactly, do you intend an apothecary and werewolf to do, sir?"

Simon shrugged. "If I knew exactly, I wouldn't have need of your expertise, would I?"

"They won't give them willingly," Luthor reminded Simon.

"Nor should they, if the constables are worth their salt."

Luthor frowned, aware that his point was lost on the Inquisitor. "What I mean to say, sir, is the constabulary won't provide them, which leaves us taking them of our own volition, which, unless I'm sadly mistaken, is greatly frowned upon. Stealing in general is hardly acceptable but stealing directly from the constables… well, it seems they'd be rather unforgiving on the subject."

"Then be creative, my dear chap." Simon frowned and stopped pacing. "On second thought, they do seem rather inflexible."

"That seems a bit ironic coming from you."

"Whatever do you mean?"

Luthor chuckled. "You're not exactly known for your flexibility. Need I remind you that you once shot a man simply because he wasn't listening to you?"

Simon furrowed his brow. "When?"

"Walker's Bay."

The Inquisitor waved his hand dismissively. "I told that man repeatedly not to move. He chose to disregard my commands."

"He was reaching for a handkerchief."

"It could have been a gun. How was I to know?"

"The man was suffering from terrible allergies."

Simon waved his hand dismissively again as he walked toward the liquor cabinet. "I'm sure you'll think of something. It's why you're paid so well."

"We have very differing definitions of 'well paid', sir."

"And you, Simon?" Mattie asked. "What shall you be doing during all this burglary and subterfuge?"

"I'll be tending to Veronica, of course," Simon replied with an arched eyebrow. He dropped an ice cube into his glass before returning to his friends. "The woman is clearly distraught and in need of compassion. When you return, I'll set to work at once divining the true criminal. Once I've solved the crime, which I can't imagine taking longer than a few days, everyone's minds will be, once again, set at ease."

Luthor and Mattie both frowned as they exchanged glances, certain that they were not receiving the better end of the deal.

CHAPTER

Ten

VERONICA TOSSED AND TURNED THROUGHOUT THE
night. Simon woke up repeatedly to muffled sobs as she cried into
her pillow. He wanted to hold her tighter, but there was little he
could do that hadn't already been done. Instead, he resolved to get less
sleep throughout the long night, instead taking the time to caress her arm
or rub her back until she fell back into a restless sleep.

By the time the sun rose the next morning, Simon was exhausted
but was able to slip out of bed while Veronica slept fitfully for the first
time in hours. Spending the night alone with his thoughts, he finally understood Luthor's frustrations. Stealing from the constables wouldn't be
easy, especially for someone as morally upright as Luthor. An official request from the Royal Inquisitors would go a long way toward assisting in
his mission. Simon was committed to visiting the Solomon's Way station
early that morning, hopefully quickly enough that he would be home
before Veronica awoke. Detective Sugden may not accept Simon's word
that the request for the files was official, but he had to at the very least try.

He took his clothes and dressed in the bathroom, ensuring that he
made as little noise as possible. When he looked at himself in the mirror,
he frowned at the gentle bruising beneath his eyes and his haggard ap-

pearance. He splashed cold water on his face, helping him wake and removing some of the flush from his face. An application of shaving cream and a straight razor left him fresh-faced and gave him a more youthful appearance. Finally, wax fixed his hair and moustache, smoothing both into place and giving him at least a semblance of being put together.

Fixing his tie, he knew that he had done all he could. He strode down the stairs, again avoiding the creaking steps, and walked into the parlor. His gaze fell on the liquor cabinet, and he considered fixing himself a drink. His task at hand wasn't one that excited him. Dealings between the constables and the Inquisitors were always, at best, strained. Sugden would take every opportunity to remind him that the Inquisitors had come to him for assistance and not the other way around. Moreover, Simon hated being emotionally attached to an investigation. Normally, his only emotions during an assignment were irritation at those around him or anger at personal attacks. Compassion, empathy, and sympathy clouded his judgment; all three of which would be present while investigating Gloria's murder.

He forewent the alcohol, instead pouring himself a glass of water. It wasn't nearly as refreshing and did little to calm his nerves. As he set his glass in the sink and turned toward the foyer, there was a loud knock at the door.

Simon cringed and glanced nervously above him. He didn't hear Veronica stirring, nor were any footsteps heard upon the upstairs landing. The Inquisitor hurried toward the door, hoping to intercept the visitor before another knock was warranted. Sadly, he fell short. The visitor knocked again, louder and more prolonged than the first. Simon scowled, at both the noise and the silhouette he could see through the refractive glass set in the door. The visitor's hand was reaching toward the cloth rope dangling beside the doorframe, one that would sound a most annoying bell throughout the house.

Grasping the door handle, Simon threw open the door, to the surprise of the messenger standing on his front landing. The man's hand froze on the cord as Simon grasped his wrist.

"Pull that rope and I swear you will lose that hand," Simon threatened.

The young man, who could be no more than eighteen, blanched at the sight of the angry Inquisitor.

Simon waited a second for the messenger to say something, but the young man appeared to be in shock. "Why are you here? Out with it, boy."

The young man let go of the rope and Simon, in turn, let go of his wrist. The messenger cleared his throat. "Your presence has been requested by the king. I'm here to escort you to the castle... sir."

Simon furrowed his brow as the young man stepped aside and gestured toward an awaiting automobile, idling in front of his house. A valet was standing beside the back door, which was open. In the darkness of the car, Simon could see a robed figure, sitting opposite the backseat. Simon glanced at the boy, who seemed to have nothing else to add to his proclamation.

"This way, if you please, sir," the valet called from the end of Simon's sidewalk.

Hesitating would do Simon no good. If the request for his presence truly was from the crown, his only option was to move with all haste toward the castle. Simon's mouth suddenly felt dry. Had the boy said that the king had requested his presence? Had he done anything wrong, especially something that might draw the ire of the throne of Ocker?

His previous mission forgotten, Simon leaned into the foyer and retrieved his top hat from where it had been hung on the coat rack the night before. He wondered whether it would be better to leave his pistol behind as well, though he hardly had time to go back inside and properly change. With a final glance toward the stairwell, he hoped he'd be finished and home before Veronica awoke, though that possibility was looking slim.

Closing the door softly behind him, Simon hurried down the stairs and to the black car. The valet stepped aside, granting him access to the interior. Slipping inside, Simon took his place on the backseat, facing the driver. There was a second seat in the rear of the long car, this once facing Simon. Sitting upon it, dressed in his gold-embossed robes, was the Grand Inquisitor.

Simon froze, sure now more than ever that he was in trouble. Why else would the Grand Inquisitor be accompanying him to the castle?

"Sir?" Simon asked.

"You may relax, Simon," the Grand Inquisitor told him. "Your presence has been requested because you're being honored by King Godwin. Apparently, words of your deeds and the victories you've made against the mystical forces have reached his ears."

Simon sighed. "Well, that's certainly a relief. I was certain we were driving toward a hangman's noose."

"Not at all, unless we're both to be hanged this day."

As the car pulled away from the curb and rumbled along the rough street, Simon's gaze drifted out the window. The Grand Inquisitor seemed content to ride in silence, which suited Simon fine. As he had seen when last he drove these very streets, Simon watched the Callifax Abbey drift by the window, its massive, pointed structure looming over the nearby buildings. The car turned before the Grand Hall, its white marble dome glistening in the early morning sun. Beyond the Hall, however, Simon was far less familiar with this part of the city. A hill rose sharply to his left, atop which was the castle. Its many turrets and tall stone walls overlooked the Upper Reaches.

It wouldn't be long before they stopped at the lower gate, a two-story guard tower, complete with heavy, wooden doors and iron portcullis. Long before they reached their turn, however, they stopped amidst a web of traffic. Closer to the castle proper, there were far more cars, all of which were forced to a stop as vehicles attempted to merge through the busy road.

Knowing he would have few other opportunities to engage the Grand Inquisitor without other distractions, Simon looked away from his window and glanced toward his mentor.

"Sir, if I may?" Simon asked.

The Grand Inquisitor opened his eyes and arched his eyebrows. Though he didn't say anything, Simon presumed that was his acknowledgment.

"Have you made a decision about…?" Simon paused, glancing through the small window separating the rear of the car from the driver.

The Grand Inquisitor glanced over his shoulder before turning back to Simon. He gestured for Simon to continue.

"Miss Hawke is eager to hear if you've thought more about her predicament?" Simon asked, trying to remain as vague as possible.

The Grand Inquisitor frowned at the question. Simon knew he'd struck a point of contention, one that his mentor would rather not address at this time. Despite the man's obvious discomfort, the Grand Inquisitor shook his head.

"Forgive me, Simon, but I haven't yet. There has been much on my plate since last we spoke, and issues like your wayward friend have fallen to the wayside."

It was Simon's turn to frown. He leaned forward so that his elbows rested on his knees. "Sir, she begs me daily for an answer, and I find it hard to be reproachful and tell her to be patient. She endured Whitten Hall, knowing it was a chance for you to consider her situation in private."

The elder statesman glanced out the window to the pedestrians walking past their stalled vehicle. "Are you familiar with what is transpiring on the southern continent, throughout the Kingdom of Kohvus?"

"The Kohvelian Knights are fighting against a magical army that emerged from the Rift," Simon remarked. "It's been well publicized."

"Indeed it has," the Grand Inquisitor said with a sigh, still looking out his window. "I assume you are also familiar with the reputation of the Knights?"

Simon shrugged. "Luddites, mostly, but more than capable warriors. The Kohvelian Knights, if rumors are to be believed, have never been defeated in combat, their swords and shield defeating even more technologically advanced armies."

"It's more than rumor, Inquisitor. The Kohvelian Knights are a bastion of warrior spirit, undefeated in combat, and the true first and last line of defense against the invading forces of the Rift."

"Yet, despite that acknowledgment, you still seem troubled, sir."

The older man turned toward Simon with worried creases across his forehead. "The Kohvelian Knights have failed. King Artiland is dead and his son assumed the mantle of leadership. The forces of the Shadow Lord crushed the Knights on their own lands, driving those that survived—which, if the intelligence escaping the wanton destruction is to be believed, wasn't many—to the coast."

Simon wasn't sure how to feel. He felt nearly nothing for the dead knights, having known little of them besides rumors and reputation, no matter how truthful. However, their defeat meant terrible things for Ocker. For years, the Inquisitors had protected the kingdom's interior while the crown's privateers protected its borders from incursions. Their missions had been light due, in large part, to the defenses of Kohvus. With the Knights defeated, there would be little to stop the army of the Rift from marching toward the northern continent.

"The leadership of the Knights has taken refuge in the Golden Isles, a chain of islands off the western coast of Kohvus, though their numbers are far too few."

"What can be done?" Simon asked.

The Grand Inquisitor shook his head. "We can do nothing for them, not now. The nobles are suing for peace."

"With the monsters?" Simon incredulously asked. He found it hard to believe that anyone would broker a peace with the monstrosities from the Rift.

"What choice do they have?" the elder man asked, stroking his beard. "Their forces are destroyed or scattered. Their ancestral home was overrun. They have only the smallest of contingents of Knights with them in the Golden Isles, but our spies tell us that the nobles fight as often with one another as they do the enemy. Kohvus is lost."

Simon leaned back heavily in the uncomfortable backseat. "There will be more incursions, of course. The monsters of the Rift will push north at their earliest convenience."

"Of course. They'll move west as well, toward the Caliphate and south into Vox. Unchecked, they intend to conquer the world. As we speak, the king is meeting with the privateers, telling them of the need for increased vigilance."

The Inquisitor rubbed his forehead. It was all too much to process. He had chosen a life as a Royal Inquisitor for its simplicity – find a monster and destroy it – and the fact that it catered to his unique skill set. Global strategy was far beyond his abilities or, frankly, his interest.

"With so much happening to our neighboring kingdoms, for what reason does the king want to see me?"

The Grand Inquisitor smiled. "We shall see when we arrive."

The car lurched as the traffic began to move. The vehicle rumbled along the road, slowly passing the nearby businesses and great meeting halls of the different guilds and factions within Callifax. Eventually, the car turned and rolled to a stop before a towering gate. Armed sentinels emblazoned with uniforms of red and gold, stood guard. Though Simon couldn't see the tops of the nearby towers, he could practically feel the devastating cannons and plethora of rifles targeting their automobile.

A guard approached, and the driver lowered his window.

"State your business."

The driver retrieved an envelope from the seat beside him. As he lifted it, Simon noted the broken red seal on the back of the parchment, the royal oak leaf and shield of Ocker. The guard unfurled the note and read it quickly before returning it to the driver. With a wave from the guard, other red-and-gold clad guards hurriedly opened the gargantuan wooden doors, revealing a steep and winding road that led in a series of switchbacks toward the castle's main gate.

Though absurd to drive, Simon respected the design of the winding trails. Nothing other than men on foot could traverse straight up the side of the steep hill, leaving carts, vehicles, and pack animals to maneuver the troublesome road, during which the castle defenses would rain death down upon the invaders. It was simple, yet ingenious, though Simon quickly tired of the crawling pace the car had to maintain to properly make the turns.

Eventually, they passed beneath a vaulted entryway, the paved road turning to large cobblestones, artifacts from an ancient time before the world of modern technology. The car rocked unsteadily as it rolled through the deep ravines worn between the pavers and came to a rest in a parking spot designated by the guards nearby.

The driver quickly exited the vehicle, once again showing the royal invitation to the guards, before opening the rear door. The Grand Inquisitor exited first. Simon was sliding toward the door when he paused and reached beneath his coat. As discreetly as possible, he removed the pistol concealed within and placed it underneath his seat, hoping it was out of view. On his first visit to the king, he preferred not to initiate an incident between him and the guards.

They were led through the inner courtyard to the base of a two-story building resting at the heart of the castle. The stonework was far older than the rest of the city, a strange dichotomy between the modern marvels of the city below and the ancient stronghold overseeing it all. It had the same gray, weathered appearance as the Callifax Abbey, as though the two structures were the only staunch remainders of a time long past.

Stained glass windows lined the sides of the building, recent additions after the removal of the narrow arrow slits that had once decorated the structure. As their group climbed the stairs leading into the royal chambers, Simon drank in the sight of the broad, ornately carved doors marking the grand entryway. Motifs of fairy tales—of knights on horseback fighting against fire-breathing dragons while helpless princesses cowered in the monster's homes—were carved into the door. He frowned at the sight. Years ago, when the doors were first carved, he would have assumed they were carved reliefs of nothing more than children's stories. Knowing now that there was a basis of truth to every tale he'd ever heard, he wondered if the original artists knew far more than even the kings of old realized.

As the doors opened at their approach, Simon walked from the stone stairwell into the cool, tiled interior. Electric lights burned in sconces along the walls, illuminating the intricate paintings that hung upon the wooden paneled walls. Statues in varying sizes, from busts to larger-than-life men, rested in nearly every visible corner. The entryway, for that was all this was in such a grandiose structure, properly portrayed the wealth and decadence enjoyed by the King of Ocker.

A second set of great doors stood closed before them. Their guide led them to the side of the doors and whispered quietly as he spoke. Even so, his voice echoed around the chamber.

"His Highness is currently in chambers. We will wait here until summoned, if you please. The chamber is yours to explore as you see fit, but you will need to return at all haste once his current meeting has concluded."

The two Inquisitors nodded before turning away from the doors. They could have walked together, but Simon opted to explore the room alone. A few other doors led from the wide entryway, but they were closed and Simon's curiosity was already well sated just by his arrival. Instead, he examined the paintings. They were portraits of previous Kings of Ocker, each in a regal pose with a crown, heavily laden with assorted gems, resting upon his head. Starting from the far left, which was the most faded and therefore the oldest, Simon examined each in turn, reading the small plaques beneath telling the name and dates they ruled. For as long as Ocker had been a nation, named for Ocker Godwin the Wise nearly eight hundred years before, there had always been a Godwin upon the throne. Theodore Godwin the Brave, who slew the barbarian hordes from the frozen west, stemming from lands that would later be renamed Haversham. Samuel Godwin the Divine, who destroyed the pirate armada in the Battle of Persher, nearly two hundred years ago. Simon frowned. It seemed the Godwins had a history of violence.

Near the far right of the chamber, he found names that were far more familiar. Rogan Godwin the Pious, one of the only kings who wasn't known for the wanton destruction of his enemies. King Rogan had wide eyes that were slightly too close together and a hooked nose. He looked surprised in his painting, as though he had heard unfortunate news just before the artist arrived. The Inquisitor knew it was far more likely that the man suffered from generations of noble inbreeding, but the result was a comical expression.

Simon smirked at the next painting. The genetic features—specifically eyes that were far too close together—were still present, but King Yolland Godwin also suffered from a weak chin. Though shadows had been added beneath the chin to give the illusion of a jutting, proud expression, it was clear that the shadows were added after the fact.

The last two paintings left Simon with mixed emotions. The second to last was Bruce Godwin, known only as the Vile. He was a short-lived king who had been dethroned shortly after the appearance of the Rift. He had been violent and cruel, though his laws of isolationism still held through the rein of his son Uriah, who currently sat upon the throne. Simon scowled at the painting of the inbred but ruthless despot, who had been responsible, though indirectly, for Simon's arrest roughly ten years prior.

It had been Uriah who usurped his father in a bloodless coup; bloodless, Simon reminded himself, except for Bruce himself, who lost his head in the process. He hadn't been sad to see the Vile King gone, and Uriah's actions had immediately endeared him to the Inquisitor. Though the painting still showed the effects of long-term genetics on a very small gene pool, Uriah appeared kind in his portrait.

A creaking of the doors opening startled Simon, and he turned abruptly as the throne room doors swung wide. He hurried back toward the Grand Inquisitor, who remained patiently beside the archway.

A series of privateer captains exited the throne room, talking in hushed tones amongst themselves. They appeared dashing in their royal navy uniforms, red jackets with white lapels and cuffs and golden epaulets upon their shoulders. Most wore the blue sashes, upon which assortments of medals had been pinned. Simon knew little of their meaning, other than that he assumed they had been issued for defense of the kingdom.

Near the rear of the group, as Simon waited for them all to pass, a familiar face caught his eye. The tall, bald man towered over the privateer captain with whom he spoke. Raised scars, forming pattern-like tattoos, marred his nearly black skin, protruding from underneath his collar and creeping up the back of his head. He spoke casually with the other captains, smiling broadly as he revealed pearly white teeth.

Simon revealed his teeth as well, though in a snarl of disdain. The Grand Inquisitor noticed his markedly different posture at nearly the same moment as the captain. The dark-skinned man excused himself from the other captains and approached.

"Simon Whitlock, as I live and breathe," the captain said, his chest loaded with medals.

He approached as though expecting a familiar hug, but Simon's expression stopped him cold. "Javin Dane," Simon remarked. "You've come a long way for a pirate."

"Privateer now," Captain Dane corrected, tapping the epaulets on his shoulders. "I'm amazed, Simon. You've hardly changed in the past ten years. Have you found a fountain of youth?"

Simon took a deep breath, calming himself. "No, Javin, I've found an outlet for my frustrations."

"Yes?" the captain asked inquisitively.

"I find that every time I get too terribly upset with someone, I merely shoot them. That way, I ensure I don't surround myself with too much negativity."

The captain's smile faltered for a moment, and the Grand Inquisitor took Simon by the arm. "We have a meeting with the king. We must be off." The older man turned toward Javin. "Forgive our abrupt departure, Captain."

"Think nothing of it, Grand Inquisitor. Do take care, Simon. I hope to see you again soon."

"No," Simon corrected. "No, you don't."

As Captain Dane hurried away to catch up to the rest of his cohorts, Simon turned and followed the Grand Inquisitor.

"Is that the same man with whom you once—" his mentor began to ask.

Simon nodded, stopping the Grand Inquisitor from finishing his sentence. Wordlessly, they followed their guide into the throne room.

CHAPTER

Eleven

WIDE PILLARS ROSE TOWARD THE VAULTED CEILING overhead. They walked along an intricate red-and-gold rug, but their footsteps still echoed throughout the chamber. Simon turned his head, glancing left and right, following the raised walkway that ran the perimeter of the rounded room. Small hallways exited from the cushioned walkway, disappearing deeper into the labyrinth of passages and rooms that lay buried in the heart of the castle.

Light flooded into the room through hundreds of small windows covering the walls. It poured in long beams, making the far end of the chamber hard to see. Simon could see a raised dais and the outline of the throne resting atop it, but he could make out little of the details.

The rays of light left the room abnormally warm. Simon could feel sweat beading on his brow, though he wasn't sure if it was from the heat or his nervousness. The Grand Inquisitor had been intentionally vague in discussing their meeting, though he didn't seem quite as nervous as Simon did. That did little to set the Inquisitor's mind at ease, however.

As they passed through more of the light, persistently following their guide, the details of the throne grew more pronounced. The gilded gold chair rose taller than a man, its trim inlaid with gemstones of assorted sizes. The gold of the chair itself changed abruptly into red velvet cushions sewn into its back. As they grew closer, Simon could see the man upon the throne.

King Uriah Godwin was small in stature and, in many ways, reminded Simon of Luthor. He lacked an impressive physical demeanor and being in his presence, aside from his position as ruler of Ocker, hardly left Simon feeling intimidated. He had the same narrow, wide eyes and weak chin of his ancestors. The king had a full head of hair, as far as Simon could discern, though much of it was concealed beneath a heavy crown. He carried a hooknose that left him unattractive, but he wore a kind expression, one that immediately put Simon at ease.

"Your Highness," the guide announced in a voice that echoed around the chamber, "I present to you Grand Inquisitor Ulster Highworth and Royal Inquisitor Simon Whitlock."

The three men bowed deeply, as was the custom, their eyes cast upon the floor. They knew not to rise until the king bade them. For a long moment, Simon wondered if he ever would, though he didn't know the king's custom.

"Rise, please," the king replied, his voice far stronger and deeper than Simon would have believed from such a diminutive man.

The three men stood once more and looked upon King Godwin. The king adjusted his crown, which seemed a touch too large for his frame. Simon realized the man carried a golden scepter in his hand, which he fiddled with absently as he spoke to the Inquisitors.

"You're dismissed," the king said to their guide.

The guide bowed deeply once more before retreating. He hurried from the room, closing the door behind him. Once the guide was gone, the king turned his attention toward the two men.

"Thank you for responding to my summons," the king said, his voice not nearly as stern once the guide was gone. "I know the work of Royal Inquisitors, especially those as renowned as the two of you, must keep you busy."

"Think nothing of it, your Highness," the Grand Inquisitor replied. "We live to serve."

The king waved his hand at the older man's remark. "There is no need for such formality. I didn't call you here to praise me. I have more than enough men in my retinue to do such things. You two serve a far more important role to the kingdom. In fact, I had the stuffiness removed from this very chamber because it was far too intimidating to those holding court. Large suits of iron armor, heavy and cumbersome, used to line the catwalk. I think it looks far more approachable without it."

Standing, he walked down the few steps until he was on the same level with the Inquisitors. Simon realized that, with his hat, he towered over the small king. Closer and out of the glaring light, Simon noticed that despite his abnormal facial features, the king looked very young, far younger than Simon himself. He didn't know exactly how old King Uriah had been when he ascended to the throne, but the years had left him young.

"Royal Inquisitor Whitlock. You've done many great services for the crown. The Grand Inquisitor has told me of your exploits against the werewolves, and most recently against vampires. You've even slain a demon. No small challenge, I'm sure."

Simon cleared his throat. "My thanks to you, Your Highness. I was merely doing my duty to the crown."

"That is exactly why I've called you here. I presume the Grand Inquisitor has told you of the troubles to the south?"

Simon glanced cautiously toward his mentor, but the older man merely nodded.

"Yes, your Highness. He's informed me that the Kingdom of Kohvus has fallen to the army of the Rift."

The king turned away and paced his chamber. "Yes, the army of the Rift. My spies inform me it's led by a single dark figure, a lord of shadows, if you will. His very description made me think of the demon you slew, not its physicality, mind you, but his ability to command great forces."

"You believe it to be another demon?" the Inquisitor asked.

"I do," the king said quietly. "Can you imagine if another demon has escaped the Rift? How many more could have followed suit, infecting the lands? Without the Kohvelian Knights to retard their conquest, I fear we may be seeing a flood of abominations attempting to enter our lands."

King Uriah turned and walked back to the two men. "That is why I've called you here. Grand Inquisitor Highworth has served the crown admirably these past ten years, but he grows older, though still spry, I'm led to believe."

The Grand Inquisitor bowed slightly. "Your Highness flatters me."

"Someday, he will need a successor. After much deliberation between the Grand Inquisitor and after hearing of your numerous exploits, we believe you to be that man."

Simon was dumbfounded. He didn't know quite how to respond. Of all the reasons to be called to the throne room, being granted the mantle of leadership for the Royal Inquisitors hadn't made his list.

"I'm... well, I'm honored, of course, Your Highness," he stammered.

The king smiled. "Well, you can't very well have it until the current Grand Inquisitor retires, of course. You'll have to wait your turn."

"Of course. I never meant—"

"This will be a great opportunity for you to learn from him," the king continued, and Simon realized he would be better suited remaining silent. "Your duties from this point forward will be solely at the Grand Inquisitor's side, learning the nuances of leadership and the more businesslike components of leading my Royal Inquisitors. It's surprisingly complex but due to the Grand Inquisitor's professionalism, virtually invisible to the naked eye. Let's not forget," he said, glancing at the elder statesman and winking, "that the duties also include managing relationships with the Order of Kinder Pel."

Simon frowned for a number of reasons. The mention of the Order of Kinder Pel left an ache in his chest. The counterpoint to his sect of Royal Inquisitors, the Order served the crown with the same responsibilities, yet far differing means to reach the same ends. Whereas the Inquisitors were a surgeon's scalpel, investigating magical outbreaks and removing them where necessary, the Pellites were a mallet, indifferent to the collateral damage they caused.

His true displeasure, however, came from the mention of staying close by the Grand Inquisitor's side. He was a field investigator and, was he to be honest with himself, one of the best. He and Luthor had solved a number of cases, and though many turned out to be charlatans or tomfoolery, they were effectively and efficiently handled. Leaving the field to become a permanent fixture at the Grand Hall was, frankly, depressing.

He wanted to voice his dissent but knew better. The king had spoken and his word was law. Instead, he bowed deeply. "Thank you, Your Highness."

The king smiled warmly. "I will be keeping my eye on you, Inquisitor Whitlock. I expect great things from you in the future."

Simon and the Grand Inquisitor noted the change in the king's tone, signifying the end of their conversation. King Uriah immediately turned and walked back up the steps to his throne, where he sat. As though on cue, the throne room doors behind them opened and their guide reappeared. Simon and his mentor both bowed deeply before excusing themselves from the grand room. As they passed beyond the throne room, the doors quickly shut behind them. Their guide bowed to them both before vanishing through a side door, leaving both men alone in the castle's atrium.

They walked toward the front doors, which were pulled open for them by guards. Through the open portal, they could see their car already pulled around, the back door open, awaiting their return. The two men hurried inside and took their customary seats before the driver pulled away from the curb.

Neither man spoke until they were beyond the guard tower and back onto the main roads of Callifax.

"This is a great honor, I hope you realize that," the Grand Inquisitor said.

Simon nodded, though he already wondered how he'd break the news to Luthor and Mattie. The apothecary was only allowed on missions because of his working relationship with Simon. Without it, Luthor would return to a much more mundane life of a city apothecary, filling prescriptions and treating the typical maladies. It was for Matilda that Simon had far more concern. She was a werewolf, a secret that he, Luthor, and the Grand Inquisitor seemed keen to keep. Her presence in the city was on behalf of her people, as she sought to keep them safe against the Inquisitors themselves. He shivered at the thought of what would happen without his protection.

"I'm well aware that this isn't the life you would have chosen for yourself. I apologize that I couldn't have given you a better warning prior to our arrival at the castle. Frankly, I thought you'd be flattered."

"I am." Simon sighed, though that was mostly a lie. "I just worry about my friends and their ongoing... predicament."

The Grand Inquisitor nodded. "I understand, and I promise you an answer before the week is out."

Their car rolled to a stop before Simon's townhouse. The Inquisitor retrieved his top hat from the seat beside him and his pistol from underneath before nodding to the Grand Inquisitor.

"Take the next week to set your affairs in order," the older man said. "After that, come to the Grand Hall and we shall discuss our way ahead."

"Very good, sir," Simon morosely said.

He slipped from the car and climbed the steps. His mind was awhirl with the events that had transpired, so much so that he was nearly to his door before he noticed it slightly ajar. Instinctively, his hand fell to his waist and he slid his silver revolver from its holster.

The door opened quietly; it was well oiled for just such a purpose. The foyer was dark, but he could see lights pouring from the sitting room and the kitchen beyond. There were voices, muffled but audible, coming from the far rooms. Simon stepped into the study, noting the teacups setting on the table and a thick pile of folders resting on one of the empty chairs.

Luthor stepped around the corner of the kitchen and nearly dropped the teapot in his hand, as he noticed Simon and his threatening weapon. He let out a faint yelp, which caused Mattie to rush to his side, teeth bared. Both his companions relaxed as they realized who it was.

Simon sighed and lowered his pistol, slipping it back into its holster. "I nearly shot you both, I hope you realize."

"Oh, trust us, we realize," Luthor said breathlessly.

"The door was ajar and..." Simon said in a mumbled form of apology.

"That would be my fault," Mattie said. "We had such exciting news that we figured it best to wait for you at your home, rather than try to catch you upon your return."

Simon furrowed his brow, wondering what news they could be bringing. He suddenly remembered the mission he had sent them on, searching out case files for Gloria's death, along with any other similar cases the constabulary might be investigating.

"You acquired the files?" he asked excitedly and, he admitted to himself, a little surprised.

"We didn't have to," Luthor admitted. He stepped aside, revealing a tall man leaning against a countertop in the kitchen. "The files actually came to us."

Doctor Youke Casan stood and walked to Luthor's side, blushing slightly.

CHAPTER

Twelve

"**W**HY ARE YOU HERE, DOCTOR?" SIMON ASKED, PER-
plexed.

Doctor Casan walked past Simon and collected the stack of
files resting on the chair. Lifting the topmost, he laid it on the table and
opened it. Within, a grainy photo of Gloria—her skin pale and waxy—
stared up at him. Intrigued, the Inquisitor walked to the sofa opposite
the doctor and sat.

"You were right, of course," Casan said. "I was forbidden from men-
tioning it while the detective was present, but your friend was murdered."

Simon glanced over his shoulder toward the stairwell. Luthor sat
across from Simon and shook his head. "Don't worry, sir, she's not upstairs. Miss Dawn went out for a walk shortly after our arrival. It was
actually she that let us in."

Frowning, the Inquisitor turned back toward his friends, even as
Mattie sat on the couch beside him. "You let her leave? You know that
she's not well."

"Should we have restrained her?" Mattie asked.

Simon paused before shaking his head. "No, of course not. Forgive
us, Doctor. Let's return to the issue at hand. How can you be sure Gloria

was murdered?"

Casan glanced nervously between the two men before his gaze settled on Mattie. "Perhaps this is a topic better discussed somewhere where a lady isn't present?"

Luthor laughed, but Mattie replied before he could. "If you think I'm that sort of a lady, then it merely proves you know nothing about me."

"She's quite correct," Simon confirmed. "I dare say she has a better constitution for such discussions than even Luthor or I."

The doctor ran a hand over his short-cropped hair before nodding. Standing abruptly, he walked to the window that overlooked the street below. He quickly pulled the curtains, blocking the view either in or out of the townhouse. "Forgive me," he said as he returned to the armchair, "but what I'm showing you isn't entirely legal. I could lose my job or worse if Detective Sugden discovered my whereabouts."

"Have no fear," Simon replied. "You have our complete discretion."

Casan cleared his throat. "I confirmed your friend's death was a murder at the scene, even before conducting my autopsy. Your friend's leg was…" He glanced awkwardly once more toward Mattie, who met his uncertain gaze with a stern one of her own. "Her leg was amputated just below the hip."

Despite being told that Veronica was on a walk, Simon still glanced cautiously toward the front door before their conversation continued. "Could it have been post-mortem?"

"She died of extreme blood loss," Casan said, shaking his head. "The incision and amputation was done while she was still awake and with surgical precision."

Mattie covered her mouth in surprise. Even Luthor blanched at the thought. Simon leaned back into the sofa and stared down at the pale-faced woman in the black-and-white photograph.

"Wouldn't she have screamed?" Mattie asked. "Wouldn't someone have heard her assault and come to her aid? Certainly Callifax isn't so callous a city that people would amble past so vicious and violent an attack."

Casan spread the photos, revealing a page of small, tight handwriting beneath. The words were printed so small that they were hardly legible but were written in nearly perfect straight lines across the yellowed page. From beneath it, Casan pulled another photograph, this one of the side of Gloria's neck. Despite the low quality of the photo, Simon could still see the tight blond curls splayed beside her head. Circled in red wax pencil in the middle of the photo, the doctor pointed to a slightly discolored dot on the page. Had he not drawn Simon's attention to it, the Inquisitor would have dismissed it as a blemish on the photograph's printing process.

"You can read my full autopsy if you so desire, but I've taken the liberty of answering many of your questions here and now. As you can see highlighted here on the photo, your friend—Gloria, if I may—had a puncture wound on the side of her neck, just below her left ear, a clear mark of a low-gauge needle, perhaps a syringe. Upon discovering the mark, I took it upon myself to run a full-spectrum analysis of her blood, at which time, I found large quantities of Curare in her system."

Simon sat upright and glanced toward Luthor, who seemed equally intrigued. "Curare, you say?"

The doctor nodded, though he seemed confused as to everyone's sudden interest. "You seem familiar with the drug. I had thought it a rare find."

"It is," Simon confirmed. "It's a very rare find indeed. I've only seen it in use once before, quite recently in fact."

"It paralyzes the muscles while—" the doctor began.

"While leaving the victim fully aware of their surroundings."

"That means she would have been aware of her mutilation," Mattie said breathlessly. "Even as she was bleeding to death, she would have known. How horrible."

Simon had to agree with her. He couldn't imagine a more horrid way to die than to be fully aware and cognizant of your brutal attack. However, the use of Curare had to be more than just a mere coincidence. Luthor may have become familiarized with the drug as a result of his apothecary studies, but it was hardly known to the general populace. It couldn't be mere coincidence that so rare a drug was used first by the mysterious troll cannibal and then by a murderer, with both events happening in Solomon's Way. Did Simon miss something by turning over the case to the constabulary rather than further investigating the troll and his hovel?

"Your autopsy is very thorough," Simon remarked as he pushed the file aside. "Top marks for your attention to detail."

Casan nodded as though expecting the compliment. "I pride myself on my work."

"This was not the only case, I presume," the Inquisitor said, pointing to the remaining files. At quick glance, there seemed to be over half a dozen more resting on the floor.

"No, you were quite correct about that as well." The doctor lifted the files and set them on the table between them. "Though the good detective is hesitant to link all these murders together—and rightfully so, as there are serious differences between the methodologies—I find too many similarities to simply ignore the potential connection."

"Let's start with the most recent," Simon said. "While we were in your morgue, Detective Sugden seemed to insinuate that there had been another murder shortly before Gloria's untimely demise."

Casan lifted the top file and set in before the Inquisitor. Flipping the file open, he pointed to the picture pinned to the inside flap. "There was, indeed, a murder nearly a week before your friend."

Despite the deathly pallor on the woman's face, he recognized her immediately. Simon had a remarkable knack for recalling faces and names and, though he only saw her for a moment, her face looked practically unchanged. His gaze drifted to the handwritten notes, where her name was printed across the top of the page.

"Abigail Traunt," he muttered.

"The woman attacked by the troll on the bridge?" Luthor asked.

"One and the same." Simon read the autopsy, and his frown deepened. "Killed no more than a day after her miraculous rescue. Also paralyzed by Curare, I see?"

"Very similar circumstances between the two deaths," Doctor Casan confirmed.

"Indeed, though it was her left arm that was removed in a similar fashion?" Simon asked.

"As I mentioned before, it was a very similar crime with comparable techniques employed but just slightly different facts. However, those two are the only ones in which you will find drastic similarities. Each lady was dismembered in some fashion, though the method of removal often varied, as did the method for subduing the woman."

"I read about these crimes in the newspaper," Mattie said. "It stated that they were all ladies of the night."

Simon frowned as he glanced at her, not eager to begin their heated debate once more.

82

"Believe me, madam, the actual crimes are far more violent than the newspapers would have you believe."

"They usually are," Simon remarked.

He opened the files one at a time and examined their contents. Doctor Casan was correct that the crimes were similar but with drastic differences as well. The earliest crimes were savage, often committed on women who weren't subdued so much as beaten to unconsciousness. The removal of limbs was actually ragged and coarse, not refined like the later crimes, often leaving torn sockets and loose sinew at the site of extraction. One of the crimes had no name associated, other than "Doe, Jane". The woman's head had been removed, and there had been no other method through which to identify the body.

"Save Gloria," Simon began, "they were all ladies of the night, attacked at late hours when there wouldn't be many witnesses roaming the streets of Solomon's Way. It appears almost that the crimes evolved as the killer's technique improved. Even the technique for subjugation changed, from physical violence to chloroform to Curare. What I don't understand is the count. Thus far, there have been three severed legs, four arms, and a head. For what purpose would someone need such a bizarre assortment of body parts?"

"I couldn't begin to surmise," Casan said as he glanced toward the others, inviting a differing opinion. Luthor and Mattie, however, remained silent.

"Is there at least continuity with the murder weapon?" Simon asked. He flipped through a couple of reports, skimming the doctor's atrocious handwriting.

"Weapons, plural," the doctor corrected. "Aside from the more garish rending of limbs in the first victims, the rest have been fairly congruent. One blade was used to sever flesh and sinew, a fairly long one and smooth on its edge. Once our killer reached bone, he switched to a serrated blade, one capable of cutting cleanly through. Based off the length and direction of the cuts, I would venture a guess that it was a bone saw, similar to one I would use during an autopsy."

"Then our killer has received medical training?" Luthor asked, adjusting his wire-frame glasses.

"Or, at the very least, has access to medical supplies," Casan confirmed.

Simon waved his hand dismissively. "That's hardly helpful. The medical profession and its related supplies aren't exactly held in high esteem. No offense, Doctor."

Casan seemed insulted but refrained from replying.

"The use of a bone saw doesn't make this case any clearer, though the techniques do lend itself toward a doctor of sorts, or a veterinarian at the very least. In a city of this size, though, that still leaves a vexingly large number of potential suspects. Vexing, indeed."

Simon stood and walked around the table, stopping at the liquor cabinet. "I find a drink clears my mind and helps me think. Would anyone else care for one?"

Luthor and Mattie politely shook their heads. "Doctor?" Simon asked.

"Forgive me for begging off, but no and thank you," Casan replied. "I don't partake."

Simon arched an eyebrow. "If you don't drink, then perhaps you have an affinity for the fairer sex? Do you frequent these dens of iniquity, the ones from which a fair number of our victims have originated?"

Casan blushed furiously but shook his head. "I most certainly do not."

"Every man has a vice," Simon explained as he finished pouring his drink. He walked back to the sofa and sat before the open files. "If a man claims to have none, there's no way I can properly trust him."

"The constables," the doctor said, pointing at the files and clearly trying to change the subject, "are as confused as you and me, Inquisitor."

"Well, of course they are," Simon remarked as he took a sip of his scotch. "What they gain in sheer numbers, they clearly lack in intellect and a discerning eye. In fact, your skills would clearly serve you well should you desire a position as a Royal Inquisitor."

"You flatter me, sir," Casan replied, "but my true passion has led me to where I am now, though I thank you for the offer."

Simon eyed the autopsy reports on the table before him and frowned as he absently swirled the brown liquor in his glass. "Do you, perchance, have any files or evidence pertaining to the crime scene?" the Inquisitor asked.

"Sadly no. I was only able to bring my personal reports. Detective Sugden is in direct control of the actual police reports."

Simon frowned deeper and returned his attention to the files. The crime scene reports, even written in a sub-par manner by the constabulary, would be greatly beneficial. After perusing a few more of the coroner's reports, one of the names listed gave him pause. He stared at it for a few moments before recognition spread across his face.

"Did you find something, sir?" Luthor asked, noting the familiar expression.

Simon quickly concealed his excitement and glanced apologetically toward the doctor. "Thank you very much for your assistance, Doctor, but I need to confer with my associates in private."

The doctor appeared stunned. He opened and closed his mouth a few times as he sought the words. "I don't understand. Have I offended you in some way?"

Simon shook his head. "Nothing of the sort; in fact, quite the opposite. You've been instrumental in starting our investigation. However, what transpires from here is solely in the realm of the Inquisitors, of which you are not. Good day to you, sir."

The Inquisitor stacked the folders neatly before handing them to the startled doctor. Casan stood hesitantly, clearly unused to being so readily dismissed. Luthor stood as well and ushered the man toward the door. Simon smiled at the sight; the diminutive apothecary leading the towering doctor toward the foyer. Doctor Casan stole another glance, his arms laden with folders, as Luthor opened the door and gently ushered him outside. As the door closed, Luthor sighed and turned back toward his friend.

"That was a bit callous," he said as he returned to his seat. "He was only trying to help."

"Help he did, most assuredly," Simon replied.

"Was Luthor right?" Mattie asked. "Did you note something?"

Simon smiled. "I did. One of the victims was Katheryn Harder-Schauer, a married woman from Solomon's Way who, until recently, worked at a bakery. She was hardly a woman of the night."

Luthor frowned, feeling as though Simon's great realization did little to advance the investigation. "Then we have no common thread tying the victims together. The crimes are, more or less, random."

"On the contrary, my dear apothecary, there is a most distinct pattern for those willing to see it. All the victims were young women between the ages of seventeen and thirty, attractively built and of remarkable beauty, lived or worked within Solomon's Way, and had occupations that kept them out until the wee hours of the morning."

"From what I've seen, you've just described a vast majority of the women within Solomon's Way," Mattie replied, "including, I might add, your own fiancée."

Simon paused, his hand half-raised, and took in a deep breath. He was about to reply when the door swung open and Veronica appeared in the foyer. The men quickly stood and Veronica, startled that everyone was present in Simon's sitting room, paused halfway through the doorway.

"Veronica." Simon sighed, genuinely glad to see her again. "Welcome back. I was worried when I returned and you were gone."

Veronica rubbed underneath her eyes, smoothing away the puffiness that resulted from her crying. Her eyes were red and swollen and her cheeks flushed. The half veil concealed much of the evidence of her tears, but it was still obvious on a simple observation that she was distraught.

"Forgive me," she said hoarsely. "I didn't realize everyone would still be here. I had just gone out for a walk, to get some fresh air."

Simon walked past the others and stepped into the foyer. "How are you, my love?"

She glanced over his shoulder, to where Luthor and Mattie watched them both. "I'm doing well," she replied, though Simon could sense she wasn't saying all that she wanted to. "If you'll excuse me, all the walking has left me tired. I think I'll go lay down upstairs."

"Of course," Simon replied. "My home is your home."

Veronica stopped as she was about to climb the stairs. "I think it would be better if I returned to my apartment, perhaps tonight. It would be unsightly for us to be living together before our wedding."

Simon furrowed his brow. "Are you certain? I didn't think you'd want to go back any time soon, what with the apartment being a constant reminder of... well..."

"I know very well what you mean, and I appreciate your consideration," Veronica said. "However, I have work and a life beyond just my time with you, Simon. It won't do for me to have to travel from the Upper Reaches to the Ace of Spades every night just to go to work."

"Of course, you're right," he replied.

She smiled softly and touched his cheek before turning and climbing the stairs. He watched her disappear onto the second-floor landing and waited for the click of the bedroom door to close before turning back toward his friends.

"She really is the spitting image of the victims' descriptions," he said as he returned to the sitting room. "If she's intent on returning to Solomon's Way, she certainly won't be doing it alone."

"She seemed fairly adamant that you and she weren't going to be living together before the wedding," Luthor replied.

Simon smiled. "Which is exactly why I won't be the one accompanying her." He turned toward Mattie. "You will."

"Me?" Mattie asked in surprise. "Why me?"

"She won't live with me, and it would be uncouth to have Luthor staying with her. You're the only viable option. Regardless, you're both women. I'm sure there are plenty of things you have in common."

Mattie scowled. "I don't know if you recall, but I'm not exactly the delicate female type. I don't know the first thing about makeup or fixing hair. I'm a werewolf, for crying out loud. What good would I be to such an effeminate woman?"

Simon smiled as he sat on the sofa beside her. "You being a werewolf is exactly the reason I want you to keep her company. Someone may be brave enough to attack even the two of you together, but I can guarantee it'll be the last thing he does in this life."

Luthor and Simon both looked at her hopefully, but she merely crossed her arms and continued to scowl at them both, a low growl rolling from deep in her chest.

CHAPTER Thirteen

WHEN MATTIE WAS PACKED, SHE AND VERONICA SET off toward the apartment. Neither woman looked pleased with the arrangement, but Simon had been very convincing when explaining it was for her protection. Until the killer was caught, he wanted to ensure her safety.

"She'll kill you in your sleep some day for this, sir," Luthor said through his broad smile as he watched the two women climb into a taxi.

"Veronica or Matilda?" Simon asked as he waved to the ladies.

"Both, I'm sure."

The black car pulled away from the curb and merged into traffic. They watched it turn at the next intersection and disappear from view before they turned to one another.

"They're gone now, sir, so what is it that we will be doing in the meantime?"

Simon stroked his chin. "We, Luthor, will be investigating a murder. Doctor Casan's notes were thorough enough to name the location in which Gloria's body was found. We will examine the scene for clues."

"Didn't the constabulary already do that?"

"Assuming the constabulary were as thorough as a Royal Inquisitor merely because they were there first is like saying the city butcher is as qualified as the king's personal chef merely because he handled the meat beforehand. We will find clues that they overlooked."

Luthor sighed and reached inside, retrieving his bowler's cap from the hat rack. He placed it on his head, pressing down his unruly hair. Simon canted his top hat before they set off, walking toward Solomon's Way rather than take a taxi. He said it was so that he would have the proper time to think, but Luthor assumed it was so that Mattie and Veronica would be well at home before they arrived in the city district, especially with the crime scene so close to the apartment building.

The walk during the day was uneventful. In contrast to nighttime, it was the Upper Reaches that was so very alive during the day, with politicians and workers meandering the streets at all hours. By the time they reached the bridge, the crowds had noticeably thinned. A few people passed the pair, but otherwise, they were left to their own devices.

During the day, Solomon's Way looked unkempt. Clothes hung from lines draped between the buildings, drying in the warm sunshine. Refuse and debris was left on the sidewalks, sometimes in metal bins but more often than not just resting on the ground, to be swept away by either the breeze or unruly children. A few people were outside, grocery shopping or the like, but most were inside asleep. Solomon's Way was a district that thrived at night, and the businesses therein catered to their night-owl populace.

The main thoroughfare from the bridge quickly transformed from apartments and townhouses into nightclubs and music halls, the greatest of which stood at the end of the road: the Ace of Spades. They were closed during the day and looked sadly depressing. Without the fluorescent lights illuminating their brightly painted walls, they looked wildly out of place and mildly decrepit. The bright paint looked garish and comical in the daylight.

Simon led Luthor from the main road and down a side street, filled to capacity with rows of townhouses. The homes were far narrower than the ones in which Simon and Luthor lived. The apothecary frowned at the sight, wondering exactly what could be fit inside a building that was only wide enough for a doorway and a single narrow window that he assumed looked in on a living room of sorts.

Past the terrace of townhouses, taller apartment buildings rose over the street. A wooden sawhorse, painted blue in the constabulary colors, blocked an alleyway nearby. It was shaded, even in the bright sunlight. As they approached, they noted that someone had gone through great pains to clean up the blood that had marred the ground, though their efforts were in vain. A dark brown stain, nearly black in the shade, was still visible. Rather than being in the shape of an amorphous blob of blood, it was now spread wider in slowly widening circles, as though a scrub brush had been futilely applied during the cleaning. Simon pulled the sawhorse aside and stepped into the alley.

"What do you hope to find, sir?" Luthor asked. "They've already cleaned. I can only assume a multitude of people have passed through here, investigating the crime."

"I don't rightly know," Simon said as he knelt beside the scrubbed bloodstain. "If I did, I wouldn't have needed to come at all, would I?"

The apothecary frowned and took up a position near the sawhorse, watching for passersby. He would have little to offer the focused Inquisitor, other than a man-sized obstacle around which Simon would have to move. He was far better suited for standing at the entrance to the alley, watching for curious bystanders or passing constables.

Simon gingerly touched the bloodstain, but it was already dry. He would never admit as much to Luthor, but Simon wasn't sure what he'd find in his investigation. Two days had passed since the murder, and the ground had clearly been trampled during what he assumed was a bungled exploration for clues by the constables. Luthor often chided Simon for the Inquisitor's clear derision toward the constabulary, but Simon thought his feeling justified. There was no love lost between the two organizations—though not as much animosity as between the Inquisitors and Pellites, mind you—and Simon always felt better suited for investigating crimes, regardless of whether they were magical or mundane in nature.

There were footprints throughout the area, though a quick observation noted at least a half dozen different sizes and shapes. Most were easily identified as the shoes of constables. Despite their different sizes and widths, the constables wore police-issued shoes with identical treads. Ignoring those, Simon sought the other footprints. A smooth-soled shoeprint was visible at the edge of the bloodstain, pressed into the mud and muck. It was a well-worn heel, matching an equally well-worn toe. Harboring a guess, Simon assumed those shoes belonged to Detective

Sugden. Simon had marked the man's attire as comfortable during their past couple encounters, and he seemed the type that would wear shoes until they were unserviceable.

A few steps deeper into the alleyway, Simon found half a footprint, a long, narrow shoeprint formed when someone inadvertently stepped into the edge of the blood. It was dried the same brown as the smear behind Simon. Extrapolating the length of the shoe based off its toe print, Simon estimated the man's height and build. He frowned as he realized his description matched perfectly that of Doctor Casan, which only made sense. The doctor's notes placed him at the scene, and he would have been close enough to the body to inadvertently step in the blood.

Simon sighed as he stood. Exploring the crime scene had provided no new details, certainly nothing that he could use to further his own line of inquiry. He started to step back toward Luthor when a pile of rubbish against the alley wall caught his eye. Simon paused and turned toward it, noting that much of the refuse had been crushed near its center.

Pulling a loose piece of paper from atop the pile, Simon smiled as he revealed the coarse outline of yet another footprint. His smile faltered, however, as he realized the sheer size of the imprint. It was wider than two of the detective's prints were and longer than a cubit. If his estimations were correct, the size placed its owner at nearly nine feet in height and weighing well over three hundred pounds. A beast of that size couldn't be human, at least not any sort of human with which Simon was familiar.

"Luthor," Simon said. "Come here. I think I've found something that may require your expertise."

The apothecary seemed genuinely surprised as he stepped into the alleyway. Simon showed him the indentation; for that was what it was, since no proper footprint would have held amidst the garbage. Luthor's eyes widened in surprise as Simon described the stature of the creature that would have left a print of that size.

"Have you come across anything of this magnitude in your studies?" Simon asked.

Luthor shrugged. "I'd have to peruse my books, sir, but it doesn't strike me as something familiar. Are we assuming this to be our killer?"

Simon paused, hesitant to say yes. It was clearly something beyond normal human ken, but it was hard to associate something of that size with the surgical precision with which the limbs were removed. Great size and great intellect weren't usually found in a shared body.

"I can't say for certain," Simon finally replied. "A creature of this size seems more in line with the limbs that appeared ripped from the previous bodies."

"A creature that learns, perhaps?" the apothecary offered. "One of brutish strength in the beginning, but one which has learned a far greater technique over time?"

"Mere speculation, Luthor, something I try my best to avoid. I'd prefer the facts speak for themselves."

"Well, sir, we don't have much in the way of facts. One overtly large footprint hardly makes the basis for an investigation."

Simon smoothed his narrow moustache as he thought. "You're correct, of course. If we intend to investigate this further, and I do, mind you, we'll need the police reports."

Luthor sighed. "Not this again, sir. We were damned lucky that the good doctor shared his findings with us. We would never have made the first connection without it, or realized the extent of the crimes. The rest of the reports, however, will not be easy to come by."

"Of course they won't," Simon said, standing. "Which is precisely why we need an official request through the Inquisitors."

"Absolutely not," the Grand Inquisitor said. "There is nothing you've described to me that warrants Inquisitor involvement in what is otherwise the constable's investigation."

"Sir, I can't overstate the sheer size of the footprint," Simon replied as he sat in the chair opposite the Grand Inquisitor, within the older man's chambers. "It was monstrous, and I am certain the constabulary overlooked that crucial piece of evidence."

"Crucial piece of evidence?" the elder statesman incredulously said. "Do you hear yourself, Simon? It was a footprint—hardly a smoking gun or fresh blood on someone's hand. Besides, investigations like this one are outside your scope of responsibility, especially as you're assuming the role of my apprentice once more."

Simon sighed and leaned back in the chair. "Meaning no offense, sir, but you and I both know I'm not meant for duties like these. I'm a field investigator and a damned good one to boot. I should be out in the field, riding airships to ports unseen just to investigate magical maladies the likes of which would never be published in newspapers for fear of widespread panic in the kingdom. That's what I'm meant to do, not sitting behind a desk sorting through papers, reading about the wondrous exploits on which everyone else in the organization is going."

The Grand Inquisitor laced his fingers before his face and frowned, his trimmed, white beard sagging from the effort. "You have successfully demeaned everything I do for this organization. If that was your intent, then well done."

Simon grew pale. "Forgive me, sir, I meant no disrespect. I just can't fathom why the king would wish me out of the field."

"He's recognized your potential, Simon. We all have."

"I did what any Inquisitor would have done in a similar situation."

The Grand Inquisitor leaned forward and placed his hands on his desk. The desk lamp cast strange shadows across his face. "Yet none of them did, Simon. You did. Time and again, it was you who discovered plots against the crown and ended them with all efficiency. Besides, I'm not entirely convinced others would have done what you did. It was a stroke of genius to summon the Order of Kinder Pel into Whitten Hall. I think most other Royal Inquisitors would have been blinded by their obvious biases. Most others probably would have been dead as a result."

"All the more reason to keep me in the field," Simon pleaded. "That sort of brilliance is exactly what we need in leaders conducting field investigations, not directing from an armchair, no offense meant once again."

The older man furrowed his brow, but his frown became a faint smile. "I'm not entirely convinced you aren't meaning offense. However, the king has spoken. Our discussion here is moot, since none of our voices can supersede his word. My hands are tied."

Simon huffed as he leaned further into the chair, hoping to disappear completely through it and vanish from sight out the other side. The Grand Inquisitor watched his protégé with genuine sympathy.

"What would you have me do, Simon?"

Simon bit his lip as he considered his answer. "If you're to take me out of the field and chain me to a desk—"

"No offense meant, I'm sure," the Grand Inquisitor chided.

"—Then let this be my last investigation," Simon concluded. "The evidence I've uncovered says that we are dealing with a serial killer and, if the size of the print is to be believed, one of superhuman stature. Everything about this lends itself to a supernatural phenomenon. Let me conduct a proper investigation into this, first and foremost by retrieving the police files. When it's all concluded, I promise you I will return here, ready to assume my duties."

"You promise you'll return willfully, and not kicking and screaming like an insolent child?"

Simon shrugged. "I make no such promises, but one way or another, I will return."

The Grand Inquisitor smiled as he pulled a sheet of blank paper from a stack. He retrieved a pen from his desk and began quickly writing. Simon could read the elder man's immaculate scrawl, requesting copies of the files be released to the Royal Inquisitor representative, one Simon Whitlock. When the note was finished and the ink sufficiently dried, the Grand Inquisitor blotted it once more before folding it succinctly. He raised the globe on his lamp, exposing the dancing flame within. The fire began melting a stick of red wax that the Grand Inquisitor held above it. Simon had to assume that was the only reason his mentor kept a true lantern on his desk, rather than one of the newer electric commodities. A dab of wax sealed the letter shut. The older man pressed a signet ring into the wax, forming its unbroken seal.

"This should get you what you need," the elder stated, "but once this is completed, I expect to see you returned with all haste. Am I understood?"

Simon smiled and took the note. "Perfectly, sir, and thank you."

He retrieved his top hat as he left the Grand Hall, heading unerringly toward the Solomon's Way police station.

CHAPTER

Fourteen

THE TAXI ROLLED JERKILY TO A STOP OUTSIDE THE STA-
tion. Simon climbed out, handing a coin to the driver before
closing the door behind him. Despite his residence in the Upper
Reaches, Simon was becoming all too familiar with the nuances of the
Way. He walked through the front doors of the station without pause and
approached the desk sergeant.

The sergeant looked up and nodded politely to the Inquisitor. "If
you're here to file a complaint or report a crime, please take a seat and an
officer of the law will be with you momentarily."

"Thank you, but I'm not," Simon replied. "I'm here to see Detective
Sugden."

The sergeant narrowed his eyes as he looked Simon over. The Inquisitor looked slightly out of place in Solomon's Way, especially during
daylight hours. His attire was more attuned to a man from the Upper
Reaches, which, of course, he was. It was readily apparent from the sergeant's expression that the man thought the very same thing.

"Wait here, sir, and I'll bring the detective at once."

The desk sergeant walked into the bull pit, weaving his way through
the multitude of desks and constables moving this way and that. Simon

watched him for a moment before losing interest and turning away, choosing instead to find a seat against the wall. The chairs were uncomfortable, very likely on purpose to keep people from loitering in the station's cool interior.

After a brief moment, the detective appeared at the desk. "Royal Inquisitor, what a pleasant surprise. What brings you to our humble station?"

Simon stood and pulled a note from his inside pocket. The seal of the Grand Inquisitor stood out on the back of the parchment, still unbroken. He walked to the desk and handed it to the detective.

"I have need of your police files pertaining to the murders in your district," Simon explained.

Sugden furrowed his brow as he took the note. "You'll have to be more specific, of course. There have been quite a few murders in Solomon's Way, as one would expect. Mix enough alcohol with an uncouth sort and you're bound to have some violent disagreements."

"Not to worry, Detective, I can give you a list of the names."

The detective didn't seem any more pleased that the Inquisitor had such intimate knowledge of the crimes within Solomon's Way. He stared at Simon for a long moment before glancing down at the letter. Slipping his finger under the red wax seal, he slid it along until the seal broke with a snap. The detective unfolded the letter and quickly read the Grand Inquisitor's official request for assistance.

"Everything seems in order," Sugden said slowly. "You say you know the particular cases that you'll need?"

"Indeed, I do," Simon said with a brazen smile.

A figure climbed the steps to the Inquisitor's right, emerging from the basement in which Simon and Veronica had examined Gloria's remains. The Inquisitor glanced over and noticed the familiar doctor, who looked stricken at the sight of Simon talking to the detective. Casan blanched and visibly bit the inside of his lip as he looked back and forth between the two men.

For a moment, Simon was confused as to the doctor's obvious consternation. As he quickly approached, however, realization dawned on Simon. Detective Sugden likewise glanced curiously as Casan approached.

"Are you well, Doctor?" the detective asked. "You look pale and clammy. I hope you're not coming down ill."

"No, nothing of the sort," Casan stammered as he stopped beside the two men. "Inquisitor, what brings you back to the police station?"

Simon smiled in what he hoped was a disarming way. "Nothing involving you, I'm sorry to say, Doctor. The Royal Inquisitors are requesting the crime scene reports pertaining to a string of murders within your district."

Casan noticeably relaxed. "Including your friend's death, I presume?"

"Exactly so," Simon replied. "It seems there have been a string of similar murders within Solomon's Way, murders that are potentially connected to supernatural occurrences."

Detective Sugden appeared cross. "Come again? We run a tight ship here, Inquisitor, and I'd be the first to know if there were supernatural murders occurring within the Way." The detective's face flushed, and his voice rose both in tone and volume as he continued. "In fact, were there to be such murders, it would be this station that would file a report through the Royal Inquisitors. I would damn well not be notified by someone from *outside*, coming to my station and giving me what for."

Simon arched his eyebrow, refusing to rise to the detective's obvious ire. "No one is giving you what for, Detective. I'm merely making an official inquiry, which, as I'm led to believe, is the only way to receive police reports. My information may be unfounded. If that's the case, then you and the rest of the constables have little to worry about."

Sugden glared at the Inquisitor before his gaze drifted toward Casan. "Where, pray tell, are you receiving such information?"

"My dear detective," Simon said, drawing the man's attention away from the nervous doctor, "you more than anyone appreciates the necessity of the privacy of informants." Simon also glanced toward Casan. The doctor wouldn't need Simon pointing fingers. He looked so pale and sickly that even a detective of mediocre skills like Sugden would notice something amiss. "Perhaps you could lead me to your files and we can begin pulling records?"

The detective clearly looked unhappy but after another look at the formal request from the Grand Inquisitor, he conceded and pointed toward the back of the room. "If you'd come this way, Inquisitor."

Simon glanced again toward Casan and smiled softly. "It's a pleasure to see you again, Doctor. Perhaps you should go home and convalesce. The detective's right; you look awfully sickly today."

Casan seemed offended as well but quickly nodded. "Perhaps you're right."

Nodding politely, Simon walked around the sergeant's desk and followed the detective toward the back of the bull pit.

———————————

"Absolute rubbish," Simon said as he threw one of the files down on his desk.

Luthor leaned back in his chair, avoiding the inevitable spread of paperwork from the discarded file. "I take it you're unhappy with the reports?"

Simon paced around his sitting room, his hands placed firmly on his hips. "It's as though the constabulary are actively trying to retard our investigation. Who writes this tripe? A primary school child with a set of finger paints could create a more accurate report."

He walked back to the table and sorted through the discombobulated paperwork that was strewn over the table. "'No evidence of fingerprints at the crime scene,'" the Inquisitor read from one sheet before flipping to a second. "'Crime scene was disturbed before the arrival of the constabulary, making collection of footprints impossible'. There's not a single mention of the oversized footprint we found at Gloria's murder scene."

"Perhaps he didn't see it, sir, or perhaps it wasn't present at the other crime scenes. It was covered and we might have overlooked it, had it not been for sheer luck on our part." Luthor perused a file in his hand and could only offer a noncommittal shrug. "This crime scene wasn't found until nearly two days after her death. I'm not trying to be inflammatory, sir, but trampling of the crime scene is entirely possible, especially by a well-intended citizen who discovered the bodies."

"Rubbish," Simon repeated as he collapsed into his chair.

"You had hoped for something a bit more definitive, sir?" Luthor asked.

"I had hoped. I knew the chances were slim, but I still hoped. I know Matilda is with Veronica and she's safe, but it would put my fiancée's mind at ease were I to come to her and tell her I'd solved the murders."

Luthor went hurriedly through the rest of the papers in his folder and shook his head. "Sadly, Detective Sugden wasn't necessarily all that thorough in this report."

"Nor in this one," Simon said, gesturing toward his strewn file.

He paused and sat upright. Pushing his paperwork aside, he retrieved the file beneath it and opened it before him. His finger traced the page until he found the signature at the bottom of the page. Charles Sugden. Sliding the file aside, he looked through the next and the next. Uniformly, each investigation was conducted and compiled by Detective Charles Sugden. Simon frowned and stacked the files neatly before him.

"Sir?" Luthor asked, after remaining quiet as Simon reviewed all the documents. He knew better than to interrupt the Inquisitor when he was focused.

"Detective Sugden investigated every murder in this stack," Simon said.

"Is it truly that unusual? He's a homicide detective, after all."

"True, but certainly not the only one in the entire district. Yet he uniformly responded to every murder involving the dismemberment of these young women. What are the chances?"

Luthor shrugged. "I don't know, but I'm sure given enough time, you could calculate the odds."

Simon frowned, knowing he was being mocked. "It's statistically significant."

"Then you believe Detective Sugden could be, what, involved in some way?"

The Inquisitor paused, unsure he was ready to make so great a leap. He slowly shook his head. "Probably not in the traditional sense, but he certainly knew about the connection between the murders, yet said nothing when I listed the names of the victims. In fact, he seemed genuinely perplexed at each of the names in turn, as though he couldn't draw the logical conclusion as to their connection."

Luthor dropped his folder on the top of the stack and leaned back into the sofa. "Then what, sir? Is he a surprisingly great actor or..."

"Or he's a simpleton," Simon concluded. "Detective Sugden doesn't strike me as a simpleton."

"Then it appears we'll have to pay the detective a visit," Luthor said.

"Indeed," Simon replied.

The two men departed the townhouse while the sun was still a sliver over the tops of the nearby buildings. Turning toward the bridge that would take them to Solomon's Way, they walked in silence, each lost to their thoughts. Simon scowled in general at the case before them. There were far too many unanswered questions, the least of which was Detective Sugden's involvement. Involvement or incompetence, either way, the detective had made a mess of the investigation.

Only a few blocks from the townhouse, a black car pulled to a stop beside the walking men. Simon thought nothing of it, other than to avoid the front bumper that jutted over the sidewalk. As the driver's door opened, however, the scowl that Simon wore deepened considerably. The bald man emerged from the car and smiled disarmingly toward the Inquisitor.

"Inquisitor Whitlock," Inquisitor Creary said. The Pellite ran a hand over his bald palate before walking around to the sidewalk.

"Inquisitor Creary," Simon said flatly. "What brings you to our neighborhood at this hour?"

"You, as a matter of fact," Creary explained. The Pellite opened the back door, inviting Simon inside.

Simon glanced toward Luthor, who could offer only a confused shrug. It was dark within the car, made more so by the setting sun. Simon could tell someone was sitting within the backseat, but he could make out none of the man's details.

"Please come with me."

Simon shook his head. "You'll have to excuse me, but I'm on a rather important errand."

"It can wait," said the person from within the automobile. A grayhaired man's face emerged from the shadows. "I would have a word with you."

Simon froze. Luthor seemed unfazed by the man's appearance, solely because the apothecary had never seen the elder man at the Grand Hall, decorated in his livery, sitting upon one of the two high-backed chairs reserved in the center of the meeting hall.

"Grand Maester," Simon said, startled.

Grand Maester Arrus motioned toward the interior of the car, inviting Simon to join him. Simon hesitated and Inquisitor Creary stepped forward, clearly prepared to invite Simon with a bit more force.

"Duncan," the Grand Maester sternly said. "Leave our guest be. Inquisitor Whitlock, you're clearly on your way to somewhere. Allow me to offer the use of my automobile. It'll give us a brief moment to talk, which is all that I require."

Simon knew that the invitation was anything but. He had no choice, no matter how the invitation may have been phrased. He turned knowingly toward Luthor and apologized. "Forgive me, Luthor, but it seems I'll be otherwise indisposed. Continue toward the police station, and I shall meet you there."

Luthor looked as though he wanted to rebut, but he kept quiet. Instead, he nodded before turning away from the car and continuing on his way. Begrudgingly, Simon turned back toward the Pellite's offered vehicle and climbed into the cool interior, choosing a seat across from the Order of Kinder Pel's leader. Inquisitor Creary closed the door before climbing into the front seat behind the wheel. With a lurch, the car rolled down the street.

"Did I hear correctly that you're going to a police station?" the Grand Maester asked.

Simon nodded. "The Solomon's Way police station, to be precise. It's not a long walk and an even shorter trip by car, so you'll forgive me if I'm eager to get to the point of this visit."

He could sense Creary's tension in the front seat but ignored the Pellite's disapproval.

"Bluntness," Maester Arrus said. "It's one of the qualities I appreciate about you, Simon. Forgive this impromptu meeting but you were so busy during the last meeting in the Grand Hall, and we never got a chance to speak. Next thing I hear, you're on your way to another assignment on the opposite end of the kingdom, this time slaying a den of vampires. You have been busy."

"I'm flattered that you pay so much attention to the goings on in my life, as mundane as they may be."

The Grand Maester laughed heartily. He seemed full of energy, such an antithesis to the Grand Inquisitor, who often seemed to bear the burden of a decade of magical inquiries. "Your life is anything but mundane. Were it mundane, the king never would have made time for a personal appearance."

Simon swallowed hard, unhappy with his life being under such scrutiny. "You do seem well informed, sir."

"When it comes to you, I am. You've done an exceptional job hunting magical creatures across the kingdom, uncovering plots that would very well endanger the crown if left unchecked. Your reputation is thus that even my Pellites have taken notice of your escapades. That is precisely why we're meeting today."

Maester Arrus leaned forward. "Do you know from where our namesake comes, Simon? The Order of Kinder Pel?"

Simon shook his head but didn't reply.

"Kinder Pel was a temple in the Kingdom of Kohvus, a religious sect dedicated to the purity of the human mind. They were monks, you see, living in quiet solitude until nearly a decade ago, when the Rift tore the southern continent asunder. The temple at Kinder Pel, a fabulous structure built by silent monks over decades, was along the very fault line which the Rift formed. The temple and its followers were swallowed whole. Only small factions of monks remained, those away from the temple proselytizing.

"When they returned, they found their temple destroyed and their brethren dead. Worse was what they found crawling from the Rift, magical abominations stealing their way into their lands. At that moment, the Order of Kinder Pel realized their true destiny, not as an order of quiet monks dedicated to the wholeness of the human mind, but as warrior monks dedicated to the purity of humanity. They could not abide the magical creature, seeing it as an affront to the wholeness of mankind."

The Grand Maester smiled wistfully at the thought. "I named our order after those very monks, the Order of Kinder Pel. With their name, we assumed the mantle of responsibility, keeping the Kingdom of Ocker likewise safe from magical creatures, by whatever means necessary."

"I have seen your Pellites in action, sir," Simon said dryly, refraining from adding any number of adjectives that were synonymous with "barbaric".

"Of course you have. You even summoned us to your aid."

"A decision I regret," Simon replied. Again, he felt Creary tense in the front seat.

"No, Simon, you don't. Hindsight being what it is, I'm sure you wish you had taken a different route, but at the time, no other means of escape had presented itself as clearly as my Pellites. For what it's worth, you were right to call us. We contained the vampire horde, something that could have been devastating to the kingdom if not destroyed."

102

Maester Arrus shook his head as the car rumbled over the bridge. They weren't far from the police station, which meant that the uncomfortable ride was nearly at an end. "None of those things are why I invited you to ride with me, Inquisitor. You have shown that your beliefs and ours are not so different. You want what we want, to contain and destroy the magical abominations."

Simon furrowed his brow. "Are you inviting me to join your order, sir?"

The Grand Maester smiled broadly. "That level of deductive reasoning is what makes you a great Inquisitor and why you would be perfect amongst our numbers."

Simon's mind spun as he sought a polite way to excuse himself from the conversation. He despised the Pellites, even if the Grand Maester was clearly unaware of his feelings. The thought of joining the Pellites made bile rise in the back of his throat. Surely, there was a way to avoid what would inevitably be an awkward conversation.

Simon smiled as he stared at the Grand Maester. "Your offer is most generous, sir, but I must respectfully decline. Part of the very meeting with the king that you referenced was an offer—an appointment, really— as the new Grand Inquisitor. I've already accepted the position and am currently apprenticing with Grand Inquisitor Highworth. So you see, it would be impossible for me to join the Order of Kinder Pel."

The Grand Maester frowned deeply as the car rolled to a stop. Simon glanced out the window and saw the front of the police station.

"If you'll excuse me, sir, it appears we've arrived at my stop."

No sooner had Simon stepped out of the car than it sped away, leaving him in its smoky wake. Luthor arrived just a few minutes later, only further proving the inefficiency of automobile transportation in Simon's mind.

"Would you care to tell me what that was all about, sir?" the apothecary asked.

"They wanted me to join their order," Simon replied, still in disbelief.

"I hope you told them to sod off. In the most polite way, of course."

"As polite as I could muster. Now, I believe we came here for a purpose. How long do you suppose it is until Detective Sugden leaves for the night?"

CHAPTER

Fifteen

VERONICA SAT ON HER APARTMENT'S ONLY COUCH and glared at Mattie, while the redhead stood by the window, staring at the street far below. Mattie wasn't sure what she expected to find or if she thought she'd see anything at all. There wasn't a telltale unmarked automobile parked beneath the glow of a streetlamp, but staring out the window meant that she didn't have to see Veronica's stern scowl.

"How long do you intend to stay?" the dark-haired woman asked, her arms crossed over her chest.

Mattie sighed and turned toward the irritated woman. "I don't know. This plan wasn't exactly discussed in great depth before I came to stay."

"It wasn't truly discussed with me at all," Veronica complained.

"Or me, either." Mattie walked away from the window, which had become her safe haven since they arrived at the apartment. "I have no intention of interfering in your life any more than necessary. I won't invade your privacy or dishonor the memory of your roommate by staying in her room. I'll sleep on the sofa, and you'll only need to see me as little as possible."

"Then you'll, what, follow me to work?"

Mattie nodded as she leaned against the wall separating the living room from the narrow kitchen. "When you're there, I'll be an invisible audience member. When you leave, I'll leave with you."

Veronica huffed loudly.

"I'm not a fan of this arrangement, trust me," Mattie said. "I'm only doing this out of a mutual respect for Simon."

Veronica placed her feet on the coffee table in a most unladylike way. "Simon doesn't trust me. Why else would he send one of his minions to watch me?"

Mattie arched her eyebrow. "Minion? I'm nobody's minion," she growled. "You think I'm here because he doesn't trust you? I'm here because someone is out there carving up beautiful young women in your neighborhood."

Veronica looked startled at the mention of the murders. The wound of Gloria's death was still fresh and painful. Mattie had just rubbed salt into that open wound. She started to speak but words failed her.

"If there's someone out to harm you," Mattie continued, "I'll make sure they live to regret that decision."

"You?" Veronica said, though her words lacked the derisive edge she desired. "You don't look like a bodyguard."

Mattie smiled. "I'm full of surprises."

Both women seemed temporarily content with a pregnant silence. Mattie walked into the kitchen and helped herself to a glass of water while Veronica turned aside and stared at the far wall. Taking deep breaths, Mattie tried to let her anger bleed away. There was a clearly poor side effect of her magical infection. She may be a violent and malevolent werewolf when transformed, but aspects of her boundless rage often bled into her life, even when in the form of the seemingly fragile human woman.

Sufficiently calmed, she walked back into the living room. Veronica was still facing away from her, but she sighed loudly enough to draw the dark-haired woman's attention.

"We don't have to be enemies," Mattie said matter-of-factly. She was sure there were more tactful ways to express her sentiments, but tact wasn't one of her strengths. Her tribesmen outside Haversham were notorious for speaking their mind. Though she'd never admit it to Simon, she longed for an inkling of his skills of diplomacy. "Neither of us wants to be in this situation, but that doesn't mean we can't make the best of it. Once Simon's certain the trouble has passed, we can go back to our otherwise simple lives."

Veronica turned and offered a wistful smile. "Do you really think I'm in danger?"

Mattie shrugged. "I honestly don't know, but there's enough evidence to make Simon worried. That's good enough for me."

Veronica slid to one side of the sofa, offering Mattie a seat. She sat and returned Veronica's faint smile.

"Why me?" Veronica asked. "For that matter, why Gloria?"

Mattie wasn't sure how much Simon wanted her to reveal, but it seemed as though their relationship was balanced precariously on a precipice. Honesty might be the best way to turn the proverbial corner.

"There have been murders in Solomon's Way, always young, beautiful women. If I may speak bluntly—"

"It does seem to be your forte," Veronica joked.

Mattie smiled. "You're one of the more beautiful women I've seen since arriving in Callifax. Simon knows that as well, and he worries about your safety."

Veronica's smile considerably broadened. Mattie wasn't sure exactly what it was that she said, since she was only being honest, but it seemed to have an endearing effect on the woman.

"That's sweet of you to say," Veronica said. She looked at the clock behind Mattie. "The sun's setting, and I'll have to get ready for work soon." She looked at Mattie's leather pants and white tunic. "Are you planning on wearing that tonight?"

Mattie glanced down at her outfit. It was practical and useful. Most importantly, she could remove it with haste during a transformation. "I had intended to, yes. Is there a problem?"

"No, of course not," Veronica hastily replied.

Mattie frowned. "There's something wrong with my outfit, isn't there?"

"There's nothing wrong, per se. It's just not very feminine."

"I prefer function over fashion."

Veronica smiled. "Oh, Miss Hawke, we can do both."

A few minutes later, Mattie stood before a mirror and scowled. Her hair was pulled up into a loose bun at the back of her head, allowing a few well-placed tendrils to drape over her long neck. She wrinkled her nose, feeling the thick makeup around her eyes crinkle from the effort. Veronica had squeezed her into a tight red-and-black leather corset, with a matching loose skirt that fell to her ankles. A pair of tall-heeled shoes, in which Mattie admittedly struggled to walk in, finished the ensemble.

"I feel that my staunch refusal wasn't as convincing as I thought it had been."

Veronica shrugged. "You put up a good fight, but I'm very convincing, just ask Simon. How do you feel?"

"Breathless," Mattie replied.

"You are looking fairly breathless," Veronica replied.

"No, I mean that I'm struggling to breathe," Mattie said.

She laughed at the comment. "It's a small sacrifice for beauty."

Veronica had changed for work, which consisted of an outfit that didn't seem nearly as restrictive as the one in which the werewolf had been stuffed. She would change at work into outfits far more revealing and, were Mattie honest, easier to slip free from than the one she was currently wearing. Mattie had personally seen how easily Veronica could slip from her clothes during their last visit to the Ace of Spades.

Turning away from the mirror, Mattie followed Veronica toward the front door. As Veronica's hand closed over the handle, she paused. Instead of opening the door, she turned around.

"I wanted to thank you, Matilda," Veronica said.

"For what?"

"I smiled and laughed just now. I didn't think that possible so soon after... well, after..."

"You're welcome," Mattie interrupted.

"Forgive me, but I knew Gloria for some time. It's hard to believe she's gone or that she was... that she was murdered."

She said the last word as though it were poison on her tongue.

"You'll have to excuse me," Mattie said, "but I don't have any tissues on hand. If you start crying now, you'll only ruin your makeup."

Veronica smiled, sufficiently distracted. "It still hurts. It's an ache in my heart that I couldn't have imagined before. I believe it'll hurt tonight, when I see her changing station at the club. It'll hurt when I come home and see her room again. I'm just very glad to have you here, a friend to help me through this time. Thank you."

"I'm glad I could help. I've lost friends before as well. It takes a while before the hurt lessens. It never really goes away; you just learn to cope with it better over time."

"You lost friends in Haversham, right?" Veronica asked. "Simon told me how your tribe was subjugated by that vile creature, that demon."

"He and my tribe were at odds," Mattie replied as vaguely as possible.

"Then I'm all the more glad that you're here. I might ask you for advice coping with the pain, should it become too much."

Mattie smiled softly and opened the door. "Are all women in Callifax this emotional?"

"Excuse me?" Veronica asked as she led them down the hall to the elevator. When she pushed the call button, a loud buzz echoed through the elevator shaft.

Mattie chuckled. "You'll have to excuse me, but I'm not used to spending so much time talking about my feelings."

"You are an odd one, Miss Hawke," Veronica replied.

"The feeling is mutual, Miss Dawn."

The elevator stopped, and the liftman pulled the metal accordion doors aside. As the two women stepped onboard, he closed the doors and pulled the lever. With a lurch, the elevator dropped toward the first floor.

The two women walked mostly in silence toward the club. The sun still glowed over the buildings, and Solomon's Way was in transition. Those who worked in the district during the day were meandering home while those who worked the nights were emerging. The dichotomy between the two groups—one group dressed in laborer's clothes while the others were dressed in eveningwear—was striking. Soon, the crowds from the other districts would flood the streets. The clubs and bars that were just now opening their doors would be filled to capacity, and debauchery would begin on nearly every street corner. Mattie reveled in the relative quiet of the Way during the workmen's transition. The city had never been her place of choice, even one as small as Haversham. She felt positively lost within the massive confines of Callifax.

Veronica led them to the Ace of Spades, which was just beginning to glow from its exterior floodlights. No crowds had lined up outside behind the velvet ropes, though a bouncer was already stationed by the door. Rather than scantily clad ladies opening the large doors, the bouncer opened them instead, letting Veronica and Mattie pass.

Unlike their last visit, the interior of the burlesque house was empty.

A couple of cleaning ladies swept between the tables while a host straightened tablecloths. Veronica walked toward the door beside the stage, but Mattie hesitated.

"Where shall I wait?" she asked.

"You can always come into the back with me," Veronica chided, giving her a once over. "You have a wonderful figure. I'm sure we could find you a job."

Mattie frowned, though she knew it was only a joke. Veronica pointed toward the table normally reserved for Simon. "You can wait there, if you'd like. I'll have someone bring you a drink."

Mattie sat in the booth and tried her best to disappear. Nothing seemed simple, however, in the constricting corset. She knew immediately that it would be a long night.

CHAPTER

Sixteen

ETECTIVE SUGDEN EMERGED FROM THE SOLOMON'S Way police station completely unaware that he was being watched. He donned his overcoat and placed a fedora low over his eyes before descending the few steps to the street. The sun had set less than an hour before and already the district was coming alive. The roads were far more crowded than they had been a few hours earlier, with ladies and gentlemen filling the streets to capacity.

Sugden frowned as he forced his way into the crowd. The throng of people pressed around him like an envelope, driving him onward down the street. Though the night was dark, the Way was well illuminated by gas and electric streetlamps intermixed with brilliant fluorescent lights splashing across the sides of the buildings.

Fighting his way free of the flow of pedestrian traffic, Sugden turned down a side street, one that would lead eventually to his small flat. There were people on this street, but not nearly in such large numbers. The fluorescents, likewise, were gone, leaving only dripping pools of light every ten feet down the road.

He walked with his head down, feeling the fatigue of a long day's work. The Inquisitor had taxed him, asking probing questions about cases he had worked before abruptly departing, his arms laden with files. His was a face the detective wasn't eager to see again. More vexing was his intimate knowledge of which cases in particular about which to inquire. Sugden presumed the nervous doctor had let slip information he clearly shouldn't, but without evidence, the detective wasn't keen on confronting Youke Casan.

As he glanced up from his musings, Sugden noticed a short man in a bowler step into the light before him. The man's hands were concealed in his pockets, and thick muttonchops framed a sour expression. Sugden glanced over his shoulder, but he saw no one behind him. The diminutive man had clearly come to speak to the detective.

Not eager for a confrontation, Sugden turned abruptly and began walking back toward the street from which he'd just emerged. No sooner had he turned, however, than Inquisitor Whitlock stepped out from the shadows, barring his path. The detective came to a stop before the mustachioed man and frowned.

"Inquisitor," Sugden said, trying to remain calm. "What a pleasant surprise."

"Detective," Simon replied. "I wish that our visit were pleasant."

The detective glanced over his shoulder and saw the shorter man standing behind him. "What's this all about then?"

"This? This is nothing. This is just a chance at a private conversation, just you, me, and Mister Strong."

Sugden turned toward the street and began to step away. "If you want to speak with me about cases, you'll have to come by the station tomorrow at a more reasonable—"

Luthor struck the detective across the chest with his cane, not hard but intense enough to stop the man in his tracks. Sugden glanced down at the offending item and scowled at the apothecary.

"I am an officer of the law. How dare you strike me? I could have you arrested."

Simon placed a hand on the detective's shoulder while using his other hand to push away Luthor's cane. "Were that the case, we would save you a seat in our cell. It seems you're not just an officer of the law, you're also a liar."

Sugden blanched and tried to step into the street, but Simon tightened his grip painfully on the portly man's shoulder.

"Forgive me but I have no idea of what you speak," Sugden stammered.

"I think you do," Simon replied. "The files that I procured from you today were very telling, so much so that you could imagine my surprise when I discovered that you had personally investigated every one of the cases."

"I'm a homicide detective. I investigate any number of cases. It's sheer coincidence that the files about which you inquired had my name upon them."

Simon stepped into the road and blocked Sugden's way. The Inquisitor stared sternly at the nervous man. "If that were true, then what possible reason would you have to be so nervous? You're practically dripping with a cold sweat."

The detective huffed. "You and your goon accosted me in the middle of the street on a dark road. You'll have to pardon me for feeling a bit out of sorts."

Simon stroked his moustache and nodded. "Let me explain what I consider the source of your obvious discomfort. I believe that the charade you put on in the police station, in which you feigned ignorance of any connection between the cases, has been revealed. You know now that I know that you knew all along."

Luthor furrowed his brow as he tried to count back and forth which man knew what about whom. Sugden looked likewise confused.

Simon shook his head. "You knew there was a connection between the cases, very likely the same killer, yet you chose not to reveal any of the pertinent facts to me during our conversation. I ask you why."

Sugden noticeably slumped, his shoulders drooping as his gaze fell to the road. "I did know and was caught completely unaware when you inquired, quite specifically, about every file pertaining to what I believe to be a serial killer within Solomon's Way."

"If you knew that our investigations were so obviously crossing paths, why didn't you share your speculations?" Simon asked, shaking his head.

Sugden raised his gaze, his expression stern. "Because this killer is mine to catch and mine alone."

Simon was taken aback by the change in demeanor. "Perhaps you'd better explain."

"Perhaps we'd better discuss over a pint," Sugden countered.

Simon could find no fault in the man's logic and offered to follow the detective. Sugden didn't walk far, taking them back to the main thoroughfare and leading them to the closest pub. There were quite a few open seats at the bar. Solomon's Way was coming alive slowly as the night progressed, but few patrons were ready to sit in a dingy pub, drinking away the night just yet.

Taking their seats, Simon and Luthor on either side of the skittish detective, they ordered drinks. Sugden and Luthor both took their pints of beer while Simon ordered his ever-present scotch. Though Simon was eager to hear the explanation, the detective quickly drank half his glass before offering even a word to either man.

"Tell me what this is all about," Simon demanded. "At this moment, it seems very much like you're somehow complicit in these murders."

Sugden looked up and frowned. "I'm no such thing. I want this murderer caught as much as you do. It's just... it's complicated."

Simon looked around the half-empty pub and shrugged. "We have nothing but time."

The detective looked back at the pint glass held tightly between both hands. "I don't know if you recall or not, but when we first met on the bridge, I told you about my son."

"He was murdered, was he not?" Simon asked, recalling their previous conversation.

Sugden arched his eyebrows. "I'm genuinely surprised you remember."

"Don't be," Luthor said from the detective's other side. "It's what he does; frankly, it's what makes him such an exceptional Inquisitor."

The detective nodded. "My son was murdered by what I still believe to be supernatural means."

"How was he killed?" Simon asked.

"I don't know exactly."

"Yet you believe the cause to be supernatural?"

Sugden looked up, tears welling in his eyes. "His chest was torn open as though by razor-sharp claws, like those of a giant wolf."

Simon and Luthor exchanged nervous glances. "Was that all the damage that was done?"

The detective slowly shook his head. "I don't know. I'll never know, since his head and both arms were removed as though by a blade of some

kind. We never found them. I was only able to identify his body because…
because of a tattoo on his chest."

Though the detective seemed overwhelmed at the memory, Simon
pressed the conversation. "Severed in a similar fashion as the newest
murders?"

"Exactly the same," the detective nodded. "Doctor Casan even believes it could have been made by the same blade."

Simon started to nod but then furrowed his brow. "Did you say that
your son had been murdered nearly two years ago?"

Sugden glanced over and nodded.

"The technique may be the same, but nothing else matches up with
our current killer's methodology. Your son was male, whereas the current
victims are female. A blade severed his extremities, but the first women's
deaths were by brute force rather than the clean separation of the knife.
Why all the variations?"

"I don't know, but now you understand my desire to find this killer.
When the murders began and the bodies of the women began appearing
in the morgue, I knew right away that my son's killer had returned. Not
at first, mind you, because of the rending of the limbs, but once the blade
was applied, there was no doubt in my mind that it was the same killer."

"That is why you've been the detective on scene for all the subsequent
murders."

Sugden nodded. "As soon as I discovered the similarities in the cases,
I made sure my constables contacted me immediately when another case
presented."

"How close are you to finding the murderer?" Luthor asked.

The detective frowned and shook his head. "I'm not. Solomon's Way
is a terrible location for physical evidence. Drunkards urinate in dark al-
leyways, often unaware that a corpse rests not three feet from their shoes.
They unwittingly and unknowingly trample crime scenes, leaving the
constabulary to discern pertinent evidence from the multitude of rubbish around the bodies. It leaves my reports—"

"Woefully inadequate," Simon said.

Sugden was clearly unhappy with the interruption, but he nodded
just the same. "The killer is still loose within my district, and I fear that
I'm no closer to catching him now than I was two years ago."

"Had you been honest with us from the start, we could have been assisting you in your investigation," Simon explained. "Due to my own personal ties to these cases, I will now be assisting you in your search for this killer."

"I mean no disrespect, but I don't need—"

"Of course you do," Simon interrupted, to Sugden's growing displeasure. "You haven't been able to catch this killer without my help, so clearly you're no worse off with a Royal Inquisitor at your side."

"And an apothecary," Luthor added.

"Of course," Simon replied, talking around the stunned detective.

"I don't suppose I have a say in the matter?" Sugden bitterly asked.

Simon shrugged. "The request from the Grand Inquisitor trumps any of your arguments as to why we should not be assisting in this investigation. So, no, you really don't."

The detective finished his beer in two long gulps and set the empty glass down on the bar. "Then, if you'll both excuse me, I'll be going home. I might as well get as much sleep as possible if I'm to deal with the two of you for the foreseeable future."

"That's the spirit," Simon cheerfully replied.

The detective frowned as he climbed from his seat and walked hastily toward the door. The door opened and shut with a bang, drawing the attention and ire of the rest of the patrons.

"He didn't pay for his drink, did he?" Simon asked as he stared at the closed door.

"No, sir, he did not," Luthor replied as he took another drink from his own beer.

Simon sighed and turned back toward his friend. "This will be a difficult working relationship."

"What do you think of the man's story?"

Simon stroked his chin. "Sugden's personal interest in the case is evident but what isn't as transparent are the facts. Why would the killer change his methods from blade to superhuman strength and back to blade? Why change from killing a man and then switch to women? Most killers would do the opposite, refining their skills on the more defenseless gender before progressing to killing the sturdier male."

"Let's not forget about the claw marks on his son's torso. Do you really think it could have been a wolf, like the detective believed?"

Simon shrugged. "Were there werewolves in Callifax—well, werewolves that we didn't personally bring into the city—I'm sure their presence would have been more evident. There would have been more cases of bites or rending, which, to the best of my knowledge, there hasn't been."

Luthor drummed his fingers on the bar. "Then you don't believe the detective?"

"I'm undecided," Simon replied, glancing over his shoulder toward the closed door. "The detective has already lied to us once. I find that lying is like an addictive drug. Once a man has lied and gotten away with it, there's no end to the lies he will perpetuate to conceal the truth." Simon took a drink from his scotch but frowned at the taste. He quickly set the tumbler down on the bar before him. "We'll keep a watchful eye on the good detective over the next few days. I'm far more concerned with what occurred before the death of Sugden's son."

"I don't follow, sir."

"A killer doesn't start with the slaying and dismemberment of a body, not with such violence and woeful disregard for human decency. Much like the women slain more recently, I'm sure that there were men killed in progressively worsening fashions before the detective's boy was brutalized."

Luthor ran a hand over his muttonchops. "There would be police files, were that the case. Does your letter permit you to review the other files as well?"

"Perhaps," Simon hesitantly said, "though any resistance from Sugden or any of the constabulary would halt our investigation. My letter is hardly a blank check and, upon further scrutiny, would probably be dismissed by the detective out of hand."

"Then how do we go about investigating three-year-old crime scenes without the police files?"

"We don't. All the murders occurred within Solomon's Way, which lends itself to the killer being from this district. Traditionally, a criminal will strike somewhere with which they have the most familiarity. That allows them opportunities to escape, should their crimes be discovered. Therefore, we focus on the present and the killer who is still here, somewhere in Solomon's Way. The footprint you found is enormous. Even were the killer of normal stature with just inhumanly large feet, he would appear clownish and his presence noted. More likely than not, however, he's a superhumanly tall chap. If there were a large killer about in the Way, someone would have seen him. We just need to find the man that did."

CHAPTER

Seventeen

MATTIE HAD GROWN UP IN A TRIBE, CONCEALED within the foothills of the frozen north and west of the continent. Her entire family had lived together in a fur-lined hut, eating, sleeping, changing, and bathing in front of one another out of necessity. It had been far more unusual for her to go a day without seeing someone naked than not. Furthermore, she was a werewolf, as was all her tribe. During their transformation, they were required to be naked. It was a brutal process during which bones knitted and reformed and their flesh—her flesh—was ripped from her body like sheets of paper, fluttering aside to reveal the wintery pelt beneath. She had stood beside her brethren for nearly two decades, rows of naked men and women preparing for the change. It hadn't been sexual, at least not during those times of being naked. She hadn't always associated the naked form with pure sexuality but more of a natural progression of her transformation. Never would she have believed that the naked form could embarrass her so.

After four hours at the Ace of Spades, Mattie had been thoroughly proven wrong. Naked burlesque dancers had taken the stage one after another, retiring only after reaching a certain level of undress. Ladies—and she used that term loosely—twisted and contorted their bodies into po-

THE GOLEM OF SOLOMON'S WAY

sitions she wouldn't have believed possible. More than once, she blushed and was forced to look away. She had been in the Ace of Spades before and had seen Veronica perform, never believing that her performance was one of the tamest of the night.

The men drank in the dancers' sexuality like wine. They cheered and jeered from their seats. Men of wealth lined the stages like dogs begging for table scraps. They salivated and clutched tightly to the edges of tables, watching immutably as the women gyrated and swayed. It was primal, and the air stank of sex and musk.

To Mattie's delicate senses, the scent was overwhelming. It radiated from the crowd in waves of unrequited passion. Their yells and cheers became a seamless drone where individual voices were lost to the call of the masses. After hours of being exposed to what she considered the worst of mankind, Mattie was left feeling nauseated.

When Veronica appeared, once again dressed with no lingering reminder of the naked woman who had recently taken the stage, the redhead was more than ready to leave. A few men tried to address Veronica as they walked toward the door, but Mattie's guttural growl silenced their voices before they could speak. The werewolf within her yearned to be released, despite the fact that she had no true target. If she could have ripped out their collective throats, she would have.

Exiting the burlesque house, they were struck by the cool night's air. As effective as ice water against warm skin, the cool air returned Mattie's sense of control. She took a few deep breaths and closed her eyes, blocking out even the glow of nearby establishments.

"Are you feeling all right?" Veronica asked.

"Better," Mattie replied.

"Thank you for being with me tonight," she said. "I needed an escape from reality."

Mattie arched an eyebrow. "That was your idea of an escape?"

Veronica glanced over her shoulder toward the burlesque house. "Everything about that place is an escape. It doesn't lessen the pain of Gloria's... of her not being there, but while I'm on stage, I can be somewhere else, anywhere else." She shook her head. "It's not as though I imagine she's still alive when I'm dancing, but rather that this world, the one in which she's gone, doesn't even exist. For three minutes, I'm a different person."

Mattie glanced over her shoulder toward the blockish building. Her experiences within had been far different, a cruel reminder of everything she found wrong with the kingdom.

"Is something the matter?" Veronica asked.

"I don't understand how you can work in a place like that."

Veronica slipped an arm through Mattie's and pulled her away from the Ace of Spades. "You get used to it after a while, though I'd be lying if I didn't say it scared me something awful when I first started."

"But all those *men*," Mattie said, with obvious disdain for the gender as a whole.

Veronica laughed. "They're not men; they're boys playing dress up. The men work in the Upper Reaches all day, but when night comes, the men go to sleep and release their inner child. It's the children who come to see me dance. It's the children, who no longer think with their upper-most heads and instead let their lower ones think for them, who lose sight of the value of a coin. We love the boys, since they're the ones who spend so lavishly."

Mattie forced a smile but felt rather filthy at the whole conversation. She shivered, a gesture that had nothing to do with the cold. "That room, though, was like a den of sex. You could practically see it in the air."

"You're absolutely right, and the more the other ladies and I cater to it, the more money we make." Veronica stopped and, with a hold on Mattie's arm, turned her toward her. "Listen, I know you don't approve. You seem much more grounded than Simon or Luthor—especially Luthor—but nothing I do sacrifices my morality. I would never touch a patron, and they understand that rule. There is more than their fair share of brothels sprinkled throughout Solomon's Way. If they want to put their grubby hands on a beautiful woman, they can have their pick. They come to us because we provide an escape from reality. We turn a simple dance," Veronica shimmied as though a physical demonstration was necessary, "into a fantasy world, where women grow wings."

"Even as they lose their clothing," Mattie dryly said. "It seems like a poor exchange to me."

Veronica laughed again. "You have much to learn about the civilized world."

They walked down the road, arm in arm, passing the drunkards who staggered out into the street. "Calling this civilized starts a whole new conversation for which I'm not entirely convinced you're ready to begin."

Veronica stepped over a man passed out in the street. A paddy wagon rolled slowly down the road as constables lifted unconscious men into the back. They'd sleep the night away in a cell at the police station only to be released in the morning with a headache and, more often than not, an empty purse, but otherwise no worse for the wear.

"Simon warned me that you were set in your ways," Veronica said.

"Me?" Mattie incredulously replied. "That man's a Royal Inquisitor. It doesn't get much more 'set in your ways' than that."

"I hardly think hunting down the monsters in Ocker makes him inflexible."

Mattie opened her mouth to reply but realized Veronica was oblivious to the truth. She could no more defend herself against the baseless accusations than she could transform in the middle of the city. Veronica, along with all the citizens of Ocker, had spent the past ten years fearing all manners of beasts from the Rift. It was unconscionable that the monsters might not be as evil as they had purported.

"Of course," Mattie finally replied. "He's a good man. You're lucky to have found someone like him."

They turned down a side street, one that led directly toward their now-shared apartment. The crowds thinned considerably, though it was hard to tell on the narrow road. There were a few glowing streetlamps, but most were dark despite the late hour. Mattie glanced upward and saw clouds rolling across the moon, blotting out the feeble light it offered. She had no fear of the dark; her lupine eyes saw considerably well in the gloom. She had to remind herself, however, to stumble on occasion from unseen and uneven cobblestones. Veronica was blind on the dark street, as were most normal humans, which Mattie tried to remember she was to emulate.

"Forgive my intrusion, but from what Simon tells me, I'm not the only lucky one," Veronica said, breaking the silence of the street.

Mattie glanced at the woman inquisitively, seeing her mischievous expression. "I don't know what you're talking about."

"You and Luthor live together, do you not?"

The darkness provided the perfect cover for Mattie's suppressed smile. "Mister Strong and I live together out of necessity. As you well know, I come from a tribe where money wasn't much of an issue. I had no funds with which to procure my own living arrangements. Luthor has been a perfect gentleman."

"I'm sure he is," Veronica replied, not aware that Mattie could damn well see her sly smile. "Are you telling me that he offered you his townhouse out of the goodness of his heart and not because of some... shall we say mutual attraction?"

"I'm sure I wouldn't know."

Veronica paused beneath one of the unlit streetlamps and turned toward Mattie. "Are you saying that you and he haven't...?" She made gestures of two cupped hands being pressed together.

"Copulated?"

"Done it," Veronica said. "Had sex. Made love. You can take your pick."

Mattie blushed furiously. "There are extenuating circumstances."

Mattie's experience with sex had been with other werewolves, where the act was animalistic and often involved biting and clawing. Despite Luthor's secret magical nature, she wasn't sure she was ready to put him through the ordeal. None of which she could properly explain to the inquisitive woman before her.

Veronica stifled a laugh as she took Mattie's arm once more. "Consider me the devil on your shoulder, doing my best to corrupt you."

"Better people than you have tried," Mattie replied, "including actual demons."

As Mattie stepped down, something crunched loudly beneath her heeled shoes. She pulled back her foot and glanced at the cobblestone. In the shades of gray through which she saw the darkness, Mattie could see twinkling shards of glass littering the street. She furrowed her brow as she stooped forward, examining the glass.

"What is it?" Veronica asked, practically blind on the dark street.

"Nothing, I'm sure."

Mattie touched the glass and was surprised that it was warm. She could feel the gentle curve, as though the individual shards had once composed a much greater globe of sorts. Craning her neck upward, she looked at the dark streetlamp overhead. The glass that once housed the electric bulbs had been smashed. Jagged slivers of glass protruded from its base.

She felt her heart give a lurch. If the glass was still warm, it meant that the globe had been whole and illuminated not long before their arrival. Someone had smashed the globe recently, practically just before they had made their turn onto the street. She glanced down the road and could see the dim light reflecting on similarly broken bulbs as far as she could see.

"Matilda, I can't see," Veronica complained. "What's happening?"

Mattie sniffed the air and smelled it. Faint, underneath the wafting smell of liquor and vomit, the scent of metal filled her nose, as though she tasted blood at the back of her throat. The metallic smell was intermixed with another, baser aroma—that of death and decay. The rot was dull, but ever present; the same sort of smell that had clung to Simon's clothing when he had returned from the morgue.

"I think we should go," Mattie softly said.

"We were going, until you stopped to examine something in the street."

Mattie shook her head. "No, not toward your apartment; back the way we came. Go now, slowly."

Mattie could practically feel Veronica shivering behind her. She was frightened and, as far as Mattie was concerned, rightfully so. Gloria had so recently died under mysterious circumstances, while traveling home late at night, much like they were doing now.

"Tell me what's wrong," the Veronica demanded, even as she stepped away from the broken glass.

"I don't know—" Mattie began before she caught sight of something in an alleyway nearby.

She had mistaken it for a part of the building, it had stood so tall and unmoving, like a chimney jutting from the brickwork. As it moved, however, she realized her mistake at once. The shadowy figure towered over her, standing nearly nine feet tall. As it turned, the smell of oil, iron, and rotted flesh washed over her. She suppressed an urge to vomit as bile rose in her throat.

Mattie thought of fleeing. She was quick and, if need be, could transform. Her hulking werewolf form would easily outrun even a towering figure like the one before her. Veronica, however, was her antithesis. The woman was an able dancer but lacked any true athletic skills. She'd never make it away in time.

Pulling Veronica behind her, so that the werewolf blocked the path between the monster and its target, Mattie snarled, baring her teeth. "Do you trust me, Veronica?"

"Tell me what you see," Veronica demanded, her voice quivering.

"Do you trust me?" Mattie asked again.

"Yes. Yes, of course."

Mattie let go of the woman and started unfastening the bone clasps of her corset. Even in the dim light, Veronica's eyes had adjusted enough to recognize the motions.

"What are you doing?"

"You said you trusted me, so I'll have to ask you to forgive me for what's about to happen."

Mattie slid free of the corset and dropped her skirt past her ankles, stepping easily out of both the dress and her unwieldy shoes. She growled, not a faint warning like she had done in the club, but a truly beastly snarl that startled Veronica.

"Matilda?" Veronica asked, but Mattie didn't hear her.

Mattie reached up and tore at her naked chest, ripping bloody strips of flesh from her body. They drifted to the ground in a quickly growing pile of discarded waste. Behind her, Veronica couldn't see the white fur protruding from the horizontal and vertical tears on her skin, only that the sound coming from Mattie was no longer human.

She crouched and her knees bent the wrong direction. With a final burst of her transformation, the werewolf inside was released. Snow-white fur coated her body. A long tail swished behind her as she crouched, ready to pounce on the massive beast before her. She clenched her hands into fists, wrapping her thumbs over the top until she could feel the bite of her claws in the bottom of her paw.

"You're a monster," Veronica whispered in utter disbelief.

"Run," Mattie said, her voice coarse but still her own.

Veronica was transfixed, unable to move as a much-larger shadow detached itself from the alleyway before them. The darkness had been too great without the lit streetlamps. She had been painfully unaware that such an abomination had been standing only a dozen feet from them throughout Mattie's transformation.

"Run, damn you!" Mattie yelled as she leapt into the air.

Her claws extended toward the behemoth and her maw opened, ready to bite. She was fast, a blur of white fur launching across the space between them as she prepared to rend the monster limb from limb. The monster, however, was far faster than she was. It lashed out with one of its oversized arms. The air was filled with a screeching of metal gears as the closed fist connected with Mattie's ribs. She was knocked far off course. Instead of sinking her claws deep into the monster's chest, one clawed hand only managed to rake the shoulder of the beast before the werewolf was tossed handily into the alleyway.

Ichor from the abomination splashed against the wall and clung to Mattie's paw; a viscous, gelatinous filth that stunk of dead meat. Mattie crashed into the bricks and crumbled to the ground in a heap, offering only the faintest yelp of protest. The monster turned and stomped toward her, the ground shaking with its steps. She started to rise but the monster punched downward, slamming its fist into the side of her head. Pain exploded across her cheek and top of her snout. It wasn't bony knuckles she felt beneath the skin of its hand but steel rods, capable of shattering bone on impact. The beast grabbed her by the fur on her chest and lifted her limp form slightly from the cobblestones of the alley. She looked up through one ruined eye and saw the creature drawing back for another strike. It punched down, connecting with the side of her head again.

Feeling her consciousness flooding away from her, Mattie quickly transformed. The fur in the monster's hand sloughed away from her human form before dissolving into a smoky mist. Mattie could feel anguish through her ruined face but tried to stay focused, not on the giant before her but on Veronica, still affixed to the same spot in the road.

"Run, you idiot," Mattie mouthed, though she doubted it came out as little more than a mumbled mess.

Veronica couldn't see the alleyway, other than to know that the werewolf—the monster she had so recently been calling a friend and with whom she had linked arms—had cried out in pain. The fear had kept her in place, but absolute terror begged her to move as the gigantic figure turned back toward her. She started to step away as a hand closed over her mouth and something sharp and narrow pierced her neck.

Her body went slack but was caught and supported by the person behind her. She willed her legs to move, to run from her unseen adversary, but her body refused to respond. Her eyes remained open even as she was laid gently on the stones. The gigantic abomination stomped toward her. Veronica's heart raced and tears streamed from her eyes, but only the faintest whimper escaped her lips.

Enormous hands closed over her wrists and dragged her unceremoniously toward the alley. She was dropped onto the stones. She stared at Mattie, once more in human form. Half her face was ruined; blood seeped from dozens of gashes and pooled on the ground. She didn't feel as horrified by Mattie at the moment. Within her mind, she screamed for Mattie to get up, to become the werewolf once more, to save them both, but Mattie's good eye fluttered slowly closed.

"Don't worry about your friend," a voice whispered from behind her. Hands grabbed Veronica and rolled her onto her back, where she could stare into the face of a cloaked figure. "It's not her I'm after."

The moon emerged from behind the clouds, reflecting off the long knife in the man's hand.

CHAPTER

Eighteen

S IMON LEANED AGAINST THE LAMPPOST AS LUTHOR
approached another group of Solomon's Way locals. The apothecary held up the hastily drawn sketch, that of an eight- or nine-foot
giant of a man who may or may not make his home in the Way. As had
occurred a dozen other times throughout the night, the men gave Luthor
an odd stare before shaking their heads emphatically. Frowning, Luthor
thanked them for their time before walking back toward the Inquisitor.

"No such luck, once again?" Simon inquired.

Luthor's frown remained unmoved. "You could help me, sir, rather
than just mock me upon my return. Posing the questions from a Royal
Inquisitor would carry far more weight than having them come from,
what was I just called, oh yes, a drunk git."

"How rude of them," Simon replied, though a faint smile hung on his
lips. "You clearly weren't drunk."

"You're far too kind," Luthor flatly said.

Simon pushed away from the lamppost and strolled further down
the road. Luthor hurried to catch up, not requiring much effort to match
Simon's lackadaisical stride. The nighttime breeze was warm, but Simon
still shoved his hands into his pockets.

"The hour grows late and I'd much rather be asleep already, rather than roaming the Way," the Inquisitor complained. "When even the drunkards are asleep comfortably in their beds, then clearly we've been out too long."

Luthor glanced toward the sky but it was still oppressively dark, with equally dark clouds blotting out the moonlight. He knew the sun would be rising soon, but there wasn't even a hint of sunrise on the horizon. Despite the gloom, Luthor, too, felt the fatigue of walking Solomon's Way all night.

"What of the killer?" the apothecary asked. "Isn't giving up our search a death sentence for some young woman in the Way?"

Simon shook his head as they walked. "Aside from locations of the crimes, I also took the liberty of annotating the dates of the murders while we were perusing Detective Sugden's files. The first two crimes occurred nearly two months apart. The following crime was nearly five weeks later. Each subsequent crime has occurred at a slightly elevated rate, growing exponentially closer to a single day apart. However, based off the time between the last crimes—which was six days—I estimate it'll be at least tomorrow night if not the night after before he strikes again."

"So soon?"

"It's difficult to argue with science and mathematics."

"You're quite right," the apothecary conceded. He glanced down at his juvenile sketch before crumpling the paper in his hand. "I don't think people are even taking our line of inquiry seriously, anyway. We'd be far better suited sleeping until lunch and trying again tomorrow night."

"It's frustrating, I understand," Simon remarked as they walked further down one of the main arteries through Solomon's Way. "If there's a killer on the loose, we should be expending every resource available. However, this is far from an official Inquisitor investigation. The Grand Inquisitor may have graced me with permission to pursue this on my own, but the constabulary owns this case."

"The same constabulary that you've accused multiple times of being grossly incompetent?"

"One and the same."

Luthor sighed. "That doesn't instill confidence."

"Nor should it," the Inquisitor replied, glancing over at his counterpart. "We have several distinct advantages over our killer, however, that will assist in his capture tomorrow evening. First, we know of his presence but, unless I'm wrong, the killer knows nothing of our dogged pursuit, nor of us. Secondly, we know the date and the location in which he'll strike. Finally, we know that he won't strike until the wee hours of the morning, which means we'll have the majority of the night to find him before he can kill again."

Luthor continued walking but seemed thoroughly unconvinced. "Those are all valid points, sir, unless we spend tomorrow night in much the same manner in which we spent this evening, wandering aimlessly through the Way without finding anything of intrinsic value."

"Something will turn up, I'm sure of it."

"Would that be an Inquisitor's sixth sense of which I've heard so much?" Luthor joked.

Simon smirked as he glanced toward his friend. "Miss Hawke isn't the only one with a keen sense of smell. She can smell blood in the air a mile away, which is impressive, but I can smell trouble and danger at every turn."

Luthor started to laugh as they passed a conjoining street. A crowd had gathered halfway down the dark road. None of the overhead lamps seemed to be lit, but dancing lantern lights and torches held aloft over the burgeoning crowd illuminated the area. Simon stopped in mid-stride and stared at the gathered throng. Though there were still people returning toward their homes at the late hour, it was unusual to see such a group gathered.

As a man holding a lantern turned, his flame illuminated the side of a horse-drawn truck parked on the side of the road. Simon recognized it instantly as a paddy wagon. As he narrowed his eyes, he could see the deep blue uniform of the constable holding the light.

"Something's happened," the Inquisitor said.

"How can you tell?" Luthor asked, squinting through his glasses but seeing none of the detail.

"Come, Luthor. Let's not dawdle, not when the police are out in such force."

The two men made their way down the cobblestone street until they reached the back of the crowd. The mob was an amalgamation of people, some evidently from Solomon's Way while so many others appeared to be from the Upper Reaches or the Bay. The pressing crowd was kept at

128

bay by wooden sawhorses and a row of constables, threatening with billy clubs those who tried to pass the barricade. Through the shifting crowd, it was nearly impossible to see what could only be a crime scene.

Simon pushed his way past a few men who grumbled noncommittally at his rudeness. They reached the sawhorses but still could see nothing of the alleyway beyond where the majority of commotion seemed to be occurring. The Inquisitor leaned forward for a better view but a constable appeared before him, pushing the tip of the club into Simon's chest.

"Back, you," he said before raising his voice. "All of you need to stay back. I won't tell you again. Next man who leans across the barriers will get a cracked skull."

"Excuse me?" Simon said, pushing the club away from him. "Do you know who I am?"

The constable leaned forward until Simon could smell the foul odor emanating from his mouth. "I don't care if you're King Uriah himself. I'm the law here, which makes you gobshite, as far as I'm concerned."

Simon gritted his teeth. "My name is Royal Inquisitor—"

"Inquisitor Whitlock," Detective Sugden said as he approached the barricade. "I'm genuinely surprised that you're still in the Way. I would have thought you'd have gone home by now."

"As would I," Luthor remarked.

"Mister Strong, wasn't it?" Sugden asked.

The apothecary nodded and touched the brim of his hat in recognition. The detective turned toward the constable. "Let these two through."

The constable blushed as he stepped aside, letting Simon and Luthor through a gap between the sawhorses. Simon took a step forward, following Sugden as the detective walked back toward the alley, but paused beside the constable.

"I bet you're feeling pretty small right about now. I wonder, though, what is lower than gobshite?"

The constable offered no response as Simon walked away.

"What happened here, if I may inquire?" Simon asked as he rejoined the others.

Sugden sighed. "There's been another murder."

Simon and Luthor both stopped in surprise. There should have been at least one more day before the next murder. Simon frowned. Something had happened; something had obviously changed the killer's well-laid plans.

"I guess science and mathematics are fallible after all," Luthor whispered.

"Be quiet." Simon raised his voice as he addressed the detective. "I'm surprised the killer struck so quickly after the last murder. It seems a bit out of character."

Sugden turned, clearly exhausted from a long night's work. "Everything about this attack is unusual, even when compared to the rest of the murders in this case. For starters, there was a witness, a young woman who was also attacked but not killed."

Simon pursed his lips in disapproval. Murderers and, by extension, those who contemplate murder, normally fell into one of two categories. They either killed only a certain type and rarely ever deviated from their chosen victim pool or attempted a randomization in their killings. Even the latter group, over time, created a definitive pattern in their randomness. Deviation was not as common in serial killers as stories would have people believe.

Yet, standing at the edge of the alley, Simon was perplexed. Leaving someone alive, especially a potential witness, made no sense. It violated everything Simon had gleaned about the killer. It was deviation. It was an introduction of uncertainty and chaos, whereas Simon greatly preferred order and routine.

"I'd very much like to speak to this witness," Simon said.

Sugden patted the hood of the truck beside which they had stopped. For the first time, the two partners realized it was an ambulance. "As would we all, gentlemen, but she's suffered severe injuries, including a broken jaw. She's in no condition to speak."

"Are you sure this is the same killer?" Simon asked, voicing his confusion.

"There is still a deceased woman, dismembered as were all the rest of the victims," Sugden replied. "I'm fairly certain it's the work of our serial killer."

A commotion drew their attention. Four constables emerged from the alleyway, a stretcher suspended between them. There was a woman upon it, a sheet draped over the majority of her body, allowing only her battered face and brilliant red hair to remain visible.

"We covered her with the sheet," the detective explained sheepishly.

"She was found in the nude. She'll be examined at the hospital for an assault of the sexual nature as well."

A part of Simon's mind screamed out a silent warning, one that was mostly ignored.

Simon felt a hot flush rise to his cheeks. "You won't find evidence of penetration during your examination. She wouldn't have allowed it. Luthor, if you would be so kind, accompany the detective to the slain woman."

He walked toward the men carrying out the battered woman as Luthor and the detective disappeared into the alleyway. The shock of red hair caught Simon's attention as it bounced with each measured step of the litter bearers. Holding out his hand, he begged the constables to stop. Stepping between them, he drew back the sheet slightly, exposing the rest of the redhead's battered chin and neck. A deep bruise had spread across the left side of her face and the swelling left her looking monstrous, but there was no denying the woman's identity.

"Matilda?" Simon asked.

Mattie's eyes fluttered open, one fully and the other only to a sliver, as much as the swelling would allow. For a moment, her expression was clouded in confusion, as though she didn't recognize Simon. Eventually, her eyes widened further and she moaned softly.

"Hush, now," the Inquisitor said, resting a hand on her shoulder. An unheard voice screamed loudly in his mind that something was amiss. "You've been through significant trauma and need time to heal."

She shook her head, despite the obvious pain it caused. Tears welled in her eyes as she tried to speak, but her fractured jaw sent lances of pain throughout her face. She moaned louder and began to thrash on the litter.

"Calm yourself," Simon demanded, his voice sterner than it had been. He knew he was overlooking something, as though part of his mind had intentionally silenced itself as he spoke to Matilda. "You need to relax before you do further damage."

"I'm... sorry," she mumbled, moving her jaw as little as possible.

Simon knew she would heal quickly from her wounds, a blessing that accompanied the curse of her lycanthropy. Her insistence on moving and attempting to speak would only prolong her pain and healing process.

"Forgive us, sir," said one of the constables holding her aloft, "but we must get her to the hospital. Did you say her name was Matilda?"

"Matilda Hawke," Simon said, nodding.

"Very good, sir. She'll be at the hospital shortly. You'll be able to visit her there."

The men started to walk away. From the corner of his eye, Simon saw Luthor walking hesitantly toward him, his face deathly pale in the warm glow of the lanterns. Simon turned away from him and hurried toward Mattie once more.

"Stop. Stop," he demanded of the constables. With a begrudging sigh, they stopped once more.

"Matilda," Simon whispered. "Where's Veronica? Where's my fiancée?"

"I'm… so… sorry," she muttered again, tears streaming from her eyes.

"Sir," the constable said curtly, "we need to leave."

Simon stepped out of their way and turned toward the alley. Luthor stood at the mouth of the alleyway, fidgeting uncertainly with his hands and staring morosely at his mentor. Simon stepped forward, his gaze past the apothecary, fixed solely on the dark sheet draped over the corpse. His steps were halted at first, but grew brusquer as he grew closer.

"Sir, I don't think you should go back there," Luthor said.

Simon chose not to hear him. That same voice in the back of his mind whispered what he had chosen to forget all along, that Mattie hadn't been alone, that she had been sent with the sole purpose of guarding Veronica.

Luthor held up his hands as he stepped into the Inquisitor's path. "Sir, don't do this. You don't have to see this."

Simon didn't stop. He lashed out with his hand closed in a fist and his thumb extended. He drove his thumb into a pressure point on Luthor's hip, and the apothecary's leg immediately went numb. He collapsed to the ground even as Simon unapologetically stepped over him.

Detective Sugden saw the Inquisitor approaching but was wise enough to step out of the way. "I had no idea you knew the victims. Had I known, believe me, Simon, I never would have let you past the barricade."

Simon said nothing, merely knelt at the side of the bloodstained sheet draped over the body. With a quivering hand, he clenched the sheet tightly and slowly pulled it down. Raven hair was spilled across the stones haphazardly, like Medusa's snakes writhing away from the head. Her eyes were closed, but he could see the look of anguish painted across her face.

He should have cried. Simon knew that was the appropriate response, but he couldn't find it within him. It wasn't sadness he felt at seeing Veronica's body. It wasn't anger at Matilda for failing in her sole mission. It wasn't even a general apathy that normally accompanied a sense of shock. All those emotions would come later, he knew, when the realization of what had occurred finally settled over him like a blanket. For the moment, he felt none of those things, save one.

It was emptiness.

All Simon felt was nothing at all.

CHAPTER

Nineteen

"SIMON," LUTHOR SAID SOFTLY. "SIR, I THINK WE should leave and let the detective do his work."

Simon didn't reply, merely remained beside Veronica's corpse, staring at the pale, bloodless remains that had once been his vital and beautiful fiancée. Luthor was right. They should leave. Every moment he remained, staring at what was left of the woman he loved, he felt the fingers of depression creeping into his mind. Yet he couldn't bring himself to go.

"I won't leave her," Simon said, shaking his head.

The apothecary placed his hand on his mentor's shoulder. "There's nothing more we can do here, sir. Let's get you home."

Simon angrily shrugged Luthor's hand from his shoulder. The diminutive man crouched beside his friend and lowered his voice to a harsh whisper. "Sir, I don't want this to become a scene."

The Inquisitor felt a flare of anger, the first real emotion he'd felt since stumbling upon the murder, but his frustration was immediately squelched by a realization. "It is exactly what this is, Luthor: a crime scene. You may tell me that there's nothing more we can do, but you're so very wrong. This is a murder, one of many perpetrated by the same villainous man. A crime such as this deserves the best possible investigator and that isn't the detective or anyone else in the constabulary, it's me. I'm here, the murder is fresh, and I will do everything in my power to solve this crime right here and now."

The strength of his resolve left Luthor at a loss for words. The apothecary stood and shrugged apologetically toward Detective Sugden, who had heard the exchange, to include Simon's underhanded insult. The detective shook his head, as though no apology were required.

"The severed limb seems to match the description of the previous cases," Simon muttered mostly to himself. "A match of the striations would provide a more definitive answer." He turned abruptly toward the detective. "Will Doctor Casan be joining us?"

Sugden nodded. "A constable has already been dispatched to retrieve the doctor. He should be here shortly."

"Excellent," Simon replied before returning to his investigation. "Ver—" he began before his voice failed him. He cleared his throat loudly before continuing. "Due to the pallor and rigidity of the victim, along with the severe blood loss, it's a safe assumption that the cause of death was exsanguination."

"What does that mean?" Sugden asked.

"It means she bled to death," Luthor said helpfully.

The detective frowned. "I know what the word means. What I meant was how does it affect our—"

"It means," Simon interrupted, "that the limb was removed perimortem." Simon turned his upper body so he could face Sugden. "It means, Detective, that she was still very much alive when the leg was severed."

Simon turned back toward Veronica's body as he swallowed a wellspring of emotion. His voice had been steady as he spoke to the detective, but every word had been like acid in his mouth.

A headache was forming at his temples. It seemed to muddle his thoughts as he tried to decide what he should do next. Everything seemed equally important, but he knew his own mind. Whatever ill effects he would suffer as a result of Veronica's death would happen sooner rather than later.

The Inquisitor glanced around the alleyway, though it was still dark. The meager light from the lanterns did little to illuminate the long alley. He stared into the darkness past Veronica's body as another lance of pain rolled across his forehead.

Detective Sugden and Luthor merely watched, unsure if their assistance was wanted, much less needed. Simon stared down the alleyway for some time as though entranced.

"Should we do something?" Sugden quietly asked, so as not to disturb the Inquisitor.

"What, pray tell, would you have us do?" Luthor replied curtly, his only concern for his friend who was doing all he could to contain the obvious devastation he was feeling. "Is there something you can think of that a Royal Inquisitor could not?"

The detective frowned sharply at Luthor and turned away, walking brusquely back toward the awaiting police cars. The apothecary glanced over his shoulder, feeling guilty for his treatment of the detective. He hadn't intended to be so harsh, but he could equally feel the tension of Veronica's death. Luthor didn't want to be in the alley, standing over the corpse of Simon's fiancée. Truthfully, he didn't even want to take the Inquisitor home. Mattie had been taken to the hospital, having been severely beaten. Despite knowing that her werewolf metabolism would heal her far quicker than a normal human, he couldn't help but feel great concern for her well-being. Not only was she injured, but healing too quickly might also draw unnecessary attention from the hospital staff. It was best if she was retrieved from the hospital to convalesce at their shared townhouse.

A man stepped up beside Luthor. For a moment, the apothecary merely assumed it was Detective Sugden, returned from his brooding. As he turned, however, he realized the man was far taller and skinnier than the robust detective was. Doctor Casan's gaze was locked ahead, watching Simon at work.

"Forgive me for interrupting your thoughts," Casan said. "You seemed thoroughly lost in them."

Luthor shook his head. "There's nothing to forgive. Better I don't spend too much time alone with my thoughts right now."

Casan watched Simon, who remained transfixed in place. "Detective Sugden stopped me as I entered and warned me that you knew the victim personally?"

"In more than a passing fancy," Luthor replied. "She and Inquisitor Whitlock were recently betrothed."

136

Casan glanced around Simon, who was blocking the victim from sight. The doctor's mouth opened slightly as his brow furrowed. He quickly leaned back to Luthor's side. "That's Miss Dawn?"

Luthor nodded. "I'm afraid so."

"You have my condolences; you both do."

The apothecary nodded but had nothing else to say. He removed his bowler and ran a hand through his sweaty hair. The night might be cool, but the entire situation left him hot and bothered.

"What is he doing?" the doctor asked, gesturing toward Simon. The Inquisitor had slid forward, oblivious to the discomfort as his knees scraped across the cobblestone pavers. Simon appeared to be examining the ground near Veronica's head.

"He's conducting an investigation," Luthor replied matter-of-factly.

Casan stroked his chin thoughtfully. "Is that wise, considering his personal involvement?"

Luthor gestured toward the Inquisitor. "You're more than welcome to try to dissuade him."

"Luthor," Simon said, his voice growing progressively more unsteady. "I need your assistance."

The apothecary hurried to his mentor's side. "What is it, sir? Have you found something?"

Simon shook his head. "I haven't, and I fear my time of rationality is dwindling rapidly. Miss Hawke was severely beaten during the altercation. No normal man could have committed such a crime, which leads me to believe that the owner of that oversized footprint was involved in this crime as well. Search the alleyway and surrounding streets to the best of your ability. Take samples of anything you may find, no matter how seemingly insignificant."

"And you, sir? What would you like to do? I can escort you home, if you'd like."

"No," Simon adamantly replied. "No, I will accompany the coroner back to the police station and assist in the autopsy. If this is the same killer, the proof may still very well be on her... remains."

Luthor appeared ready to argue, but Simon glanced past him toward Doctor Casan. "Doctor, if you're ready, I believe we can now remove the body."

"Of course," Casan replied. The doctor gestured toward a pair of constables, who hurried forward with a gurney.

"Find whatever you can and then meet us at the precinct," Simon said before following the sheet-covered body toward the awaiting horse-drawn wagon.

The apothecary watched Simon climb into the back and the door swing closed behind him. He knew what had been requested, but his friend temporarily stupefied Luthor. His fiancée had just been slain and another good friend badly beaten. A normal man would have collapsed to his knees and wept like a child and, as far as Luthor was concerned, rightfully so. No one would have thought less of Simon had he cried, the tears justified after so traumatic a loss. Yet Simon didn't cry. He spoke only haltingly at times, as though the human emotions existed within him but were so foreign he didn't know how to cope with their swelling to the surface. The apothecary had thought Simon an automaton before, an unfeeling, uncaring mechanical creation no more human than an automobile, but tonight made him think his simple jest held far more truth than Luthor would have liked.

Detective Sugden noticed Luthor standing at the mouth of the alleyway and hurried over. "Forgive me, Mister Strong, I didn't realize you were still here."

Luthor's gaze followed the retreating coroner's wagon for a moment longer before he replied. "We're all a bit surprised by my continued presence here."

"Then you'll completely understand when I tell you that your presence isn't needed?" Sugden asked, though it was hardly a question.

Luthor frowned. "I made a promise—"

"You made a promise to a man who had no jurisdiction to investigate this crime in the first place," Sugden interrupted. "I was ordered by his superiors to deliver case files, not to invite him into my investigation. You, being an underling for the Inquisitor, have even less right to disrupt my crime scene. Now, if you'll excuse me, I must brief the actual crime scene investigators. By the time I return, I assume you'll be gone?"

Luthor's frown deepened. He had known since the beginning that Detective Sugden wasn't a stupid man, but he hadn't pegged him for being so abrasive. The detective turned away. Luthor sighed and glanced around cautiously, ensuring no prying eyes were looking. The constables had done a remarkable job dispersing the inquisitive crowd. Only a few hangers on were still watching from a distance, though much too far away to see anything as discreet as what Luthor intended. Using just his index finger, Luthor traced a symbol into the air between the two men. It flashed silver for a moment before fading completely, leaving just an afterglow in the apothecary's vision.

Detective Sugden stopped, only a few paces away from Luthor. The detective shook his head slowly before turning around. "Forgive my rudeness. I don't know what came over me. I know how personally attached you are to this case and welcome your assistance. Would five minutes be enough time before I bring over the constables?"

"More than enough," Luthor quietly said, feeling heavily taxed after expending his magic.

As Sugden turned away once more, Luthor's shoulders sagged. His spell gently nudged Sugden's thoughts in a more amicable direction, but the effects wouldn't last long. Within the hour, the detective would be sitting in his office, wondering what possessed him to allow the apothecary to stay. With the fading of the spell would come a bit of resentment, as though the apothecary had made him do something against his will, which in fact he had, though Sugden would never know exactly how. Luthor very much doubted the next meeting between the two of them would go so smoothly.

"Excuse me, Detective, but would you have any vials or containers with which I might collect samples?"

The detective retrieved some glass vials along with a pair of tweezers and handkerchiefs that Luthor could employ. He happily handed them to the apothecary, as though sending gifts to a long-lost friend.

As the detective departed once more, Luthor turned toward the alley. Retrieving one of the nearby lanterns, he held it aloft as he walked into the alleyway. He avoided the rivers of blood that were still seeping between the stones, soaking into the dirt and mortar along the narrow path. Like most other alleys in Solomon's Way, garbage littered the ground; some contained within bags but more often than not just piled freely. He also smelled the unmistakable scent of human waste. It stung his nostrils and forced him to stoop lower as he walked, watching carefully for undeterminable piles of refuse.

He could see nothing worthwhile near the mouth of the alley or even a few feet into the gloom. Simon was right that the large accomplice had to be present at the crime scene. Mattie had been naked when she was recovered, which meant that she had transformed during the fight. No normal man would have withstood the full wrath of a transformed werewolf, especially when caught unaware. Knowing the larger monster had to be present did little to help his investigation. There were no obvious footprints that he could find near where Veronica had been found, even when he pushed aside piles of garbage.

Luthor knew time was short. His five minutes would pass quicker than he'd like. He wasn't concerned about constables entering the crime scene. He was more concerned about the magical effects he had placed on the detective wearing off sooner rather than later. Sugden had shown himself to be just as strong-willed as Simon at times, which was a precursor to a man shrugging off the effects of the spell quicker than anticipated.

Walking deeper into the alleyway, Luthor continued to search the ground for clues. It felt like a hopeless endeavor, his lantern light bobbing and splashing against the raised stones but revealing nothing. Near the far end, Luthor came across a manhole cover. Steam rose from the small vent holes, a white cloud of putrescence that made the apothecary's eyes water. He started to turn away when something caught his eye. Beside the cover was a smear of dark brown, nearly black mud. Pressed firmly into the mud was the toe print of an abnormally large shoe.

Smiling excitedly, Luthor crouched and removed a vial. Using a handkerchief, he pushed a pinch of the mud into the glass container. As he withdrew the cloth and placed a stopper into the bottle, Luthor frowned. The handkerchief was nearly black from the mud, but the edges of the stain were marred a dark red, as though mixed with old blood.

Hearing the constables' footsteps quickly approaching from the far end of the alley, the apothecary stepped out, exiting from the end opposite the crime scene. As the sun began to crest over the tops of the nearby buildings, Luthor hurried toward the police station.

CHAPTER

Twenty

OCTOR CASAN GRASPED THE TOP OF THE SHEET
covering Veronica's head, but his hand paused. He glanced toward Simon, who stood a good distance away from the metal
slab on which her corpse had been placed, clearly unnerved by the situation.

"You don't have to be here for this," Casan offered. "I could just as
well complete my report and bring it to you at a later date."

Simon ran his tongue nervously over his lips but shook his head. He
could feel the same beginnings of a headache that had plagued him since
the alley. He knew he should be in bed recuperating. By all rights, he
wanted to be in bed, sleeping away the wellspring of emotions that roiled
through his body and settled in his chest. He wanted nothing more than
to go home but being here, being with her during the autopsy, was too
important.

"No, Doctor, please proceed."

Casan stared at the Inquisitor a moment longer before his gaze returned to the sheet. He slowly drew back the cover until Veronica's face
and shoulders were exposed but revealed nothing else, maintaining her
feminine decency, even in death. Her body had been stripped of clothing

upon their arrival. Simon had wisely chosen to wait beyond the doors of the morgue during the procedure.

Stooping, the doctor felt Veronica's hair and ran a gloved hand over the skin of her face. Gentle pressure smoothed the wrinkles on her forehead, clear marks that she had been under duress at the time of her death. He glanced cautiously toward Simon time and again, ensuring the Inquisitor wasn't offended by his handling of her remains. The Inquisitor stroked his chin repeatedly in a nervous gesture but remained silent.

With a deep breath, Casan tilted the corpse's head from side to side, feeling the initial onsets of rigor mortis and the resistance now evident in her muscles. He stooped even lower until his nose was only an inch from the flesh of her neck, and he could see his breath dancing through her hair.

"It's here," the doctor commented, staring intently at a red mark on her neck. "Much like our previous case, there's a small puncture wound on her neck. It appears to be a low-gauge needle, judging by the diameter and inflammation around the injection site."

Simon took an unsteady breath. "Is it Curare, as with Gloria?"

Casan straightened and shrugged his shoulders. "I'll take a blood sample as part of the autopsy, but it'll be a day or more before we can properly receive the results. Though it won't be included in my professional report, I would say that Curare is a safe assumption in this case. There are... indications that she was alert during..."

The doctor faltered, unsure of the words to use. The clinical precision with which he normally spoke seemed heartless when discussing the death of Simon's fiancée.

"I understand all too well," Simon replied, saving Casan the discomfort.

"Of course." The doctor turned away from the Inquisitor and retrieved a metal tray, on which surgical instruments had been arranged.

At the sight of the tools, Simon felt anguish piercing his temple, a headache the likes of which he'd never encountered before. Bile rushed into his throat as his stomach churned. He knew what was to come next, being well versed in forensic medicine. He had personally conducted autopsies in the past, but he approached those instances with the same clinical detachment he had maintained in his work as in Inquisitor. Bodies were faceless lumps of flesh, no longer housing the spark of life that made them unique. It was simple to draw a scalpel across their chests in the pursuit of the truth. They didn't feel the pain; therefore, it meant nothing to Simon to conduct the autopsy.

Staring down at Veronica's face, however, he knew the same wouldn't be true this day. Her angelic face was at peace, the doctor having smoothed away the lines of discomfort. Her eyes were closed as though merely asleep. It was easy to forget she wasn't just sleeping naked on the cold, metal slab. More than anything, Simon wanted to believe she was asleep. He wanted to believe that any moment, through a true miracle from the God she believed in so much, she would open her eyes, her body whole once more.

The scalpel that Doctor Casan lifted from the metal tray was the vessel that would make her death all too real. The second it touched her flesh, drew beads of whatever blood still remained in her exsanguinated body, her death would be real. He'd have to face the realization that the woman he loved, the only woman he'd truly loved, was dead.

His mouth felt parched as he swallowed down the mixture of acid and depression. He wanted a drink. No, he *needed* a drink.

"Are you sure you're all right?" Casan asked, his scalpel hovering inches over Veronica's exposed collarbone.

Simon shook his head. "I'm most decidedly not all right. Forgive me, Doctor, I don't believe I can stay for this. I—"

His words failed and he turned quickly, fighting strongly against the urge to vomit. Once clear of the room, Simon took a deep breath and wiped his eyes with his handkerchief. The cloth came away damp, but Simon maintained his composure as he walked toward the stairs leading to the police station's main floor.

He met Luthor halfway up the stairwell, the apothecary carrying a glass vial full of an indeterminate viscous muck. Luthor started to give his regards, but Simon ignored him and continued his climb.

Luthor watched his mentor's hasty departure. He wanted to stop him, to ask if he was feeling well. He couldn't imagine Simon's loss or how it might impact the man. The Inquisitor was strong, both physically and emotionally, but the expression on his face as they passed one another spoke of a man on the brink of crumbling.

Rather than follow his friend, Luthor turned toward the basement and finished his walk to the morgue. He opened the doors and entered but immediately regretted the choice not to announce himself. Veronica was lying on the metal slab, the skin of her chest peeled away, exposing the sinew and white ribs beneath. Doctor Casan held a bone saw in his hand, angling it appropriately to crack the sternum.

Casan looked up at Luthor, a bit apologetically as he noted the apothecary's pale demeanor. "I wish that I could offer to do this at another time, but I've already opened the body. Time is of the essence."

Luthor nodded but found a hundred other interesting items scattered through the morgue at which he could look.

"If it would be better, you could return in two hours or so," the doctor offered. "I should be done by then."

"No, no," Luthor quickly replied. "I have some other things to discuss with you that could occupy my time and, God willing, my attention."

The doctor smiled. "You seem rather squeamish around the sight of blood. I would have thought you desensitized to the sight, being partnered with a Royal Inquisitor."

The sound of the metal saw teeth cutting through bone temporarily stole Luthor's response. He eventually cleared his throat. "Blood doesn't bother me at all. On the contrary, I've seen more than my fair share, often covering Simon. Sometimes the blood even belongs to someone other than the Inquisitor."

Casan laughed, which seemed even more off-putting for Luthor, as though humor and autopsies had no place together. The doctor seemed within his element, a far cry from the nervous man who had sat in Simon's sitting room, nervously describing a multitude of murder victims.

"There's a personal attachment that I'm not used to, is all," the apothecary continued. "I know into whose chest you're cutting right now. That makes it all a bit unnerving."

The cutting stopped, and Luthor stole a glance. The sternal saw was still firmly in place, having not completely severed the sternum, but Casan was watching with genuine concern.

"I wish there was a simpler way for me to conduct this autopsy," the doctor explained. "If there were a way to merely echo what we already know—that her leg had been severed, leading to severe blood loss and death, most likely, as a result of shock—than I could forego the formal autopsy." He grasped the saw once more, and Luthor looked away. "Unfortunately, I would also then lose my job, which is instrumental in me maintaining my meager way of life. Therefore," a long saw stroke filled the room, "I must continue my work. I did offer for you to leave during these formalities, however."

"You did and it was most kind of you," Luthor meekly replied. He held up the vial in his hands. "I did find this at the crime scene. I was going to give it directly to Simon, but he seemed a bit out of sorts when we passed on the stairs. Perhaps you could have a look at it when you get a chance?"

"Of course," Casan said. Removing the saw, he picked up a hammer and chisel.

Luthor immediately regretted his decision to stay.

The next two hours seemed to drag on for Luthor. The sawing eventually gave way to the careful removal of organs, all of which were weighed and annotated before being placed in jars. Luthor allowed a deep sigh of relief when Doctor Casan finally began sewing Veronica shut. After two long hours of the forensic autopsy, the apothecary was having trouble seeing the dark-haired woman as the lady he had met so often, rather than just a corpse on a slab.

"We're done, finally," Casan said, sounding as drained as Luthor felt. "I will perform a toxicology test on her blood to identify the agent used, but I still believe we'll merely be confirming the use of Curare."

"You have my many thanks," Luthor said as the doctor walked around the gurney, stripping away his blood-soaked gloves. He walked to Luthor, picked up the vial, and held it up to the light. "What do you suppose this is?"

"Mud would be my assumption," Luthor replied, "based solely off the location where it was found, though it's far darker than I would expect from normal mud. Perhaps this will be the one clue that helps solve the string of murders."

Casan smiled. "One can only hope." He set down the vial, and his smile faded. "Forgive me, but I must ask a more serious question regarding her remains."

Luthor glanced over the doctor's shoulder.

"Is there someone to whom I can release the remains?" Casan asked.

The apothecary let his gaze drift to the door, out of which Simon had retreated a few hours earlier. "Is it possible for you to hold the remains here temporarily as we make proper arrangements?"

The doctor nodded. "Of course, though I can only keep it—her—for a short while."

"Hopefully a short time will be all we require," Luthor said, his gaze still on the closed door.

Simon walked into his house, closing the door quickly behind him. Without turning on any of his lights, he paced slowly into the sitting room, reveling in the darkness. The table was still littered with folders of previous victims. Aside from Gloria, they had mostly been faceless names to Simon before now. He had examined their pictures with as much interest as someone examining a caricature drawn by one of the carnival folk at a circus. They seemed unreal, as though the people behind those faces, the women who had died, weren't real.

Now each face seemed to stare at him accusingly, reminding him of their parents or spouses or children who had been left behind with their murder, as he was now left behind. The eyes of the women's faces followed him around the room, their mouths pursed in silent whispers, calling him a failure.

Simon bit his lip until he could taste copper in his mouth. His eyes drifted to the liquor cabinet, and an insatiable thirst seemed to wash over him. He quickly turned away, focusing instead on the files. Walking to the table, he lifted the closest report and began reading it anew.

He had told Luthor that her investigation deserved the best. Simon knew that with enough time and determination, he could find what the constabulary had missed. It was here, within the files, concealed amongst Detective Sugden's crude handwriting, the one clue that would tie the murder scenes together, that would reveal the identity of the murderer. He would find Veronica's killer, of that he had no doubt.

He dropped the first report on the table and lifted the second. His eyes darted over the files but the words seemed to slide across the page, elusively avoiding the Inquisitor's gaze. He could feel it again, the headache behind his eyes and the weight in his chest. It was a burden tied around his neck as he stood on the precipice of a proverbial cliff, threatening always to pull him over and drag him down.

Dropping the second report, he grabbed the third and then the fourth. Tears stung his eyes as he tried to find the evidence, the something that he had missed during his first examination of the reports. It was there; it had to be.

Simon felt the welling of anger within him. The answer wasn't in the reports, at least not that he could see. Sugden's reports had been incomplete. That had to be the answer because the alternative was that Simon just wasn't good enough to follow the clues. The only other option was that Simon wasn't competent enough to find Veronica's killer.

Lifting the stack of files, Simon roared in anger and threw them against the wall. The folders exploded open, showering the far side of the room in loose-leaf parchments. Black-and-white pictures fluttered end over end as they fell to the floor.

Huffing heavily, Simon turned away from the table and walked to the liquor cabinet. Retrieving a bottle of scotch and a tumbler, he uncorked the bottle with his teeth and, with shaking hands, poured himself a glass near to overflowing. Drinking half in a single long gulp, Simon refilled his glass before retreating to the nearest chair, tumbler in one hand and bottle in the other.

CHAPTER
Twenty-one

AINT DONOVAN'S HOSPITAL WAS A TWO-STORY
bleached white building that sat on the divide between Solomon's
Way and Eden's Grove, a district of Callifax best known for its
debtor's prison and Saint Midridge's Asylum for the Mentally Impaired.
Luthor approached the glass-inset front doors, through which he could
see only a single receptionist's desk. Opening the front door, he realized
that the room was far more crowded than he had first believed. Rows of
chairs lined either wall, most of which were filled with people in some
stage of illness or injury. The tiled floor was stained with spots of dried
blood. A man in the corner, keeping as much to himself as the crowded
room would allow, coughed loudly into a handkerchief that was marred
with bright red blood every time he withdrew it from his lips.

The receptionist, a heavyset woman with a dour expression, raised
her gaze to the newcomer. "What is your illness?"

Luthor removed his bowler's cap and held it protectively before him,
as though it offered a shield against the myriad of illnesses around him.
He knew, instinctively, that the tattoos running the length of his spine
protected him from any normal and, to some degree magical, malady,
but he still felt uncomfortable around such brazen sickness.

"I'm actually not here to be seen but rather to see someone already admitted," Luthor offered.

The woman's expression changed not at all, even as her gaze dropped to a ledger before her. "What is the name of the patient?"

"Mattie, or rather Matilda Hawke."

The woman ran a portly finger along the page until she found the name. She glanced up once more toward the apothecary. "Are you family?"

Luthor shrugged. "As close to family as she has in Callifax."

"I can only admit family to visit an admitted patient. It's hospital rules."

"Then I'm her brother," Luthor bluntly stated.

The woman stared at him impatiently before eventually shrugging. "She's in room 205, up the stairs behind me."

"Thank you kindly, madam." He leaned in closer so that he could speak in a whisper. He pointed toward the man in the corner. "Are you aware that the man there is exhibiting all the signs and symptoms of consumption? It's highly contagious."

The receptionist narrowed her eyes. "Are you a doctor?"

Luthor realized it was not so much a question as a direct insult to his credibility. Rather than reply, he nodded toward the woman before hurrying toward the stairwell, stealing only the quickest glance at the man suffering obvious respiratory distress.

The second floor seemed far quieter and more reserved than the lobby. Only a few patients were out of their rooms, most in various stages of convalescing. Some walked with the assistance of canes while others were wheeled about in wheelchairs. Mostly, however, the patients were quarantined within their rooms and interacted solely with the doctors and nurses.

Room 205 was easy to find, not so much by the haphazard numbering system employed by the hospital but rather by the uniformed constable standing guard outside its door. As Luthor approached, the constable nodded to him politely.

"Can I help you, sir?" the policeman asked.

"I'm Miss Hawke's brother," Luthor lied once more, figuring a consistent lie was better than a mixture of lies and truth. "I hurried here once I was informed of her attack. Is she all right?"

"Forgive me, sir, I wasn't told to expect any family for the lady."

Luthor shook his head. "Think nothing of it. I'm as surprised as you are."

The constable glanced through the small glass window set in the door. "The lady is currently resting. Perhaps you could come back after she's awoken?"

"I'd rather I see her now, if it's all the same. I promise not to be a bother or wake her."

The bobby seemed conflicted as he looked Luthor over. As he glanced over his shoulder toward the room once more, Luthor looked quickly about and then traced a small rune in the air. The constable shook his head as he turned back around.

"I should think paying your respects wouldn't hurt her none," the guard replied. "It would probably do her some good to awaken to a friendly face." The constable politely opened the door. "Do be sure to be quiet while she rests though, sir."

"Of course," Luthor replied.

The apothecary stepped inside, and the guard gently closed the door behind him. The room was dark with the curtains drawn. The only light in the room came through the narrow window in the door. It took Luthor's eyes a few moments to adjust to the gloom. In the meantime, he merely stood by the door.

"Are you going to come in or are you going to keep standing there wide-eyed?" Mattie asked hoarsely from her place on the hospital bed.

"Mattie? I was told you were asleep."

"I was," she replied. He could begin to make out her outline as his eyes adjusted to the darkness. "As soon as you entered the room, however, I could smell you. It woke me up right away."

Convinced he could see well enough, Luthor walked toward her bedside. She raised a hand and he immediately took it, holding it close to his chest. He couldn't see the details of her face but could feel her wince as she moved about on the bed.

"How are you?" he asked. "No, that's a stupid question. Of course you're not all right. You were just beaten by a monster. What I meant to ask was—"

"You're rambling," she said. "I'm healing miraculously well, if you would believe my doctor."

Luthor smiled. "Somehow, I'm not at all surprised."

"Perhaps not, but they are," she said, gesturing toward the doorway. "I can't help but feel they'll be terribly suspicious when I'm nearly completely healed within a day or two."

"We will worry about that problem when we come to it."

Mattie's eyes widened suddenly, as though the memories of her encounter came rushing back to her in a tidal wave of horror. "Veronica. Oh God, I'm so sorry—"

Luthor quickly placed his finger over her mouth, feeling terrible even as he felt the scab running across her split lip. "No, I won't let you concern yourself about that now."

"But she died," Mattie sobbed, tears welling and leaking from the corners of her eyes, leaving trails down both cheeks. "I tried to stop him, but I couldn't. I saw the sheet as I awoke, draped over her body."

Luthor grasped her shoulders, though he dared not squeeze too tightly. "Now is not the time for talk like that, Mattie. You need your rest."

"I failed her," she wailed. "Now she's dead."

Luthor shook his head. "You didn't kill her. In fact, you did all you could to save her. Right now, I want you to forget about Miss Dawn and worry, instead, about yourself."

She took a deep breath. "I should be helping with the investigation, not lying in a hospital," she defiantly said. "I clawed the beast during our struggle. My hands and nails were coated with whatever passed for its blood. I could have shown you if this accursed hospital hadn't scrubbed my skin so thoroughly." She held up her spotless hands. "There's nothing left for our investigation."

"The investigation is better left for the constabulary."

"They know even less than you," she explained.

Luthor arched a brow. "Have they already spoken to you?"

"As soon as I awoke in the hospital. A detective asked me some preliminary questions. I told the truth to the best of my ability but left out some of the more egregious facts. Luthor, we can't leave this investigation in their hands. Veronica died and the constabulary will never catch her killer."

"Don't worry yourself about the investigation. You need... I need you healthy if you're to help us, but for right now, leave the investigation to... to Simon and me. I promise you we're doing all we can to find the killer."

She reached up and wiped her cheeks. Luthor hated to see her so vulnerable. She was a werewolf; she transformed into a creature that tore men asunder. Yet now, as a woman, she seemed incredibly frail and frightened. As she was, he didn't have the heart to tell her that Simon seemed too distracted to properly investigate the crime at hand.

"I need you to do something for me," she said, her stoic self returning.

Luthor took her hand and squeezed it once more. "What can I do for you?"

She looked at him sternly. "Get me out of this hospital. Take me home where I can heal with some semblance of dignity. Here, I have a nurse or a doctor disturbing me every few hours to take my temperature or check for signs of infection. They'll never find one, but they don't know that."

"I'm not sure—"

"Don't patronize me, Luthor," she said, her voice strong and confident. "Take me home."

He nodded, not seeing that he had much choice. As she began drawing back the covers, Luthor realized she was still very much naked beneath the sheet and quickly turned away, blushing. Mattie walked to an armoire nearby and opened the cabinet doors, revealing her outfit from the evening hung within.

"They were kind enough to retrieve my things when they brought me here," she explained as she hastily dressed. "I don't know if it didn't dawn on them to ask why my clothes were so far away from where I had been beaten or if their sense of chivalry forbade such questions, but I'm thankful either way." After a moment's pause, where she groaned as she clasped the corset over bruised ribs, she continued. "There. I'm done. You may turn around now."

The apothecary turned and was surprised by what he saw. Mattie was dressed in fine eveningwear, clearly an outfit chosen not by her but, more likely than not, by the recently deceased Miss Dawn. Regardless of the source, she looked stunning. The ensemble nearly offset the dark bruises across the side of her face and now-exposed shoulder and the gashes marring her cheek, brow, and lip.

As he stared, the door opened behind him and the doctor turned on the electric lamp overhead. Luthor squinted at the sudden light, raising his hand to shield his eyes.

"Where do you think you're going?" the doctor asked as he glanced past Luthor and saw the dressed woman.

"Home," she replied, "where I can get a full nap without being perpetually interrupted."

The doctor shook his head as he searched for the words. "You can't leave. You're unwell and certainly unfit to be out of a hospital bed."

Mattie smoothed the front of her corset, which hugged her curves flatteringly. "You told me during your last visit that I'm recovering exceptionally well. 'Miraculously,' I believe, is the word you used."

"Healing quickly is not quite the same as being healthy enough to leave the care of a doctor."

Mattie shrugged and glanced at Luthor. "Shall we, Mister Strong?"

"You can't leave!" the doctor said, raising his voice and drawing the attention of the constable stationed beyond the door.

"You can't stop me," she replied, brushing past the stunned physician.

They opened the door only to find the uniformed policeman barring their way. The doctor gestured toward the pair. "Constable, I'm ordering you to stop them at once."

Luthor smiled at the man. "Keeping us here is just more work for you and, unless I'm mistaken, there are far better things you could be doing with your time."

The constable smiled dreamily as Luthor's magic continued to course through him. "I'm sure you could heal just as well under the supervision of your... brother." The guard motioned toward the stairwell. "Shall I call you both a taxi?"

"That would be delightfully helpful," Luthor replied.

The constable turned down the hall and walked away. Luthor offered Mattie his arm for support as they walked slowly from the room, the redhead flinching with every painful step.

"If you leave, you're doing so against my expressed recommendations," the doctor yelled after them.

Mattie, to her credit, suppressed the urge to visually express exactly what she thought about the doctor. By the time they made it down the stairs, which took far longer than it should have, there was already a taxi idling by the curb beyond the hospital's front doors. Luthor helped her into the seat even as the constable politely held the door for them both. When Luthor was seated within, comfortably beside Mattie, the guard closed the door and patted the roof of the automobile. With a jerk, it sped away from the whitewashed building, driving hurriedly toward the

Upper Reaches.

The ride was blissfully quick and smooth, ending as the taxi pulled to a stop before Luthor's townhouse. As before, the apothecary helped her from the car. He could see her expression of dread as she noticed the six steps leading to his front door. Any other day, the steps would have been nothing more than a minor inconvenience. Today, however, they appeared as nothing short of a mountain that must be scaled, pain and discomfort be damned.

With great effort, they reached the landing and Luthor unlocked the door. As Mattie stepped inside, the apothecary let his gaze drift to the neighboring townhouse. No lights shone through the windows, though the heavy curtains were drawn. The building's façade had an overwhelmingly uninviting appearance, despite Luthor knowing that his mentor was at home.

He followed her inside, closing the door behind him. Mattie was standing transfixed in the foyer, staring in horror at the staircase leading to the second floor and her bedroom. A faint whimper escaped her lips at just the thought of climbing more steps today.

"Can you not simply magic me up the stairs?" she pleaded.

"If I had that in my repertoire, I most certainly would."

She shook her head. "I can't climb stairs anymore. Not today. Perhaps tomorrow, but even then I make no promises."

Luthor glanced into the sitting room, to the cushioned couch. "Would you accept mediocre sleeping arrangements today? The sofa is surprisingly comfortable."

Mattie smiled. "Bring me a pillow, a blanket, and a hot cup of tea and I think we might have come to some sort of an accord."

Once Mattie was comfortable on the couch and had finally fallen asleep, Luthor quietly left the townhouse and walked next door. The windows were still dark, even in the narrow slats between the curtains. Luthor knocked loudly, loud enough to raise the dead, but he heard nothing from within. Simon didn't yell out for him to go away, as Luthor had presumed he would, nor did he hear the shuffling of furniture as Simon stood to check on his unannounced visitor.

If Simon was home, and Luthor had no reason to doubt that he was, he clearly had no interest in being disturbed. Begrudgingly, Luthor turned away and returned home.

CHAPTER

Twenty-two

BY THE TIME LUTHOR CAME DOWN THE STEPS THE
next morning, Mattie was already awake. The sound of sizzling
bacon came from the kitchen, mixing with the harsh whistle
of the teakettle. The apothecary rounded the corner and found Mattie
standing before the stove, already dressed for the day. Gone were her fancy clothes, the corset and wide skirt traded for a simple button-down
shirt and slacks.

"I didn't expect to find you up," he remarked as he entered the kitch-
en.

"Well, I seem to be feeling much better today," she said, turning toward him with a knowing smile. "Like the doctor said, it's miraculous."

She looked considerable better than she even had the day before. A
few bruises remained along the side of her face, and she opened her jaw
gingerly as she spoke but most of the swelling had receded. The deep
gashes on her cheek and brow had begun to close, leaving behind puck-
ered scabs that would turn to scars within a day or two. Luthor frowned,
hating that even simple scars would mar her face, leaving constant reminders of her attack, but he was thankful for her werewolf physiology.
A normal woman would have most likely died in the alleyway that night.

If she had survived, she would be bedridden for weeks as she recovered from her wounds. Mattie, to the contrary, was walking about the very next day.

"I took the liberty of cooking breakfast," she said.

"I can't thank you enough for it," Luthor replied. "I'm famished. I don't believe I ate anything at all during the day yesterday. My stomach seemed turned after…" He stopped himself, leaving the rest of the sentence hanging pregnant in the air.

Mattie shook her head. "We seem so intent on not stating the simple facts. Veronica is dead and, to a degree, I'm to blame." She held up her hand, silencing any objection. "I couldn't keep her safe, which was my task. I accept that blame, but let's not pussyfoot around the subject any longer."

Luthor nodded and took the plate of food that she offered. The aroma was enough to make him temporarily, and willingly, forget their conversation. She led them from the kitchen and they sat at the small table, enjoying their meal.

"Did you speak with Simon yesterday after I fell asleep?" Mattie asked, wincing as she sat, straining the still-healing ribs. "I heard you leave but lacked the energy to ask where you were going. I must have been completely asleep by the time you returned."

"No, I didn't," Luthor replied, taking a bite of his bacon. "I knocked on the door and am pretty sure he was at home, but he refused to answer."

She shrugged. "His behavior seems a bit childish, ignoring his friend."

"Simon's a private man under the best of circumstances. Now he's mourning his loss as he does best, alone in the darkness."

"You don't mourn alone," Mattie explained, wagging a strip of bacon at him for emphasis. "You find your friends, you pour yourselves drinks, and you celebrate their life."

Luthor cringed. "I'm pretty sure that he's doing all those things, save spending time with friends."

Mattie had set down her food and lifted her cup of tea but paused. "Do you think he's all right, drinking alone in the dark? Any scenario that begins that way usually ends poorly for all involved."

"I've seen him drink men twice his size under the table," Luthor replied unapologetically. "Let's allow him to mourn in peace for a bit, and then we'll invade his privacy once more."

Mattie took a sip before setting down her cup. "Celebrating his drinking prowess is not a very glowing endorsement of his state of mind."

"Perhaps not," Luthor replied absently. "I know this is a delicate subject, but if you feel up to it, I need you to recount the events in the alleyway."

Mattie frowned. "You certainly know how to ruin a breakfast." She sighed. "Very well."

Luthor stared out the window as Mattie described the night of Veronica's death. Her words droned on as Luthor's mind wandered to thoughts of his friend. He agreed wholeheartedly with Mattie. Simon drinking alone in his townhouse was a potentially dangerous situation, but there was little to be done. If Simon wanted to ignore the world for a day or so as he coped with the loss of his fiancée, who was Luthor to try to dissuade him? The Inquisitor would come to his senses eventually, and everything would return to the way it had always been between them.

"Have you heard a word I've said?" Mattie curtly asked.

Luthor arched an eyebrow as he glanced toward the irate woman. "Every articulate word, but forgive me all the same, my dear. My mind was elsewhere."

"Continue ignoring me and I'll send your head to join your thoughts."

He smiled but glanced back out the window. Parked in front of Simon's walk, there was a black automobile idling. Concentrating, he could hear its engine rumbling and could just make out a driver sitting in the shadows within. Luthor furrowed his brow as he gently moved aside the curtain.

"What is it?" Mattie asked, craning her neck to look out the window as well.

"There's a car parked in front of Simon's door."

"What do you suppose they want?" she asked.

Luthor released the curtain and turned toward her with a frown. "Well, I haven't the foggiest, now do I? Clearly, someone wishes to speak to the Inquisitor."

"He won't answer for them either," she replied, taking another sip of tea. "If he wouldn't open the door for you, then certainly he wouldn't open the door for a stranger."

"Perhaps not, but they certainly seem persistent," he remarked. "Maybe I should go and see who is paying Simon a visit this early in the morning?"

"Do you think that's wise? Perhaps Simon asked someone to come."

"Then he'd just be ignoring me and that's rude," Luthor chided as he stood. "I think I'll go see what this is all about. If you'll excuse me."

He leaned forward and kissed Mattie on the cheek before walking toward the door. Taking his bowler from the hat stand, he placed it atop his head as he opened the door. The morning was bright and clear, though the faint haze of smog hung in the air above him. He stepped onto his landing and glanced to the townhouse next door. A young man—clearly a messenger by his formal attire—stood by the door with a folded parchment in hand.

"You, boy," Luthor said, catching the messenger's attention. "What's your business with Inquisitor Whitlock?"

The boy looked flustered, his hand hovering inches from the door as he prepared to knock again. "I have an urgent letter from the Grand Inquisitor. Do you know if the Royal Inquisitor is at home?"

"Are his lights off and curtains drawn?" The boy nodded, and Luthor sighed. "He must be away on official business. I'm Luthor Strong, Inquisitor Whitlock's partner. Any correspondence can be left with me. I'll be sure to pass it along to the Inquisitor upon his return."

The messenger seemed unsure, going so far as to glance toward the awaiting car parked on the curb. "I was told specifically to deliver this to Inquisitor Whitlock."

"I've already informed you that I can take custody of the letter," Luthor said with far less patience. "Bring it to me and be gone."

Hesitantly, the boy glanced once more at Simon's door before hurrying down the steps. He came around to Luthor's walk, and the apothecary met him halfway down his front steps. The messenger held out the note, which Luthor gladly took from him. The front of the letter was emblazoned with the red wax and official seal of the Grand Inquisitor.

Fishing around in his pocket, Luthor withdrew a silver coin and begrudgingly handed it to the boy. Luthor had far less disposable income than Simon and every coin spent offended his frugal sensibilities. Giving the messenger a silver coin, however, ensured the boy left with no questions asked and would, presumably, tell his boss that the task had been completed satisfactorily.

With a tip of his hat, the boy returned to the automobile. As soon as his door was closed, the vehicle pulled away from the curb and sped down the street. Luthor watched it leave for a moment before glancing down at the note in his hands. Simon would be infuriated if he discovered that Luthor had stolen a letter addressed to him, but the apothecary was sure Simon was in no condition to handle any such correspondence.

He slipped back into the townhouse, closing the door firmly behind him. No sooner did he hang his hat on the rack than Mattie addressed him.

"Who was his visitor?"

"A messenger, with a note directly from the Grand Inquisitor."

Mattie frowned. "Is it wise to have taken that letter yourself?"

Luthor was still looking at the Grand Inquisitor's seal as he walked back to the table. "I was just asking myself that very thing. The immediate answer is yes, as I worry about Simon's state of mind at the moment, though I think I might very well change my answer in the foreseeable future."

"Roughly around the time Simon discovers what you've done?" she knowingly asked.

Luthor glanced up at the woman. "Yes, right about at that moment."

He stood impassively and glanced down at the note once more, as Mattie waited impatiently at the table. He bit his lip as his finger hovered at the edge of the seal. It seemed like a great leap of faith, as though he wouldn't understand the implications of what he'd done until he finally broke the seal.

"Will you be keeping me in suspense all day?" she asked brusquely. "At some point I'll have to excuse myself to use the loo, but I don't want to miss something important."

Luthor glanced toward her derisively over the top rim of his glasses. Without a curt reply, he slipped his finger beneath the seal and broke through the wax. Unfolding the letter, he read the short note.

"The Grand Inquisitor is requesting an update on Simon's investigation into the murders," Luthor dryly explained.

Mattie set down her teacup and crossed her arms over her chest. "Clearly they don't know about Veronica as of yet."

"Clearly."

"They're expecting a response from Simon. You'll have to take the letter to him and explain your interference."

Luthor arched an eyebrow. "Are you mad? I'd rather swallow a hot coal than admit I intercepted a letter meant for him and opened it, all the while as he was recovering from so grievous an event."

Mattie lifted her napkin from her lap and dabbed the corners of her mouth. "What's the alternative?"

Luthor set the letter on the table as a faint smile spread across his lips. "Magic. It's always the answer, isn't it?" He hurried from the room. She could hear him in the study next door, searching furtively through his belongings.

"It only seems to be the answer when you're up to no good," she replied, frowning. She raised her voice to be heard over the din. "Much like the incident with the guard at the hospital. Don't think I didn't notice something amiss."

"And Detective Sugden," Luthor called back.

"You magicked the detective?" she replied in disbelief. "Are you mad?"

"No," Luthor replied as he walked proudly back into the room, a quill and sheet of parchment held in one hand and an inkwell in the other, "but he will be next time we meet."

"You seem to be taking this all in stride."

"Mattie, my love, I have more things to worry about than I currently know what to do with. I take each problem as they arise and don't concern myself with the others until they become a bit more pertinent."

She pushed back her chair and stood, collecting the empty plates from the table. Stacking them, she carried the dishes into the kitchen. "That's an absolutely awful way to go through life."

"The doily, too, if you please," was his only reply.

She walked back into the room and pulled aside the lace doily, leaving him a clear spot on which to work. He laid the parchment on the table before him, smoothing the corners until it stopped trying to curl on the edges. Holding the quill between the fingers of his right hand, Luthor drew a nearly invisible rune onto the narrow rachis. Burning red, it smoldered on the quill even as Luthor held the writing instrument aloft once more. He dipped the quill into the ink and began writing, muttering to himself as he did so.

"Dear Grand Inquisitor," he said, echoing the words he wrote on the page. "My investigation goes well. My collaboration with the local constabulary has produced numerous pieces of evidence, the most important of which I pursue even now."

Mattie glanced over his shoulder, and her eyes widened in surprise. She had seen Luthor's more sprawling script but what she saw produced on the page looked nothing like his handwriting. Instead, she saw tight and succinct writing, each letter meticulously drawn. She had, likewise, seen that handwriting before. The writing on the page clearly belonged to Simon, though it came from Luthor's hand.

"How are you—?"

"Magic, my dear," he said. The quill wrote those very words onto the page, and Luthor scowled. "Erase that, damn you!" The words vanished, evaporating into the air. Looking up apologetically, he offered no other response before turning his attention back to the page.

Luthor continued the letter until it was complete, including a very convincing signature at the bottom, clearly belonging to the Inquisitor. The apothecary leaned back in satisfaction and examined his handiwork as he allowed the ink to dry.

"That's very impressive," she said.

"It won't fool them for long, unfortunately," Luthor replied, shaking his head. "Eventually Simon and the Grand Inquisitor will speak once more, and the deception will be revealed. This will hopefully satisfy the Inquisitors long enough for us to solve these murders."

"How, if I may ask? Simon is an integral part of our investigation, but he won't answer his door."

Luthor shrugged. "Then I'll knock until I become so bothersome he'll have no choice but to let me in."

"Sorry for being a naysayer, but what if that fails as well?" she asked.

"Then we'll have to solve this crime in spite of the Inquisitor."

CHAPTER
Twenty-three

"**T**HEY'LL BE EXPECTING AN ACTIVE INVESTIGATION,**"** Mattie exclaimed as Luthor folded the letter and handed it to her. "Regardless of what your forged letter reads, there is no active investigation."

"Not yet," Luthor explained, "but there will be. The first step will be you delivering that letter to a courier and ensuring it gets into the hands of the Grand Inquisitor. I'd rather trust you to take it directly yourself, but I dare not leave you alone in the Grand Hall."

"I appreciate your concern and application of common sense, not that I have any urge to step foot into that building again. While I'm busy delivering messages, what shall you do?"

Luthor straightened his tie and adjusted the shoulders of his suit jacket. "Isn't it readily apparent? I'm going to go see Simon and ensure we didn't outright lie in that letter."

Mattie pursed her lips, cringing slightly at the strain on her healing split lip. "Good luck, Luthor. You'll need it."

Leaning forward, he kissed her on the cheek, avoiding the myriad of injuries on her face. She turned abruptly and hurried from the townhouse, eager to have her part of the plan completed as quickly as possible.

In contrast, Luthor followed her slowly out the door, taking the time to close it completely behind him. As much as she dreaded being anywhere close to the Grand Hall, he dreaded trying to convince Simon to forget his morose self-deprecation and rejoin their investigation. It was an up-hill battle, the apothecary knew, like trying to carry a drunken man up a flight of stairs. Everything about his task seemed like an uphill battle, in which the simplest of tasks would be the deadweight he was trying to maneuver up the stairwell.

Walking to the end of his sidewalk, he turned sharply and entered the very next gate leading up to the Inquisitor's home. The curtains were still drawn, despite the early morning sunlight reflecting off the front of the stone townhouse. With great trepidation, the apothecary climbed the stairs and knocked loudly on the door.

No one answered, nor did he hear movement within, though he was certain Simon hadn't left. He knocked again, louder than the first time, but heard no response.

Taking a deep breath, Luthor yelled at the closed door. "I know you're in there, sir. Please open the door."

For the first time, he heard shuffling from within, though it was muffled and it went as quickly as it came. Still, it was enough to convince him that Simon was, in fact, at home.

"I can hear you inside, sir. You should know that I won't leave until we've spoken. If I have to stand here all day, banging incessantly on your door until you concede defeat and open it, so be it."

He raised his hand to knock again but paused as the door handle rotated slowly. He hadn't heard Simon moving within the home, but the Inquisitor was now clearly standing on the far side of the door. It opened a sliver, and Simon's ragged face appeared in the crack.

"What do you want, Luthor?" Simon muttered. "Can't you see I'm busy?"

The smell of alcohol radiated from the Inquisitor, as though it were oozing from his very pores. His breath stunk of heat and scotch, a terrible combination that made Luthor wither in his presence.

"I can see that you're drunk, sir."

Simon's head nodded slowly. "Good. Now we've spoken, so you can depart from my front step and leave me in peace."

The door started to close, but Luthor shoved his foot into the crack.

He winced as Simon threw his shoulder into the door, crushing the apothecary's foot between the door and its jam. With some force, Luthor pushed the door aside and Simon with it. The Inquisitor stumbled into the foyer before catching his balance.

"I don't recall inviting you into my home," Simon curtly said.

Luthor stared at his mentor in disbelief. The man's hair was disheveled, draping over his eyes rather than slicked back across his head in its normal coif. Stubble lined his cheek and dark bags hung under his eyes, though Luthor couldn't tell if that was from lack of sleep or intoxication. Likewise, Simon's bloodshot eyes could have been the result of either malady. As the Inquisitor stared angrily at the apothecary, Simon's nostrils flared with each deep breath.

"Sir, you're a mess. Have you slept at all?"

Simon shrugged. "I'm sure that I have, not that it's any business of yours."

"You're drunk," Luthor said, his voice condescending, as though talking to a child. "Don't you think it's a bit early in the morning for scotch?"

"I wouldn't know, Luthor," Simon replied as he walked back into the sitting room. "I've been drinking the alcohol so as to not be inconvenienced with problems like thinking,"

The room was incredibly dark, lit only by the slivers of light that slipped unbidden between the heavy curtains. No lights were lit, though Luthor's eyes adjusted quickly to the gloom. The Inquisitor sat heavily into a cushioned chair. Beside his seat, a rounded end table stood, on top of which stood a half-emptied bottle of scotch and a nearly empty tumbler. As though noticing the bottle, Simon refilled the glass and took another drink.

"For what reason have you invaded my sanctuary this..." Simon glanced out the window inquisitively, "this morning?"

Luthor took a seat on the sofa across from the Inquisitor. "The Grand Inquisitor has been attempting to contact you, sir. It seems he's quite intent on finding out how goes your investigation into the murders."

"And what did you tell him?"

"I lied and told him we had the investigation well in hand," Luthor explained.

"Excellent," Simon blurted. "Then you clearly don't need me. You seem to have this well in hand."

"On the contrary, sir, we need you now more than ever. I lied to the Grand Inquisitor, but there will come a time in the near future when he sees through my ruse. We need your help."

Simon took another long drink, draining a full quarter of the tumbler. "No, Luthor, you don't. You are more than capable of conducting this investigation on your own. Leave me be to wallow in my self-pity."

"That's a surprisingly clear interpretation of your current predicament, but I can't leave you be. We need—"

"No, you don't," Simon sternly replied, his gaze matching the intensity of his words. "I don't know what you don't understand, but I've just lost someone very near and dear to my heart. I don't think I'm asking too much to be left alone." He threw up his free hand in disgust. "Dear God, why is it so difficult just to be left alone, to mourn in peace without being constantly interrupted by people thinking they are deserving of my time?"

Luthor was stunned by Simon's outburst. For a moment, he wasn't sure how to respond. "This isn't you, sir. This is the liquor speaking."

"The liquor may have lowered my inhibitions, allowing me to speak far more freely, but this is the most brutally honest version of me you're likely to see in your lifetime."

"What I know, sir, is that no matter the pain you're currently in, alcohol isn't the solution."

Simon chuckled. "My dear Luthor, you're a chemist at heart and in chemistry, alcohol is very much a solution. Now go away, I don't want to see you."

"I know you better than to believe that."

Simon shook his head before taking another drink, his eyes never leaving Luthor. "Maybe you just don't know me as well as you assume."

Luthor felt entirely on the defensive. When he had come to visit Simon, he hadn't expected to be attacked at every turn. Every response he gave felt like that of a petulant child, refusing to believe the facts presented so clearly before him. "I don't believe that."

Simon smirked condescendingly. "That's the wonderful thing about the truth, Luthor. It's like gravity, evolution, or the planet's rotation around the sun. You don't have to believe it for it to be true."

A silence stretched between the two men. Luthor had trouble matching Simon's piercing stare, which hardly seemed to waver, regardless of how much alcohol the Inquisitor consumed. Eventually, Luthor stood, though he had no intention of so readily leaving Simon's home.

Correctly guessing Luthor's persistence, Simon sighed. "I'm quite busy, Luthor. What do you need?"

Removing his glasses, Luthor pinched the bridge of his nose. He could feel his ire rising at Simon's clear ambivalence. "What do I need, sir?" he incredulously replied. "Your fiancée was just murdered. I want to know that you're okay, rather than just hiding yourself in your home, drinking yourself into a stupor."

Simon quickly drained the remainder of his glass before setting the tumbler down heavily on the end table. "I'm not just drinking. I'm... I'm keeping myself busy."

"With what, pray tell?" Luthor asked, his patience quickly reaching its end. "It looks like you're wallowing."

"Just because your mind doesn't grasp the subtle nuances of my profession, don't presume I'm not occupied with my work."

Luthor threw his arms up in disgust. "Your work be damned, sir! You've just lost someone you love. It's okay to *feel*, to be saddened by her loss. No one will blame you if your cold exterior cracked with some semblance of feeling morose."

Simon drummed his fingers impatiently on the table. "Forgive me, but what good would that accomplish?"

"It would remind people that beneath that impenetrable exterior beats a real heart," Luthor explained as he leaned toward the Inquisitor. "It lets people know that you're a human and not merely an automaton."

Simon glanced up at his friend, but Luthor didn't see empathy reflected in his eyes. The Inquisitor's eyes were glassy and dark. He lifted his arm from the chair and for a moment, Luthor believed Simon was reaching out for him. The apothecary extended his hand, but Simon reached past Luthor and retrieved the open bottle of scotch.

Infuriated, Luthor lashed out, knocking the bottle from Simon's hand. It crashed to the floor, its contents spilling onto the rug. The apothecary immediately regretted his outburst, and he raised his hand to his mouth.

"Forgive me, sir. I don't know what came over me."

Simon, his hand still outstretched, glanced at the ruined scotch. "That bottle was a gift from the Grand Inquisitor himself. I had been saving it to celebrate my pending nuptials but instead now drank as a consolation." His glossy gaze rose to the embarrassed man. "I shall say good day to you."

"Sir," Luthor stammered, "please accept my deepest apology—"

Simon rose quickly from his chair, practically yelling at him. "I said good day, sir!"

Seeing no other recourse, Luthor hurried from the townhouse.

CHAPTER

Twenty-four

LUTHOR RETURNED SOLEMNLY TO HIS TOWNHOUSE. The foyer was dark as he entered. He removed his hat and jacket and placed them on hooks. Dismayed, he walked into the sitting room and collapsed into a chair. In a fit of irony that wasn't lost on the apothecary, he immediately felt that the situation demanded a drink.

He had barely moved from his chair when the door opened once more and Mattie appeared. She looked slightly flushed from the heat of the day and the walking, and she stood rigidly in the doorway as her eyes adjusted to the gloom. Eventually she glanced over and noticed Luthor resting in the sitting room, his fingers laced before his face. His expression told Mattie all she needed to know as she entered. She shook her head in dismay.

"He won't be coming, will he?" she asked.

"At the rate he's going, I'd be damned well surprised if he was still breathing by this time tomorrow. No, Mattie, he most certainly won't be coming."

She walked hurriedly toward him, pausing as she stopped beside him. Her brow was furrowed in concern. "What are we going to do? If the Grand Inquisitor wasn't expecting an eventual conclusion to the investigation before, he most certainly will thanks to the letter I just delivered."

"We'll have to conduct the investigation ourselves."

Mattie laughed softly. "You'll have to excuse my laughter, but what do either of us know about conducting an investigation?"

Luthor looked genuinely offended. "I've accompanied Simon on countless investigations over the past two years. I think I'm qualified to conduct this investigation on my own."

Mattie sat on the arm of the chair and patted Luthor's shoulder. "Do you honestly believe that?"

Luthor frowned. Admittedly, he lacked Simon's abilities of deductive reasoning and interrogation, a keen mastery of observation by which the Inquisitor could discern lies from the truth. Still, he wasn't sure he and Mattie were completely helpless. Her supernatural senses and his magic might very well span the gaps left in the wake of Simon's departure.

"We need Simon," she said.

"He won't come."

She slid from the chair and knelt before Luthor, taking the apothecary's hands in hers. "Luthor, we need Simon."

Luthor failed to meet her gaze, looking instead toward the window. Though he wasn't sure she was right, he knew that the investigation would be a hundred times easier with Simon by their side. His detective skills and seemingly infinite knowledge would be invaluable.

The apothecary smiled. "We don't need Simon. We need someone just like Simon."

Mattie arched an eyebrow. "I assume you know someone who meets those qualifications?"

"A forensic scientist equally versed in the ways of the constabulary? I have just the person in mind."

———————— ⚙ ————————

Luthor stood outside the Solomon's Way police station, feeling apprehensive about entering. Doctor Youke Casan would be in the basement, toiling away in the morgue as was his wont, but prior to reaching the morgue, Luthor would have to pass, and potentially confront, Detective Sugden. A spot of magic at the crime scene had convinced the detective to allow Luthor to remain, despite a complete lack of credentials. Sugden had been cordial, to the point of outright friendliness toward the apothecary at the time. However, like all mind-influencing magic, the effects were short lived. Moreover, the person, upon shrugging off the effects of the spell, was filled with quite a different series of emotions. Namely, the victim of the spell maintained a general loathing toward the wizard in question. There was nothing that Luthor could tell the detective that would dissuade the man's swelling urge to shoot him on sight.

Taking a deep breath, Luthor climbed the steps and entered the precinct. As before, a police sergeant manned the front desk, looking mildly disinterested in his line of work. He raised his gaze as Luthor entered. Recognizing him, the sergeant's eyes widened as Luthor approached the table.

"I'm here to see—"

"You'll need to wait here," the sergeant interrupted before standing and hurrying toward one of the many offices lining the wall of the expansive floor behind him. Luthor cringed as the sergeant reappeared, with Detective Sugden in tow. The detective smiled wickedly as he hastily approached the apothecary.

"Mister Strong," the detective reproachfully said.

"Detective Sugden," Luthor said, smiling in what he hoped was a disarming way.

"Do you have a moment to speak?"

Luthor gestured toward the stairwell. "I have a meeting with the doctor in a few moments, and I would hate to keep him waiting."

Glancing toward the stairs, the detective scowled. "I don't think I need to remind you that neither you nor Inquisitor Whitlock have any formal authorization to be investigating these murders. This is a business best left to professionals like the constabulary."

"I understand completely," Luthor lied.

"What's your business with the doctor, then?"

Luthor cleared his throat. "Strictly a personal visit to a newly acquired friend, nothing more."

Sugden nodded before motioning for the sergeant to leave them. When the policeman was gone, the detective leaned closer so he could speak in a low but harsh whisper. "I don't know what you did in the alleyway to convince me to let you stay, whether it was hypnosis or something far more—"

"Let me stop you there, Detective," Luthor interrupted loudly enough that it drew the attention of the other constables sitting nearby. "If you are insinuating in some way that I used sorcery, then I would advise you to choose your next words very, very carefully."

The detective blanched. The spell's aftereffects might leave the detective heated but not in complete disregard of his faculties. Both men knew the risk of making an accusation of witchcraft. A false allegation would bring nearly as deadly repercussions to the accuser.

"I believe you're going to be late for your meeting with the doctor if you don't go at once," the detective said, though Luthor could hear the ire in his voice. "Have a good day, Mister Strong."

Luthor didn't offer a reply as he walked toward the stairwell. His heart pounded against his ribs and his stomach leapt into his throat. He wanted to vomit. It had been a dangerous gamble, placing the detective on the defensive. Though it had worked, Luthor thought it in his best interest to avoid the police station for the foreseeable future. Forever seemed like the right amount of time.

He maintained his composure as he descended the stairs, waiting until he was out of sight before wiping the sheen of sweat from his brow. The basement was far cooler than the upstairs, the cold seemingly radiating from the frigid morgue. The doors were closed, but the cold seeped from around the edges of the doorframe.

Remembering his last experience, Luthor opted to knock before entering. Doctor Casan quickly invited him to enter, and Luthor pushed through the doors. The doctor was seated at his desk, files spread before him as he annotated notes from his recent work. The floor of the morgue was gratifyingly empty, the corpses all housed in their shelves along the walls.

"Luthor, it's good to see you again," Casan said, setting down his pencil. "To what do I owe this unexpected visit?"

"I've come to ask for your help."

Casan raised his eyebrows. "I have the impression that this help exceeds that of a simple mortician."

Luthor ran a hand over his muttonchops. "I need your help solving these murders."

The doctor's eyebrows fell as he furrowed his brow. "I thought that was exactly what I'd been doing."

Luthor gestured toward the empty chair across from the doctor. "May I?"

"Where are my manners? Of course."

Luthor sat and leaned forward, resting his elbows on his knees. "I need you to take a more active role in the investigation, to become more than just the forensic doctor on the case. I need you to be an Inquisitor."

"Correct me if I'm wrong, but that position is already filled."

Luthor glanced over his shoulder, as though expecting Detective Sugden to burst through the doors at any moment. "Perhaps we could talk elsewhere, somewhere away from the station?"

"It's probably for the best," Casan replied as he stacked his papers neatly on the desk before him. "Detective Sugden hasn't been very pleased with me lately."

Luthor sighed. "I'm glad to know it's not just me."

"There's a pub across the street," the doctor said as he stood, took off his lab coat, and draped it over the back of his chair.

"Perfect."

Luthor followed the man from the morgue and up the stairs. Sugden still stood in the doorway of his office, watching the two men pass with a look of great disdain on his face. Luthor tried to avoid making eye contact, instead following the doctor—who seemed all the more oblivious—out of the station.

The two men weaved through the slow moving automobile traffic and entered a pub across the street. It was quickly approaching lunch, and Luthor's stomach growled at the smell of cooking stew filling the room. Patrons were filtering in and tables were quickly filling as working men and women prepared for a hearty lunch before returning to their various jobs. Casan and Luthor chose a table away from the door, a private affair near the back wall. Though there were plenty of people within the pub, they could talk freely without being overheard. As Simon had told Luthor many times before, a busy room allowed the greatest chances of anonymity.

A waitress came by, offering drinks. Casan glanced at Luthor, inviting the apothecary to order first. A part of Luthor wanted a pint, something hearty that would burn as it went down his throat, but circumstances being what they were, it seemed in bad taste to order alcohol.

"Just a water, if you please."

Casan nodded appreciatively. "The same, and thank you."

"Will you both be eating?" the waitress asked.

"Is that stew I smell?" Luthor asked.

"It is."

"I'll have a bowl."

"Make it two," Casan added.

The waitress nodded before departing. The smiles on their faces lingered even as they turned back toward one another.

"You seemed rather uncomfortable at the police station," the doctor noted. "I hope nothing's the matter."

"Very observant," Luthor noted. "Yet another reason I need you to accept my proposal."

"One issue at a time."

"The detective and I seem to have had a recent falling out," Luthor said as vaguely as possible.

Casan chuckled. "The poor detective has been having issues with any number of people recently."

"Even you?"

"Especially me." The doctor sighed. "I've been under intense scrutiny since Miss Dawn's untimely demise. It seems that Simon's inadvertent comments at the crime scene led the detective to believe, rightfully, that I provided the coroner's reports to you both."

Luthor was taken aback. "Forgive us, Doctor, we never meant to get you into trouble."

Casan waved his hand. "Think nothing of it. I don't blame him; he was under an inordinate amount of stress at the time and could hardly be expected to self-censor."

"I find the detective to be insufferable at times."

"Don't hate the detective too much. He's suffered great loss in his life, as well. His son was killed, a murder that was never truly solved. That loss has shaped the man he's become and made him bitter, all the more so with every passing day that he can't find our most recent murderer."

The waitress returned, placing a pair of water glasses between them and interrupting their conversation. From a tray, she produced a couple of shallow bowls of thick stew. The aroma was intoxicating, and Luthor's stomach growled in response. As the waitress departed, the apothecary took a bite of the stew and sat back appreciatively.

Doctor Casan, likewise, took a bite, though it was small and he chewed and swallowed it quickly. "Speaking of the Inquisitor, how is Simon?"

Luthor finished his bite quickly and wiped his mouth on his napkin. "He climbed into a bottle and made his bed. I shan't think we'll see him again any time soon."

Casan nodded and took a sip of water. "Losing someone you love can be hard on a man. Everyone copes with loss differently."

"You speak as a man of experience."

The doctor set down his glass and dabbed the corners of his mouth. "My father was a man of some considerable wealth. He was mortified when his only son chose a profession as pedestrian as a doctor. When I was attending university, my mother passed away quite unexpectedly. At the time, my father was alone, having lost his wife and me, their only child, miles away from home attending school. As a result of his loneliness, my father turned to drink. Eventually, he sank into a depression from which he never truly recovered."

Luthor nodded but remained quiet for a moment, feeling the gesture of silence would be appreciated. "Is your father still alive?"

Casan shook his head. "He was admitted to Saint Midridge's, here in Callifax, but never regained his faculties enough to be released. When he passed some years back, his wealth was divided first amongst his investors and, after those vultures had picked my inheritance to the bones, I was really only left with a pair of useless antique chairs and an empty warehouse here in Solomon's Way, the contents inside having already been sold off to pay his outstanding debts."

"That's a terrible ending to his story. He sounded like he was a remarkable man."

"He was, once. He deteriorated over time until dementia set upon him. I visited from time to time, but he never recognized me. His eyes were hollow and vacant, as though only enough of his mind remained to keep him breathing and his heart beating in his chest. Eventually, those parts of his mind went as well."

Casan laughed awkwardly and stirred his stew. "What a dreadful topic during lunch. The moral of that story is that, as a result of my lack of inheritance, I now find myself in a morgue, working in the basement of a police station in Solomon's Way. More importantly, I know the pain of having someone drown their sorrows in a bottle and how important it is to ensure their mental stability."

"All the more reason for you to join us," Luthor insisted. "Simon is in no condition to conduct a proper investigation, as you yourself can attest. We need someone with a keen mind and sharp powers of observation. Miss Hawke and I will, of course, assist in every way we can, but we lack your seemingly limitless capabilities."

"You flatter me."

"Only because you're deserving. Though I would be loathed to admit this in Simon's presence, you are the only man I've met that might rival his intellectual faculties."

Casan shrugged. "How can I say no to such a glowing recommendation?"

"Clearly, you can't."

"Very well, then, Luthor, what would you have me do?"

Luthor smiled. "You and I are going to solve a murder."

CHAPTER

Twenty-Five

LUTHOR DID HIS BEST TO EXPLAIN ALL THE EVIDENCE he and Simon had collected prior to Veronica's untimely death, to include the footprint in the rubbish and their estimation that the owner of said footprint stood at least nine-feet tall. As they talked, the sky outside grew dark as storm clouds gathered overhead. The pub filled with the patter of rain striking the glass windows. Luthor and Youke quickly paid their bills and walked toward the door, disgruntled yet excited. Though neither man wanted to walk in the rain—nor, admittedly, was either man dressed for the weather—they were both eager to begin the investigation anew.

Luthor turned up his collar and placed his bowler low on his head with the hopes of keeping out the rain, which had turned from a simple drizzle to an outright downpour, pelting the awning and pooling along the sidewalk. Stepping through the door, ensuring they remained in the narrow protective overhang of the awning, both men scanned the road, hoping a taxi would happen by. After some minutes of genuine indecision between the two men of whether it was worth walking through the drenching rain, a taxi happened by, one that they were lucky enough to flag down.

Even the insignificant walk from the awning to the waiting taxi left them both drenched. Such was the Callifax weather—beautiful one moment before a sudden storm cloud appeared as though by magic overhead. Luthor envied Mattie as the two men sat in the back of the car; she may lack the refinement reserved for those who were brought up within the city, but she would have had no problem shaking herself like a dog to rid herself of the accumulated water. Instead, the two dignified men sat beside one another, dripping stoically during the drive to Luthor's townhouse.

The rain had lessened considerably by the time they arrived, returning once more to a light drizzle. Luthor paid the fare as they exited and hurried up the walkway to the front stairs. Reaching the safety of the front landing, Luthor lowered his collar once more and reached into his pocket to retrieve the key. His gaze drifted to the house next door, where the curtains were drawn and still no light seeped from the dark windows. A part of him longed to knock on Simon's door once more, regardless of the abrupt ending to their last conversation. They were about to delve into the heart of the investigation, an arena in which Simon was champion. Luthor could most certainly use the Inquisitor's expertise, but was sure it wouldn't be freely given today or any day soon. Begrudgingly, he turned back toward his own door and unlocked it.

The interior was warm and well lit, a stark contrast to the gloomy exterior, where dark storm clouds had blotted out the sun, their dark edges bleeding into the black smoke billowing from smokestacks throughout the city. The rain had left them wet, and the bitter wind that accompanied the storm passed through their clothes and struck them in their very bones. Luthor stripped off his damp jacket and hat, hanging them on pegs beside the door before inviting the doctor to do the same. As they were warming themselves in the foyer, Mattie rounded the corner from the sitting room.

"I thought I heard someone come in," she said with a smile that turned up only one corner of her mouth. The other was still scabbed and healing, along with the matching bruise that marred the side of her face.

Luthor smiled, knowing damn well that she had heard, smelled, and very likely identified them individually long before rounding the corner. "Mattie, may I formally introduce you to Doctor Youke Casan? He'll be assisting in the investigation in Simon's stead."

"It's a pleasure to meet you, Doctor," Mattie replied, offering a sorry excuse for a curtsey. The unmanageable ringlets of her hair bounced as she stood.

Casan furrowed his brow as he examined her, his eyes barely leaving the exposed marks on her face. "Miss Matilda Hawke?"

"One and the same," Luthor replied.

The doctor reached out toward Mattie's cheek, but she quickly pulled away, out of his reach. Casan withdrew his hand immediately and blushed. "Forgive me, madam, I meant no disrespect. My medical curiosity got the better of me, and I forgot my manners. You are the woman that was attacked just yesterday in Solomon's Way?"

"I am," she guardedly said.

"Your wounds are healing incredibly quickly, lest the report I received overstated your injuries," he said. "From that report, I would have believed you'd be bedridden for weeks as a result of the attack."

"My physician had an inflated sense of self," she said. "I'm sure he exaggerated greatly in his report, so that he might impress upon his colleagues the depths of his surgical skills, saving the life of such a grievously wounded woman."

She ended her sentence with a dramatic flare and, for a moment, Luthor even believed she might have been that very fragile woman. The reality of her situation weighed upon him almost immediately, however, and he was eager to draw the doctor's attention away from her injuries.

"If we may," he said. "I've taken the liberty of writing some basic notes about the case, as I've observed them. I would greatly appreciate any level of insight you might provide us, Doctor Casan."

The doctor nodded but gestured toward Mattie. "If it's all the same, in such an intimate setting, I'd much prefer you called me by my given name. Calling me 'doctor' or merely by my surname seems so impersonal."

"Of course," Mattie said. "Youke, was it?"

"Indeed." He stretched out his hand again, though this time to take Mattie's rather than probe at her wounds. Taking her hand, he brought it to his lips.

"If you'd both follow me into the study," Luthor interjected, "we shall begin."

They took their seats around the central table. The warm fire roared beside them, popping intermittently as the wood blazed a cherry red. The heat soaked through Luthor's remaining damp clothing, and he felt goose flesh rising on his arms. He shook off what remained of the chill before retrieving his notebook.

"Based solely from the coroner's reports—for which we thank you greatly—and the crime scene reports lent to us by Detective Sugden, I've taken the liberty of identifying what I believe to be key characteristics of our killer. Once refined, I think this may be a thorough template that we might utilize to identify his location."

"I'm intrigued," Youke replied. "Do go on."

Glancing between his notebook and the two people seated around the table, Luthor began. "What do we know? The killer appears to be a man in the medical field, or at least someone proficient with a blade, enough that they could perform a swift and delicate removal of a limb."

"Excuse me, but why a man?" Mattie asked.

Luthor frowned, not expecting an interruption so quickly in his presentation. "Meaning no disrespect, but the women were overpowered physically before the fatal injuries were inflicted. While I have met some very sturdy women, present company included, this would insinuate a man."

He paused for a moment, expecting an argument but when Mattie offered none, he continued. "I lean toward a member of the medical community because of the use of drugs to subdue the victims."

"I can agree with that assessment," Youke replied.

"Inquisitor Whitlock also seemed keen on the idea that the killer was a resident of Solomon's Way," Mattie added. "Not only did all the attacks occur within the district but if something went sour with a victim, he—or she—would need to be able to escape quickly, which is easier to do within a district with which you're familiar."

"Logical," the doctor added. "Have you considered the differing methodologies for the murders, the unlikely transition between the rending of the limbs in the beginning to a more affluent method involving a blade, as we've seen recently?"

"I did," Luthor said, adjusting his glasses as he read further down his page. "Coupled with the oversized footprint found at the crime scene, I think it likely that we're dealing with one of two scenarios. The first of which, I wondered if we might be dealing with a copycat, someone seeking notoriety while riding the coattails of a more proficient killer?"

Casan shook his head. "The methods are vastly different, admittedly, but the theft of the limbs is a detail we intentionally left out of the papers. Were it not for the murders of your acquaintances, it's highly unlikely any of you would have become aware of that specific detail. In fact, aside from those of us in this very room, only the detective, constabulary, and Inquisitor Whitlock know those pertinent and gruesome facts."

"Then perhaps we're truly dealing with just a single killer, one who's adopted an evolving style that has grown along with his confidence?"

Again, Youke shook his head. "People, killers in particular, don't change, at least not to such vast degrees that one might go from using such brute strength to, instead, incorporating surgical precision in his," he glanced toward Mattie, "or her attacks. Besides, a single killer theory is unsupported if we are looking for someone in the medical field. By your own admission, the killer is beastly, standing nearly nine feet tall. A nine-foot-tall surgeon would surely attract unwanted attention, enough that we would easily identify our killer."

Luthor leaned back in the sofa, setting his notebook aside. He had exhausted his list of clues and was now eager to see the directions in which the inquisitive mind of the doctor would take. "I had only two scenarios, both of which you've now refuted. Do you have a third?"

Casan smiled as he leaned forward, resting his elbows on his knees. "I do. We've already mentioned that a nine-foot physician is impractical, but there is a level of medical expertise. We also know—and forgive me for bringing up such painful and recent wounds—that a tall assailant is present during the course of the crimes. I'm insinuating that there are, in fact, two killers working in tandem, one the public face and one the disfigured, shadowy figure."

"A similar thought to the one Simon shared during the early stages of the investigations," Mattie said.

Luthor nodded. "Indeed, but I remain fixated on this towering brute. I imagine him with a hunched back and limbs of uneven sizes, hobbling through the streets on his vile missions. Yet we queried the inhabitants of Solomon's Way and found no one who recognized so giant or disfigured a person. How would you hide someone like that? Even the night wouldn't conceal their movements so perfectly."

The doctor nodded thoughtfully. "I've considered this predicament and think I have a solution. When you came by the morgue earlier, you brought a sample of mud with you, in which was imprinted a similarly oversized footprint, correct?"

"I did."

"Sadly, as you well know, I haven't had a chance yet to examine the mud or make any determinations, but it's not the mud itself that struck me but rather where you'd found it."

Luthor arched an eyebrow. "In the alleyway?"

"More precisely, near a manhole cover, one that, unless I'm mistaken, leads into a labyrinth of sewer tunnels that run beneath the city."

Luthor's eyes widened, not in surprise but at his own ignorance for not making the connection sooner. "The sewers would be a perfect means for moving beneath the city without drawing unwanted attention. The public face could very easily move freely throughout the city—"

"While the beast roams its underbelly," Casan concluded.

"A brilliant deduction," Luthor complimented. "You truly are the right man for the job."

The doctor shrugged. "In the absence of someone more proficient, you mean?"

"On the contrary. You're a man of reserved sophistication, Doctor."

"Perhaps, but my deductive reasoning hasn't gotten us any closer to an identity for either of the mysterious killers."

"I might be able to help with that," Mattie interrupted. She had been quiet for most of the conversation, as was her wont, which gave her words—when she did speak—all the more weight. "I injured the beast during our struggle… a mere scratch across its stomach, hardly a hindrance to so large a creature, but enough to draw blood. I had some on my hands and under my nails until my unfortunately brief stay at the hospital, during which it was all washed away. I am sure, however, that some of its blood was also splashed across the wall of the alleyway. Did either of you happen to see it during your investigations at the scene?"

Youke narrowed his gaze. "You say you slashed the creature with enough force to drive blood under your nails and splash it across the walls? Exactly how potent are your hands, madam?"

"I didn't see it," Luthor interjected, "though admittedly, I wasn't looking to the walls during my time at the murder scene. Did you, per chance, notice the blood, Youke?"

The doctor's gaze remained on Mattie a moment longer before he shook his head. "Like you, I was occupied with Miss Dawn's remains and not examining the scene itself."

"If the constabulary also overlooked the evidence, it might still be there," Luthor said. "With these rains, our evidence is likely to be washed away if we don't act soon. Perhaps we should meet in Solomon's Way within the hour?"

Casan nodded. "If these rains hold, the water level in the sewers will have risen. I agree that we should act very quickly or not at all."

"Then it's settled," Luthor said, glancing toward Mattie. "Within the hour, then? We'll all meet at the crime scene."

"I shall see you there," Casan said as he stood.

Luthor escorted the doctor to the door, handing the man his jacket and offering to call him a taxi. The doctor, however, politely declined.

"I shall manage well enough on my own, but thank you for the offer," Youke said. "I hope we find the evidence we need."

"As do I, Youke. We shall see you again within the hour."

The doctor stepped out of the door and into the driving rain, which had increased in intensity once more. He raised his jacket until it covered his head before rushing down the front steps. Feeling sympathy for the man, Luthor watched until the doctor had turned the corner and was waving excitedly toward a passing taxi.

With the door closed, Luthor also retrieved his jacket and hat, placing it firmly on his head in anticipation for the foul weather. Mattie stepped into the foyer, crossed her arms, and leaned against the doorframe. She stared inquisitively toward the apothecary.

"Will you go to see him again?" she asked.

"It's my duty," he replied. "He has a right to remain informed."

"Even if he has no intention of acting upon that information?"

Luthor glanced at her as he opened the front door. "No, but rather because if the information I provide spurns him from his inaction, then it won't be wasted time at all."

He closed the door behind him and hurried down the stairs.

CHAPTER
Twenty-six

LUTHOR TOOK A DEEP BREATH BEFORE KNOCKING ON the door. He pulled his doctor's bag tighter to his side with his free hand as he waited. He could hear the shuffling within but, as with the last time, no one came to let him in. The apothecary knocked again, louder, rattling the door with each strike. Eventually, he heard the footfalls of someone entering the foyer and the locks being thrown. The door opened wide as Simon turned away from the door and strode unsteadily back toward the sitting room.

"How did you know it was me?" Luthor asked.

"Who else would be insufferable enough to bang on my door so incessantly?"

Luthor wiped his feet before entering, lest he track water into the house. After stepping inside, however, he resented cleaning the puddled water from his shoes. A bit of water would have done the house some good.

A pungent aroma hung in the air, a mixture of stale tobacco and food left unattended on the countertops. As Luthor walked toward the sitting room, he could see a nearly full ashtray resting beside a half-finished bottle of liquor. Thin tendrils of smoke still rose from the discarded cigarette balanced precariously on the side of the ashtray.

"For what great honor have you come to visit me a second time?" Simon asked curtly. "Did our last conversation leave you wanting?"

Luthor flushed with both embarrassment and anger. "No, sir, you made yourself transparent during my last visit. I thought you might want to hear about the progress being made in the investigation, since it's all being done in your name."

"You thought wrong," Simon replied, sitting in the chair so that his back was to the apothecary. He lifted his tumbler from the table and took a drink.

"I've employed Doctor Casan to assist in the case," Luthor continued as though the Inquisitor hadn't just chastised him. "He's an exceptionally brilliant man, not too unlike yourself, sir. His medical insight and his years working in close confines with the constabulary have given him a plethora of skills at our disposal."

"You should avoid alliteration when you speak, Luthor. It's the sign of an unimaginative mind."

Luthor frowned. "You may not be interested in actively participating in this investigation—the one in which we seek the killer of your slain fiancée—but the least you can do is speak to me with a modicum of respect, respect that I've clearly earned over our years together."

Simon turned his head so he could see Luthor. Despite his obvious inebriation, Simon still managed a piercing gaze. "Finish what you have to say so you can leave once more."

Clearing his throat, Luthor continued. "We believe we've found the means by which the beastly killer has moved so freely about Solomon's Way without being seen. I must leave momentarily, regardless, to meet with the doctor and Mattie at the crime scene. Next time we meet, I hope I'll bear news that this investigation has been brought to a close." He walked to the head of Simon's chair, so that the Inquisitor was forced to crane his neck to look at his friend. "We could use your expertise, especially as we travel into the belly of the beast."

"You have the doctor," Simon said dismissively. "For what reason could you possibly still need me?"

"Youke has proven himself invaluable, which is a fair bit more than I can say about you thus far."

Simon arched an eyebrow. "I see that the two of you are now on a first-name basis. Good for you both. If you'll excuse me, however, I grow weary of hearing of the young doctor."

Luthor stepped around the chair so that he and Simon were face to face. "He's a brilliant and engaging man, sir. Under different circumstances, I'm sure you would find him quite endearing."

Simon stood abruptly and pushed past the apothecary, his tumbler of scotch clenched tightly in his hand. He staggered to the fireplace, where he leaned heavily on the mantle for support. "Yes, yes, Luthor, the doctor is clearly someone we should immolate."

Luthor moved to speak but paused and nervously furrowed his brow. "Sir, you did say emulate, did you not?"

Simon waved his hand dismissively. "Of course I did. What else would I have said?" The Inquisitor walked immediately back toward the end table on which the bottle of scotch was perched. "I believe we've both said all that needs to be said. I'll bid you a good day, Luthor."

The Inquisitor lifted the bottle and went to pour himself another drink. The blinding ire that Luthor had felt before returned tenfold. His face went flush and his ears felt hot to the touch. He greatly disliked being so readily dismissed, but it wasn't Simon's offhanded dismissal that infuriated him. Simon was one of the finest Inquisitors Luthor had ever met, much less worked with in such intimate settings. To see a brilliant mind being muddied with an excess of alcohol was reproachful; knowing that Simon was doing it intentionally as a means to avoid his responsibilities and confronting his anguish, doubly so.

"Stop, damn you!" Luthor yelled. "Just stop!"

Simon started, the bottle bouncing in his hand at the sudden noise. He hesitated, the bottle frozen halfway through the pouring process, the brown liquor balanced precariously near its lip.

"You suffered a great loss, sir, but don't make it worse by robbing the world of your presence as well. If you could put down the bottle and clear your mind even for one second, you'd see the detriment you've caused in this investigation. You'd finally realize that the murderer very well might have already been caught if you hadn't sat here, in the dark, wallowing in your own self-pity." Luthor walked to Simon's side, though the Inquisitor never turned toward his friend. "Put down the bottle, sir, and come with me. Join Mattie, Youke, and I at the crime scene and help us bring closure to this horrific crime."

Simon frowned as he looked at the glass in his hand. He felt the burning embarrassment of his own failure more acutely than Luthor would ever realize. "I couldn't save the woman I loved, Luthor. I've saved countless lives from magical abominations, yet my own fiancée fell victim to one and I was impotent to stop it."

With a regretful sigh, Simon tilted the bottle and let the scotch pour over the ice cubes in his glass. Luthor shook his head, tears stinging at the corners of his eyes.

"You and I, sir, we've had many an adventure together," Luthor said, his voice unsteady. "Yet I tell you now, with all earnestness, that if you do not put down your bottle and help solve this murder, our partnership and very likely our friendship will come to an end."

Simon's shoulders sagged, though he still only offered Luthor his back. The Inquisitor slowly raised his head and stared at the askew paintings hanging on the wall. With a shaking hand, Simon raised the glass to his lips and took a drink.

Luthor nodded, feeling defeated. "Then I say good day to you, sir."

With his head hanging low, Luthor walked out of the sitting room, not bothering with a backward glance at the defeated man he had once admired.

CHAPTER
Twenty-seven

T HE RAIN HAD LESSENED TO A MERE DRIZZLE BY THE
time Luthor arrived with Mattie. Luthor carried his doctor's bag, as
was his wont, while Mattie's arms were laden with supplies, including a pair of torches. Doctor Casan was standing under an overhang, his
suit jacket pulled tightly around him to ward off the damp chill. Seeing
the others arrive, the doctor stepped back into the rain and approached
the alleyway.

"We're in luck," the doctor remarked, gesturing toward the walls of
the alley.

The rain had been falling at an angle, which was mostly blocked by
the high walls that formed the alleyway. Water ran in rivulets down between the bricks, following the natural channels of the mortar, yet left
most of the wall dry and untouched.

"About how far in would you say you were standing when you struck
the monster?" Luthor asked, turning toward her.

Mattie narrowed her eyes as she concentrated on the events of that
night. It was a haze, for the most part. She remembered walking back
from the Ace of Spades with Veronica, them talking rather jovially, considering the loss Miss Dawn had recently suffered. Then the towering

giant had been in the alleyway, blocking its entrance.

Mattie walked forward, retracing her steps as she stripped from her eveningwear, transformed into the werewolf, and leapt toward it. In the present, she reached out her arm in a slow swipe from left to right. Her gaze followed the arc of her swing.

"Here," she said. "I was here when I struck it."

Luthor and Youke hurried to her side and examined the walls but could see nothing remarkable. The apothecary was crestfallen. He had hoped that a sample of the creature's blood would reveal more about their adversary. "Nothing," Luthor remarked.

Mattie shook her head. "No, not there. I had leapt in an attempt to reach the giant's throat. You wouldn't find any blood at eye level."

Luthor craned his neck as the faint mist of rain settled over his glasses. He smiled broadly as he saw a smear of yellowish ooze affixed to the wall slightly overhead. Setting down his doctor's bag, Luthor opened it and pulled from it an empty vial with a stopper. Pulling the cork free, he retrieved a small, metal file with which he could scrape the brickwork. Reaching high, suddenly reminded of his diminutive stature, he scraped some of the ooze into the glass jar.

"Excellent work, Miss Hawke," Youke said, though Luthor could sense the man's hesitation at the reminder that so seemingly delicate a woman had struck such a powerful blow.

The apothecary brought the jar to his nose and breathed deeply. He could catch whiffs of something organic, with faint undertones of something that left a metallic taste in the back of his throat.

"Is it blood?" the doctor asked.

"If so, it's entirely unlike any blood I've seen before," Luthor replied, placing the cork in the end of the vial. "We'll have to examine it further under more proper settings."

Luthor gestured toward the end of the alleyway, which seemed far closer and not nearly as intimidating in the daylight. "Come on, what we're after is down here."

The trio moved to the end of the alley. The passage widened as they moved, as the buildings forming their route were set further apart. They were shorter as well, offering less protection from the elements. Luthor paused before the manhole cover and frowned. A pool of water swirled over the top of the circular cover as water poured through the small intake holes on its surface. The water had spread, backed up like a reservoir, filling most of the end of the alley. It wasn't the water that upset Luthor; it was that the moving liquid had obfuscated the muddy footprint that had existed the night of the murder. Now there was nothing, save the faintest traces of brown-black mud clinging for dear life to the cobblestones at their feet, nearly an inch beneath the surface of the water.

"We won't be finding any more samples," Luthor dryly said.

"We have one already," Casan offered. "I took the liberty of giving it a cursory glance while I waited for you both to arrive. It's clearly mud, but it's mixed with blood. Although to find out what kind, I would need more time."

"There's no way to find out who the blood once belonged to, I presume?" Mattie asked.

The doctor shook his head. "If only our scientific capabilities allowed such identification. Sadly, though, they don't. The best I can offer is a family or potentially a genus of the creature from which the blood came."

"We thank you for your assistance all the same," Luthor said. He extended his hand. "Mattie, if you will."

She set the lanterns on a crate near the wall and pulled a long crowbar from beneath her arm, handing it to Luthor. The apothecary set it into a small fissure along the edge of the manhole cover and leaned against the metal pole with all his weight. The heavy cover shifted slightly, but not enough to be fully moved aside. With a sigh, Luthor leaned back.

"Though it pains me to ask, would you two be so kind?"

Doctor Casan stood opposite Luthor and, together, they pushed their weight against the crowbar once more. The manhole cover shifted again, this time with a sucking noise as the seal was broken around its edge. The water pooled nearby rushed into the void as they pushed the metal disk aside. Far below, beyond the range of the filtering sunlight, they could hear the water splashing into the sewers.

A metal ladder, rusted from age and exposure, was bolted against one wall. The cascading water formed a waterfall around the perimeter of the tunnel, running the length of the four-foot-wide shaft. The faint rain did little to suppress the foul odor emanating from the sewer below. The wafting scent of offal turned Luthor's stomach, and he was forced to step aside to regain his constitution. He stole a glance toward Mattie and saw her blanched, her senses far more astute than his own. The smell must have been nearly overpowering, and she wrinkled her nose accordingly.

"Shall we?" Youke asked from his place beside the open sewer entrance.

Luthor nodded begrudgingly and walked to the lanterns, still resting on the crate. Lifting their glass bulbs one at a time, he covered the exposed wick with his hands as he lit the lanterns from a lighter he produced from his pocket. When the oil-soaked wicks had caught fire, he lowered the bulbs back into place, protecting the flickering lights.

"I'll go in first," Luthor offered. "Have one of the lanterns prepared to lower to me once I'm fully inside."

He walked to the edge of the opening, feeling the water sloshing into his shoes and absorbing into his socks. Frowning, he placed a foot on the topmost rung and, grasping the edge of the manhole for balance, began lowering himself into the tightly fitting shaft. Though small in stature, Luthor still felt the claustrophobia of being within such a confined space. He had plenty of room on either side but immediately wondered if they had made the correct assumption about the giant's movements. Luthor would be confined within the tunnel, and he was far smaller than the nine-foot beast. Nearly halfway down the passage, with the light still illuminating the shaft around him, Luthor knew that they had made the correct choice. A rusted nail protruded from the side of the tunnel, having worked its way free from its mooring. Slathered upon the head of the nail was the same ochre ooze they found upon the wall, from where the giant had been injured. The monster had come this way, amazingly, squeezing its bulky frame into so narrow a passage.

At the end of the shaft, Luthor's feet sank into shin-deep water. It was bitterly cold and soaked him to his bones at once. He shivered momentarily, even as the warding runes along his spine artificially inflated his temperature to combat the cold. The tunnel was an inky black in all directions, his only connection to the world of vision coming from the narrow pinprick of light high overhead.

The current was strong and tugged at his feet. He dared not step in any direction until a light was delivered, for fear that he was standing only on a narrow precipice near the wall. A step forward very well might dump him over his head in cold water and human waste. The very thought turned his stomach.

He craned his neck toward the light high above. "It's all right for you both to come down."

His voice echoed up the shaft, but he knew he'd been heard when shadowy figures suddenly blocked the light from view. Luthor felt a momentary panic as he was cast into utter darkness, no longer having his faint refuge from the manhole overhead. He calmed himself with the knowledge that he could create light at will, should it become necessary.

As the first figure grew nearer, their form grew more pronounced. The lantern was balanced in one of Mattie's hands, and she used the other for balance as she descended the ladder. Luthor looked upward but immediately blushed and turned away. Though dressed in leather riding pants and a loose blouse, Luthor still found himself looking upward at a very obscene angle toward the climbing woman.

Mattie stepped into the cold current but seemed oblivious to the temperature. She held the lantern aloft, and its light filled the sewer passages nearby. The tunnel was rounded, curving in a half-moon overhead before disappearing into the water. Tapping her foot forward, Mattie felt the edge of the ledge on which they stood.

"We're standing on a narrow ledge," she said, confirming Luthor's suspicions. "I wouldn't step in either direction, were I you."

"I have no intention of drowning in such putrescent water, thank you, though."

The water level was clearly swollen from the recent rains. Though rank and foul, it remained clearer than Luthor would have assumed, in large part due to the flooding. While it saved the group from having to move through concentrated filth, it also washed away any hopes the apothecary had harbored of finding more clues.

Doctor Casan finished his climb, a lantern in hand as well, and glanced around the rounded passage. Unlike Luthor and Mattie, the tall, lanky doctor had to stoop slightly once he stepped out of the shaft.

"The low ceiling would make moving about in the sewers difficult for so tall a creature, but not impossible," the doctor remarked.

They turned the lanterns this way and that, examining both directions. They appeared nondescript, rounded sewer passages that led away in both directions. In the distance, they could see side passages merging with the main tunnel in which they stood. The side tunnels were slightly raised and their filth cascaded from the mouths of the tunnels to mix with the swollen waters. The light glinted off metal in the distance, marking another ladder leading up to the streets of Solomon's Way. Glancing the other direction, Luthor saw the doctor's light reflecting off yet another ladder.

"If the giant came this way," the apothecary explained, "then he would have limitless access to the streets above through the multitude of ladders and manhole covers."

"It hardly helps our investigation," Casan replied. "He could just as easily have accessed the sewers through any of those openings."

Mattie slid past Luthor gingerly, careful to remain on the narrow ledge. Though concealed from the doctor's prying eyes, Luthor could see the redhead sniffing the air cautiously before shaking her head and turning an unhealthy shade of white.

"Can you smell anything?" Luthor asked quietly, the sound of his voice concealed by the rushing waters.

Mattie shook her head. "Even once I managed my way past the overwhelming scent of refuse, the smells of the sewer are too foreign. Everything has a faint ting of spoilt meat. I'm sorry."

Luthor shook his head before turning toward the doctor. "I had hoped to find more of the footprints or, at the very least, markings indicating the giant had passed one way or the other. I had thought the mud might have been from the sewer itself, though even if it had been, it's all been washed away in the deluge. I fear I've led us all on a fool's errand."

"I hardly blame you," Casan replied. "You have the fine instincts of an Inquisitor. Clearly, Simon has worn off on you over the years."

Luthor smiled. Mattie tapped him insistently on the shoulder at that moment, drawing his attention. Both men turned toward the woman.

"I don't think you're wrong at all, Luthor," she said. "I just think that the rains have hindered our search, but hardly stopped it. You said you thought you might find the same mud here in the sewers, but what if the mud didn't come from the sewers? What if it came, instead, from where the beast originated? It hadn't rained either the night of Veronica's attack nor any of the nights previous. That means that if the giant carried mud on its shoe from whence it came, nothing would have washed it away as it's doing now to us."

"You have a location in mind?" Luthor asked.

"Only generally," she replied. "These sewers have to drain somewhere, and I would venture a guess that the ground nearby would be saturated and muddy."

Luthor smiled broadly. "Miss Hawke, you are a genius," he proclaimed. "Were the situation different and I not standing nearly knee deep in human excrement, I might consider kissing you right now."

"You know where we can find the beast?" the doctor dubiously asked.

"All these sewers drain into the river," Luthor explained. "It's just like the experience with the troll and his home, which he created by breaking through the wall between a basement and the sewers. The outlets drain onto the river bank, which would be coated with mud."

Casan smiled as well. "Combined with our knowledge that the perpetrator has a working knowledge of medicine—"

"Or even veterinary medicine," Mattie added.

Both men nodded their agreement. "Or veterinary medicine," Casan continued, "we should be able to identify any doctor or veterinary practices along the banks of the river, specifically near one of the sewer outlets."

"Excellent," Mattie replied. "Now that we have a way ahead, would it be too much to ask that we leave the sewers at once?"

Both men nodded agreement once more, and the doctor began climbing.

When they arrived back at the townhouse, Mattie immediately excused herself to go bathe the foul stench of the sewers from her body. Luthor appreciated the duress she must be under, suffering the indignity of not just smelling like human waste but having it coupled with an acute sense of smell.

As Mattie climbed the stairs, the two men entered the study. Luthor pulled a map of Callifax from a shelf and laid it upon the table. With wax pencil in hand, Luthor marked the boundary of Solomon's Way, bordered as it was on its northern edge by the Oreck River. A good number of the businesses within Callifax were already marked. The castle stood atop the rising hill. The Grand Hall and Callifax Abbey were noted within the Upper Reaches. Eden's Grove claimed the debtor's prison and Saint Midridge's Asylum for the Mentally Impaired. The docks of the Gaslight District were clearly marked as well. Solomon's Way was mostly barren, with only the Ace of Spades and, more recently, the police station labeled.

"Most of these are warehouses," Casan explained, motioning toward rows of larger square buildings. "They give way to some businesses closer to the bridge, though I can't recall any medical practices in the area."

"Everything now is conjecture, at this point," Luthor said. "Without walking the area, we'll have to rely solely on our memory of the water's edge."

"Agreed. We should plan to walk the businesses soon, so that we might find the identity of our killer before he strikes again."

Luthor suppressed a yawn. "Would you think less of me if I begged off the search today? The events of the past few days have left me both physically and mentally drained."

Casan shook his head as he looked up from the map. "Not at all. You and Mattie have been both inviting to me, a practical stranger, and instrumental to the investigation thus far. Why don't the both of you rest and clean yourselves as best you can. I will conduct the search as part of my duties as coroner, though I'd be derelict if I gave you the impression it would all be completed tonight. Searching the river's edge of Solomon's Way will be a taxing journey and will probably take... would you think less of me if I said a week or more?"

"I would be lying if I said I hadn't hoped for sooner, but I completely understand. That would be exceptional. I'll continue my own investigation and hopefully when we reconvene we'll be sharing similar notes and conclusions. Thank you, Youke."

The doctor nodded and turned toward the door. "I should be off, then."

Luthor opened the door for the young doctor and saw him out. The rain had stopped, though the sky remained dark and cloudy. They stopped on the landing before the front door and shook hands.

"We're getting close, Doctor," Luthor said. "I can feel it as surely as it were one of my five senses."

"We'll reconvene as soon as I have completed my reconnaissance," the doctor said, with a broad and confident smile. "We will have our killer in cuffs soon enough."

———————— ❧⟨∞⟩❧ ————————

Simon sat at his windowsill, the window slightly open, letting in the cool breeze and airing out the stale air of the house. He overhead Luthor and the doctor's conversation and watched the young doctor depart, a knowing smile spread across his face. The Inquisitor felt an ache in his chest at the thought that so much of the investigation had been conducted without him. Moreover, he hadn't fully realized until that moment that he was expendable in his and Luthor's working and personal relationships. If their conversation was to be believed, they were close to solving Veronica's murder.

Veronica's murder, Simon thought. It should have been him investigating, he knew. While his friends were solving the murder of his fiancée, he was holed up within his home, barely seeing the sunlight, much less actually leaving the house. His inaction had made him obsolete.

No, he realized, not his inaction. He turned away from the window, the ache in his chest growing stronger until it became a physical pain that lanced through his heart. Simon picked up his nearly empty tumbler and the likewise nearly emptied bottle of scotch, holding them in his hands and staring at them. His mouth felt parched once more, a type of thirst that would never be truly satiated. It would always be a gnawing ache in the back of his throat, as though he were a man walking through the desert, never finding the water to satisfy his needs.

Wobbling on his feet, Simon took a few tentative steps toward the mantle. As he reached the fireplace, he drew back his hand and threw the glass into the hearth. It shattered, spilling what liquor remained onto the cold, gray ashes.

Simon tilted the bottle, watching the scotch slosh along the walls of the glass as it ran toward his lips. Instead of pouring it into his mouth, he turned the bottle's neck and added the remainder of the liquor to the exhausted fireplace. Absently, he set the empty bottle down on his table before turning away.

Staggering away from the smoking fireplace, Simon stumbled into his study. Rolled parchments stood from a barrel near the door. He pulled one from the barrel and unrolled it in his hands. Frustrated at not finding what he sought, he tossed it aside and pulled another free. Scowling at another failed attempt, the Inquisitor dumped the contents onto the study's table and fumbled through them. As he unrolled a thick map, he unsteadily smiled. Pausing before the overladen bookshelf, Simon ran his fingers over the spines of the novels. He blinked heavily as the words blurred in his vision.

"Oafish men of superhuman strength," he mumbled to himself. "Large, brutish, ogre-ish, I dare say." His hand paused on one of his research books. He pulled it from the shelf and balanced it in his hand as he flipped through the pages. Smiling, he snapped the book closed, though he flinched at the loud noise and the pounding it caused behind his eyes.

Stumbling back into the sitting room, book and map in hand, he paused as he realized an empty bottle of scotch blocked his workspace.

Dropping the empty bottle to the ground, Simon staggered back to his high-backed chair and collapsed into it, map in hand. His eyes glanced over the top as he watched the fireplace, as though he expected it to suddenly roar to life in protest.

CHAPTER

Twenty-eight

LUTHOR SAT HEAVILY IN THE CUSHIONED CHAIR, SIP-
ping his tea as his mind wandered. The events in the sewers weighed
heavily on his mind, as did hopes that Doctor Casan would find
the surgeon or veterinarian in question during his search. The morning
was bright, the sun having burned away the storm clouds that had lingered for nearly a week, and sun streamed through the front windows.

"You smell a fair bit better than you have in a while," Mattie remarked
as she entered the room.

Her hair was still damp from her innumerable baths since their return. Though Luthor knew they reeked of the sewer's filth, he lacked her
sensitive lupine nose. He could only imagine how malodorous they had
seemed to her. Luthor had similarly bathed, though only once each night.
Admittedly, he remained in the bath for long after the water in the porcelain tub had grown cold and the kettle of replacement hot water had been
tapped dry. Scrubbing seemed hardly good enough to remove the stench
from his skin. His clothing had been discarded as a loss. No amount of
washing would return the fibers of his outfit to a suitable level of clean-
liness.

"I made sure to wash thoroughly," he replied. "I enjoy your company immensely and would hate to lose even a moment with you due to a lingering putrescence."

"Always the thoughtful gentleman," she said as she leaned forward and kissed him upon the forehead. "Has Youke not yet shown? I would have expected him by now."

Luthor frowned and glanced at the clock resting atop the mantle. The morning was growing late, already past breakfast, but the doctor had not shown nor had he sent word of a delay. It had been a full week since their impromptu meeting in Luthor's home, and the promise of the doctor's reconnaissance weighed heavily on the apothecary's mind. "I certainly hope nothing ill has befallen him," the apothecary said, removing his glasses absently to clean the lenses once more. "I would blame myself if somehow the killer caught wind of our investigation."

"You must forgive yourself, Luthor. I know that during this past week you had hoped to reveal some great truth behind the murders. Perhaps the good doctor will have something more definitive."

Mattie walked past him and into the kitchen. Luthor could hear the clink of china as she removed a teacup from the cupboard. "Did you read the paper this morning?"

"I thought the same thing." He rested his hand on the folded paper, sitting on the table beside him. "There was no mention of our young doctor."

"Then we assume the best and that he's just delayed."

Mattie poured herself some tea before adding her sugar and milk. She stirred it gently with a spoon before returning to the sitting room, glancing at Luthor as she sat across from him. His shoulders were tight, and she could see the vein in his neck throbbing with each pulse of his heartbeat.

"You need to relax before you require the doctor for a much different reason," she said.

His shoulders dropped as he took a deep breath. "Forgive me. I'm just worried about our investigation. As far as the Grand Inquisitor is concerned, Simon is conducting a thorough investigation as we speak."

"You sent the other letter?" Mattie asked, referring to another forgery Luthor concocted to appease the Grand Inquisitor.

Luthor nodded. "With Simon otherwise indisposed, it falls on the two of us—with Youke's obvious assistance—to solve this string of murders. The Grand Hall will remain none the wiser only if we succeed."

Mattie opened her mouth to reply but she was interrupted by a knock at the door. She smiled. "You see, Luthor, there's our doctor now."

The apothecary stood and made his way into the foyer. A smile had returned to his face. Though they still had much to do, he was eager to continue their investigation. He drew back the lock on the door and opened it but immediately paused, his mouth slightly agape in a friendly welcome that never came. It wasn't Doctor Casan on the other side of the door. Standing there, in full regalia but leaning heavily against the doorframe, stood Simon.

The Inquisitor looked refreshed; a much different man than the one who had been so curt during their last encounter. He was dressed once more in his suit, the top hat canted on his head and the chain of his pocket watch hanging across the front of his vest. A rolled map was tucked neatly under one arm. Though the brim of his hat blocked the bright sunlight, his eyes were wide and enthusiastic as he stared at the apothecary.

"Sir?" Luthor breathlessly asked. "I'm surprised to see you. You'll have to forgive me for being dumbfounded, but I was expecting someone else."

"Yes, the good doctor," Simon replied. The Inquisitor gestured toward the cooler and darker interior. "Would you care to invite me in?"

Luthor regained his composure and stepped aside. "Of course."

"For some God awful reason, it's abysmally bright this morning."

Simon moved to step over the threshold, but his gait was unsteady and he had to lean once more against the doorframe for support.

Luthor frowned. "Sir, you're still drunk."

"Don't be absurd, Luthor," Simon said as he pushed himself upright once more. "I just haven't slept much lately. There has been so much to do on the investigation. I just seem to have regained my faculties far quicker than I've regained my equilibrium. I promise you I've been stone sober since some time earlier this week."

The Inquisitor stepped inside, and Luthor closed the door behind him. Mattie rose at the sight of Simon and smiled. "We've missed you, Simon."

"Finally someone who offers an appropriate welcome after my unforeseen leave of absence." Mattie walked over to him, in lieu of waiting for him to walk unsteadily toward her, and tightly hugged him. "I've missed you both as well, Matilda."

"You'll forgive my asking, sir, but what are you doing here?" Luthor asked. "I hardly expected to see you again, especially during the course of my investigation."

"*Our* investigation," Simon corrected. "You were right. I've been remiss in my duties, not just as a Royal Inquisitor but more importantly as a widower."

Luthor furrowed his brow. "I believe you have to be married for that term to apply."

"Don't interrupt me while I'm apologizing. It's bad form."

Mattie glanced at Luthor with a suppressed smile. Luthor seemed far less humored having Simon back, though the apothecary had to admit that their conversation was reminiscent of days gone by.

"Your words struck a cord within me, Luthor," Simon explained. When the apothecary seemed surprised, Simon continued, "Is that so hard to believe? I've spent the past few days taking a much more active role in solving these murders. I've done what I can on my own but could use your research as well. I presume you have notes on the cases, beyond the folders I've kept at my house?"

Luthor finally smiled and motioned toward the sitting room. "Of course, sir. They've been awaiting your intricately deductive mind. What sort of investigation have you conducted, if you don't mind my asking?"

The apothecary led Simon into the room, helping the Inquisitor past the larger obstacles against which Simon seemed keen to bump, and showed him his seat.

"I've spent the past few days walking every inch of Solomon's Way, exploring the district from every angle in an attempt to find the culprit behind these murders. I think that I'm close, but could use your book-learning—and the rest of the clues you've collected—to connect the pieces of this dreadfully complex puzzle."

From the table, Luthor retrieved the notebook onto which he had written many of the clues and his notes from the night before. He explained their findings—the footprint and mud, the sewer entrance, the ooze-like blood on the wall, and their speculation that the killer operated from the edge of the river—while Simon read through Luthor's handwritten notes. Simon nodded along intently, though Luthor wasn't sure how much the Inquisitor heard. His eyes flickered quickly over the page and the apothecary knew from experience that Simon was likely tuning out all other sounds from the room as his mind began to work.

Another knock at the door jarred Luthor from his conversation, though Simon continued reading unabashed. Mattie peered out the window and glanced toward the front stoop. She was smiling as she turned back.

"It appears our doctor has made it after all."

Excitedly, Luthor hurried toward the foyer. He opened the door, and the tall doctor stepped into the townhouse. Gesturing toward the sitting room, Luthor drew the doctor's attention to their unexpected visitor.

"It appears that the elusive Inquisitor Whitlock has now joined us on our investigation," the apothecary explained.

Casan smiled, though it seemed forced. He walked into the sitting room and paused before the table, extending his hand in greeting. "It's an honor to have you joining us in the investigation."

Simon glanced up from his reading but didn't shake the doctor's hand. Casan's hand lingered for a moment longer before dropping back to his side. Luthor frowned at the exchange and quickly interceded. "Tell us, Youke, what did you find in Solomon's Way?"

The doctor's gaze lingered on the Inquisitor, who hadn't offered another glance in Casan's direction. Turning away, the doctor smiled toward Luthor and Mattie. "I managed to isolate the blood in the sample you provided and its identity I shall reveal to you in a moment. As for the location of our killer's home, I'm sorry, but I found nothing of use. I scoured the Way from one end to the other, examining not only the businesses along the river but also those across the street, but found no doctor's offices or veterinary services in that area."

Simon set down the notebook noisily before standing abruptly. "Nor would you, since our killer is neither a doctor nor a veterinarian. Though, truth be told, I wouldn't have expected any other assumption from you, Doctor."

Casan scowled at the interruption. "Have I done something to offend you?"

Simon crossed his arms over his chest defensively, but took a deep breath and seemed to noticeably relax before continuing. "I don't much care for you, Doctor. I believe the cause is a sense of professional jealousy. Based solely from Luthor's glowing description of you, I believe you are perhaps the only man I've met recently who is my intellectual equal. However, your knowledge lacks refinement, which is why you have overlooked the more glaring possibilities in this case."

"Was that an apology?" Casan indignantly asked.

"As near a one as I've ever heard offered," Luthor interjected, again trying to diffuse the volatile situation. The apothecary glared at Simon, clearly urging him to put more effort into his halfhearted apology.

Simon cleared his throat. "Doctor Casan, I fear I have wronged you through omission. I had chosen to ignore the knowledge you possess because of your juvenile interpretations of said knowledge. Please accept my apologies."

Casan looked flabbergasted toward the apothecary.

Luthor shrugged. "I would accept the offer, were I you."

With a sigh, Youke turned back toward Simon. "Apology accepted."

"Excellent," Simon replied before dropping heavily back onto the couch, the strain of standing upright clearly overwhelming him.

Youke, Luthor, and Mattie likewise sat, encircling the small table between them. Casan leaned back with feigned disinterest as he spoke. "If we've overlooked the more glaring possibilities, as you've stated, then please enlighten us."

Simon nodded. "From reading the notes and perusing the case files hundreds of times to better understand our killer, I've come to realize that we are not dealing with a single killer, but rather two."

Casan chortled derisively. "We've already come to the same conclusion, one the public face who can move freely through Solomon's Way, while the other is the brutish thug who moves solely by means of the sewers beneath the city."

"Indeed you have, as I've deduced from Luthor's scrawled notes. However, I do not believe that both killers are human. I believe that our second killer, the giant whom attacked Miss Hawke, is something other than a man."

"We surmised as much ourselves," Luthor said. "The giant is too large to be a man. Were you thinking that he's, perhaps, an abomination from the Rift?"

Simon shook his head. "I don't believe our giant is another incursion from the Rift, but rather the work of a man's hand. Are you familiar with the tales of the Golem?"

CHAPTER

Twenty nine

"THE GOLEM OF LEGEND WAS CREATED BY RELIGIOUS zealots, persecuted for their faith but too weak to stand against their oppressors directly," Simon explained as he leaned forward in his chair. "Instead, they crafted clay into the likeness of a man, taller than any of the priests gathered. Calling upon the holy might of their God, they demanded the Golem be imbued with the spark of life, that it rise from its place of creation and defend the zealots from those who would do them harm. Such was the power of their belief that the Golem did rise. It towered over the priests, its power undeniable, as strong as ten men. It marched from the temple and slaughtered the invaders to a man before crumbling to dust."

Luthor, Casan, and Mattie seemed transfixed by the brief story, all their minds awhirl with possibilities. They began speaking at once, asking question upon question. Simon raised his hand to silence them all.

"One at a time, please."

"Are you saying that our killer is a priest?" Luthor asked.

Simon shook his head. "Don't be ridiculous, Luthor. Do keep in mind that our second killer is likely the Golem's creator. It's hardly becoming of a man of the cloth to be a cold-blooded killer. Besides, this story is just a parable, a fairy tale told to get children to sleep at night, as my own parents did when I was young. 'Go to bed or else the Golem will come for you. No locked door or window can stop a beast made of mud.'"

"Then what makes you believe this giant is a Golem at all?" Casan asked.

"I had my suspicions after perusing one of my Inquisitor tomes on superhuman beasts, but I didn't until I arrived here this very morning. It was Luthor who first made me believe that we are looking at a manmade creation, something of flesh and metal, fused together in an amalgamation of evil intent."

"Me, sir?" Luthor asked.

Simon nodded. "It was when you described for me the ooze that you discovered splattered on the alley's wall. Meat and metal was how you described it, was it not? It's even here in your notes. Do you have that sample with you?"

Luthor stood and walked to the mantle, upon which his doctor's bag currently rested. Opening the bag, he pulled from it a vial, the contents of which were ochre in color. Despite his vigorous shaking, the contents moved very little within the jar. With the stopper still in place, Luthor handed the sample to the Inquisitor.

Simon uncorked the vial at once and raised it to his nose, breathing deeply the fumes emanating from the sample. He closed his eyes as he attempted to discern its individual components.

"If this is the blood of a Golem," Luthor said, "then could this be a reagent of sorts or some other mystical component in the Golem's creation?"

Ignoring Luthor's question, Simon dipped a finger into the gelatin. Pulling his finger from the vial, he examined the sample under the electric lights. Abruptly, he brought his finger to his mouth and licked the ooze. The other three stared at the Inquisitor, appalled by what they had just seen.

"It's lard," Simon proclaimed, "mixed with a faint metallic aftertaste. It's hardly mystical in nature; more likely than not it's used as a lubricant."

"Was that absolutely necessary?" Mattie asked, her color pale. "Couldn't you have come to that determination without putting it in your mouth?"

"Of course not, Matilda. Don't be silly."

204

"You've done a masterful job of identifying one of the two culprits," Casan chided, "but we're still no closer to identifying the Golem's master, if that is what we're facing."

"On the contrary," Simon said, "all the clues we need are right here before us, for those keen enough to connect the proverbial dots. Answer me this, Doctor. The blood that you isolated from the mud, was it either porcine or bovine?"

The doctor arched his eyebrows in surprise. "Porcine. How did you know?"

Simon turned the notebook toward the doctor, on the page of which the Inquisitor had circled Luthor's notes about the killer's skill with a blade, insinuating a medical background. "Your instinct serves you well, Doctor, but the simple facts elude the complexities of your mind. You have such a high regard for the medical profession, being a professional yourself that you find it hard to believe that someone so skilled with a blade could exist outside the world of medicine. A doctor is not the only man capable of wielding a blade or removing meat from bone. Tell me, who else would be skilled with a blade and whose waste would include porcine blood?"

"A butcher," Mattie answered, sufficiently impressed.

Casan snapped in the air. "The map, if you please, Luthor."

"There's no need," Simon interjected. He unfurled his own map and laid it across the table. Numerous buildings were marked on the map, a clear indication of how the Inquisitor had spent his last few days. "I believe you'll find the answer on my map."

As the map was laid out before him, the doctor's eyes flew across the page until they settled on a square structure on the drawn map. He tapped it with the tip of his pencil. "Mercer and Son Butcher. I walked past their shop twice this week and hardly gave it a second glance. Right there on the waterfront, right in front of our collective noses the whole time."

Simon smiled. "I believe you'll find that the mud beyond the walls of the butcher's will be stained with the blood of the slaughtered animals, a match for the dark mud you discovered in the alleyway."

Casan looked up excitedly from the map. "We should take this to the constabulary at once," the doctor offered, but Simon shook his head.

"This is our crime to solve."

"What do we know about the, presumably, father and son who own the shop?" Mattie asked.

Casan shook his head. "Nearly nothing, I'm afraid. I don't frequent their business, though I know where I could find out more. If you could give me an hour to query the constables, I shall have everything we need to confront these killers."

"I agree," Luthor added. "I'm hardly prepared as I am to face such a beast."

"Very well," Simon said, turning the map toward him so he could further examine the marked shop along the water's edge. "We'll meet at the police station in one hour's time, assuming that's sufficient time for everyone to prepare."

The others all nodded their consent. Casan stood and extended his hand once more, which Simon this time took. "I'm glad to be working with you again, Inquisitor," Casan said, without the telltale sarcasm that had been in his tone previously.

"And I you, Doctor," Simon said.

The doctor hurried to the foyer with Luthor in tow. As Youke left, the apothecary locked the door behind him.

Mattie stood as Luthor walked back into the room. "If you'll both excuse me, I'd like to prepare for my second time facing this monster. He got the better of me last time, but rest assured our next meeting will be quite different."

Simon stood as Mattie excused herself. She hurried up the stairs, the sound of her footfalls following her to her bedroom overhead. When they were finally alone, Luthor walked back to the table and sat in his chair, facing the Inquisitor. He stared at Simon, though the man hardly looked up from the map.

Luthor cleared his throat to get Simon's attention. "Sir, in the heat of the moment things were said between us, things that can never be taken back once issued. I would hope that you know everything I said was done with your best interests at heart."

Simon looked up slowly from the paper before him, his lips thin and bloodless. The Inquisitor smoothed his thin moustache. "Of course. I don't hold you accountable for the things that were said in anger. In fact, your words cut through the din of my depression. I dare say I wouldn't be sitting here now were it not for your insistence."

Releasing a pent-up sigh of relief, Luthor smiled. "Beneath your gruff exterior truly does beat a warm heart, sir. No matter the words said between us, please do know that I'm dreadfully sorry for your loss, I truly am."

Simon calmly folded the map before retrieving the notebook he had cleared from the table. He stacked the papers together neatly before returning his gaze to the apothecary.

"I know that when you look at me, Luthor, you see an emotionless automaton."

Luthor nodded. "At times, sir. If I understand you correctly, though, you're trying to tell me that you're far more like an onion, with layers?"

Simon furrowed his brow in confusion. "Nonsense, my good man, I *am* an emotionless automaton, not at all much different from the Golem we seek." He shrugged as he considered Luthor's question. "Though I believe the onion analogy might be apropos, since I'm likely to make you cry."

Luthor couldn't suppress a laugh. "It's good to have you back, sir."

CHAPTER

Thirty

THE STREET IN FRONT OF THE SOLOMON'S WAY POLICE station was mildly busy by the time Simon and his cohorts reached it. People went about their business, entering the nearby pubs for an early lunch. A single man refused to move with the rest of the flowing pedestrian traffic. Doctor Casan stood stoically beside the precinct steps, craning his neck over the crowd as he watched for the others.

Simon saw the doctor before the doctor saw him and the Inquisitor led Luthor and Mattie to the tall, lanky man's side.

"Doctor," Simon said as they pressed themselves against the wall to avoid the passing people.

"Inquisitor," Casan replied.

"I do hope you're now adequately prepared for what's to come next."

The doctor nodded. He pulled aside his jacket to reveal a pistol concealed beneath. It was shoved haphazardly into the doctor's belt and jutted at an odd angle, one that Simon knew would make it hard to draw when the time came. Simon pushed the man's jacket closed once more, afraid of startling the passersby.

"Do you know how to use that?" the Inquisitor asked.

Casan frowned. "I have only the most rudimentary understanding, to be honest. I'm far more comfortable with a scalpel."

"The pistol will serve you better should we need it, though I'd prefer you remain behind us as we proceed."

"You will get no argument from me," Youke replied. "I took the liberty of querying the constables about Mason and Sons."

"What did you find about our mysterious pair?" Luthor asked as he tapped his cane impatiently on the ground, feeling that he should interject himself into the conversation at some point, rather than let the two intellectuals continue their wayward discussion. The apothecary glanced at Mattie, but she shook her head, clearly content remaining unseen near the back of the group.

"There is no pair," Casan explained, "at least not any more. Thomas Mason founded the butchers nearly twenty years ago and his son, Peter, joined him in the family business nearly a decade later. Thomas suffered a heart attack three years ago, leaving the business solely in the capable hands of his only son."

"Then Peter is our second killer?" Luthor asked.

"It would appear so," Simon replied. "Did you, perchance, learn anything more about the son?"

Casan nodded. "I did, though only the most trivial of facts: a physical description and little else. As is the propensity of his profession, he's stocky but not necessarily short. Peter is in his early thirties and is in great health for his age. Beyond that, I apologize that information wasn't very forthcoming."

"It will do," Simon remarked. "Gather your belongings. It's time to confront Peter Mason and his monstrous creation."

They pushed their way through the crowd though, admittedly, many people moved out of the way of the odd party. Perhaps it was more the determined and severe expression on Simon's face that moved people aside. In either case, the group quickly approached Riverbend Street, which ran the edge of the canal through Solomon's Way and into Eden's Grove. There was only a smattering of people in the streets this far away from the main thoroughfare. Though assorted shops lined the canal, they were mostly produce and goods that would be far more desirable after a long day's work, rather than something to be purchased during a short lunch break.

"There it is," Casan said, pointing toward a two-story building that came into view as they traversed a gentle bend in the road. A wooden plaque, weather worn and barely legible, stood above the door. The ampersand was nearly worn away, leaving only "Mason" and "Sons" visible. Even the "butchers" underneath was little more than peeling paint.

"Doctor, you and I will be entering the front of the shop. Luthor and Matilda, if you please, go around to the back. If there is bloodletting going on within the butchers, as I would presume there would be, there should be both the telltale runoff in the form of our mysterious dark mud, as well as a back entrance through which they could discard the unneeded scraps."

"You want us to wade through blood, mud, and discarded meat?" Luthor indignantly asked. With a sigh, he led Mattie into a gap between the buildings and disappeared toward the river beyond.

"I know you lack a level of comfort with your handgun, Doctor, but now would be a good time to have it handy," Simon said.

The Inquisitor led the doctor toward the front of the shop. A sign hung in the window, proclaiming the butchers was open. Simon paused at the window and stared inside but could see no one manning the counter. Wrapped meats sat within a cooling display case inset into the countertop. Cautiously, Simon opened the front door. A small bell above the door jingled as he entered, and the Inquisitor frowned at the unexpected noise. They paused in the doorway, waiting for someone to investigate the noise, but heard nothing. No footfalls seemed to come from the back of the store. The only sound to be heard was a constant hum of a generator.

Luthor and Mattie walked past the buildings and emerged onto the sloped bank that led down to the river. The ground was expectedly muddy, and it was readily apparent that the river had swelled with the recent rains. The water stain reached halfway to the backs of the stores lining Riverbend Street.

The apothecary paused at the crest of the hill and looked down on the water. Debris littered the edge of the bank, where garbage and other unmentionable refuse had gathered in swirling eddies. The water itself was muddied and discolored. The air was filled with gulls, swooping about and landing precariously on the side of the angled hill. Their cries filled the air. Those that had landed took flight at the sight of the two interlopers.

His cane sank into the loose mud, and he had to use some effort to free it. Luthor lifted his shoe and frowned at the mud likewise clinging to its sole. Noting the bird droppings cast intermittently across the ground, he hoped mud was all that was clinging to his shoe. "He sent us here on purpose, you realize."

Mattie walked past him and proceeded toward the rear of the butchers. "For a man of action, who claims to so thoroughly enjoy the Inquisitor's assignments, you certainly do spend an awful lot of time complaining about minor inconveniences."

She clapped her hands, and the brave gulls that had landed again took flight once more.

"They're not minor inconveniences," Luthor complained as he followed suit. "I expect to be muddied and soiled during an assignment in the armpit of the civilized world but not within my own city."

"An armpit like Haversham?" she chided.

"Like Whitten Hall," Luthor corrected, "and that abysmal march through its assorted ravines and cluttered woods. I fully expected to be filthy by the conclusion of that mission. Yet it's been here in Callifax that I've crawled through retched sewers and now am playing in mud."

"Blood-soaked mud," she warned. "Watch your step."

They had approached the rear entry to the building. The ground grew considerably darker from just beyond the step of the building's back door. Even without Mattie's enhanced sense of smell, Luthor could detect the wafting scent of blood in the air. Following the flow of blood downhill, he saw chunks of discarded flesh, gristle, and bone littering the hillside. The gulls watched them carefully before landing amidst the filth and continued picking at the remains. Beyond the white and gray birds, the blood melded into the river, leaving a dark red streak spreading downstream.

"Here, Luthor," Mattie remarked, gesturing toward the ground.

The apothecary crouched beside her and recognized the mark at once. A massively oversized footprint had been left in the soft ground. By the water seeping into its treads, Luthor guessed it had been left recently. As he stood, he joined Mattie at the back door. There was a hum of machinery filling the air, muffled though it was by the closed door. Cautiously, Luthor tested the door and found it locked. He gestured for

Mattie to stand aside as he carefully drew a rune over the lock. Barely audible over the hum of the generator, Luthor could hear each tumbler falling in turn. When it was done, the rune dissipated. Grasping the handle, he found it now turned easily.

Opening the door, they stepped into a well-lit butcher's workshop. Marble slabs sat on tables, their surfaces stained red. Slivers of meat clung to the drains in the center of the tables. The hum had grown louder and, turning, Luthor noted its source. The far wall had been modified. Its surface shone a brilliant silver. Windowless, there was only a single closed door breaking its otherwise smooth surface. The door was latched from the outside. A wooden staircase rested in the shadows on the far side of the odd metal wall, the stairwell's upper reaches lost in the darkness.

As the apothecary stepped forward, Mattie immediately grabbed for his arm, but she was a second too late. The barrel of a pistol was pressed against Luthor's head.

———————— ✦❀✦ ————————

Simon sighed and lowered his gun. "You ought to announce yourself better. I damn near shot you."

Luthor exhaled nervously. "Announce myself better? At what point during a stealthy incursion into the lair of a magical beast shall I clatter pans together and blow a horn? I thought discretion was the word of the day?"

"It was until we realized that no one is currently manning the shop," Simon explained. "It would appear that Peter Mason has caught wind of our investigation and disappeared."

Luthor shook his head. "There's still more to explore, sir, such as this metal contraption."

Simon turned his attention toward the unusual metallic shape.

"It's a mechanical cooler," Casan said. "It's very similar to the one we use in the morgue. It's perfect for storing and preserving corpses."

"Or, at the very least, storing their severed limbs?" Mattie asked.

Simon's expression grew very serious as he approached the door to the cooler. It was latched from the outside, presumably to ensure the door remained closed and sealed though, Simon was forced to admit, it might also serve well to keep something contained. Steel walls and a heavy locked door seemed like the perfect location to contain a gigantic abomination when its services were not needed.

"Be on your guard," Simon remarked.

Luthor pulled a sword free from the end of his cane, the narrow blade reflecting the overhead electric lights. He glanced warningly toward Mattie, but she merely frowned. She clearly wanted to transform, to use her best defensive and offensive assets, but dared not reveal herself in front of the doctor. For his part, Casan clenched his pistol tightly, though it shook unsteadily in his hand.

Simon moved forward until he was beside the door. He could feel the cold radiating from the metal walls of the cooler and knew that the doctor had been correct in his assumption. The door was latched with a simple metal pin through a much more complex lever-action handle. Grasping the top of the pin, he wiggled it back and forth until it slid free of the door. Glancing back toward Luthor and Mattie and, to a much lesser degree the doctor, Simon nodded and pulled the latch toward him.

The door released with a hiss of escaping cold air. Simon shivered involuntarily, surprised by the bitterness of the temperature within. As the door swung open soundlessly, the entryway became a dark maw, leading into a black interior. The pools of light from the meager overhead lights in the back workshop fell short of the door, much like they failed to properly illuminate the stairwell behind the Inquisitor.

Simon glanced toward Mattie, who shook her head slowly. Even with her supernatural vision, she could only see shapeless blobs of gray within the room, as though its interior was cluttered from wall to wall.

"Check for a light," Casan whispered. "I would assume there would be a switch of some sort just within the door."

Simon reached his hand inside, his body tense. He wasn't afraid of the dark—hadn't been since he was a young child—but his imagination was running away with his sensibilities. He knew that a massive hand hovered just within the cooler, ready to grasp the Inquisitor's fragile wrist and yank him into the darkness. The door would close abruptly behind him, leaving him trapped inside an arctic prison with a mindless Golem.

Sweat beaded on his brow as his hand fell on the switch. He knew his demise was imminent, but to everyone's surprise, nothing happened. Instead, he threw the switch unperturbed and light filled the cooler.

Headless pig and cow corpses hung from hooks in the ceiling. Severed animal limbs, in various stages of preparation, sat on baker's racks along the wall. The cooler was cluttered and busy, making it hard to see within its depths.

Wisely, Simon crouched and looked below the hanging meats. He saw no massive legs or oversized feet awaiting his entrance, nor was there any sign of limbs that didn't clearly belong to a slaughtered animal. Frowning, Simon lowered his pistol and stood. He turned toward the others and shook his head.

"There's nothing here, certainly not the severed remains of the women who have been murdered." Simon looked crestfallen and his gaze fell to the floor. "We've—I've clearly made a mistake."

Before anyone could reply, a loud creak sounded from the floor above them. Dust fell from rafters, drifting over the group. Simon raised his pistol once more, his expression as determined as ever. Luthor and Mattie rushed toward the stairwell, not needing to be told what to do. The doctor began forward as well, but Simon placed a hand on his chest.

"My apologies, Doctor, but you are far outside your element already. Whatever we're about to face upstairs, I can't guarantee I would be able to watch over you and keep you safe from harm. It would be far better for everyone involved if you simply waited for us here and protected the stairwell from unwanted intrusion."

Simon could see the conflicting emotions raging across the doctor's face, but Casan eventually nodded his consent. "Yell for me if you need me."

"If we have need of you, Doctor, I fear it would already be too late to save us," Simon replied curtly before hurrying up the stairs in pursuit of his associates.

Mattie led them upward, the skin of her fingers tearing away to reveal fur-covered claws beneath. Luthor had paused halfway up the stairwell and was examining something on the banister. Simon stopped behind him, close enough so that he could whisper without being overheard.

"What have you found?"

Luthor held up his hand so that, in the dim light, Simon could see the ochre colored lubricant smeared across the railing. "It's here, sir."

"Be on your guard."

The two men hurried up the stairs and entered a short hallway stretching from the narrow landing. A small window was set into the wall, streaming bright sunlight into the dusty hall. There was a door at the far end, closed tightly. As they approached, they could hear a lumbering step and muffled groans.

Mattie glanced toward Simon. The Inquisitor glanced over his shoulder to ensure the doctor had heeded his instructions and remained below. When he saw no one, Simon turned back toward Mattie and nodded his consent.

Slipping free of her clothing, Mattie quickly transformed into the white werewolf. Raising a powerful leg, she lashed out at the door handle. The frame splintered as the door exploded inward.

CHAPTER

Thirty-one

THE APARTMENT WAS DIMLY LIT, WITH ONLY A PAIR OF oil lanterns providing a weak illumination for the single room beyond. Though spacious, it was simplistic. A bed sat against the far wall, curtains were drawn around the bed, offering a small semblance of privacy within the open apartment. A meager kitchen sat off to the left and a writing desk to the right. A support pillar, a thick square shaft of wood that divided the room, dominated the center of the space.

The Golem stood beside the pillar, its face impassive as it held the butcher in its clutches. The giant was a towering monstrosity in such a confined space, its shock of dark hair brushing the ceiling as it stood unmoving. Mattie, the first into the room, frowned at the sight. In the alleyway in which she'd previously fought with the creature, it had been dark. Even with her exceptional night vision, it had been hard to discern details about the abomination.

Its head was far too small for its enormous frame; the head was normal sized for a man and still retained all the features of a normal human, albeit awkwardly when placed upon the body of a giant. Thick scars lined the creature's chest and banded around its arms and legs in rings. The torso was far wider than what could be considered natural, alluding to the creature's great strength. The Golem's height came mainly from the elongated legs, packed with dense muscles and unseen machinery.

It was the machinery that caught the group by surprise. A metal plate had been welded over the Golem's heart and seemingly screwed into place directly into the giant's sternum. It's left arm bore the brunt of the mechanical abnormalities. The skin in its shoulder and upper arm had been stretched over a series of spinning gears, though it hardly covered the mechanizations. The skin had either torn some time ago or simply lacked the elasticity to stretch over the bulging gears.

Clutched at the end of its massive arms was Peter Mason. The short man was indeed stocky but was held aloft—his neck clutched in both the Golem's hands—as though he weighed nothing at all. His face was purple and his eyes bulged slightly in their sockets. The man's tongue lolled from between his parted lips, a blue tinge painted across it.

"Drop the butcher," Simon demanded, though he was unsure the giant understood him at all, since it made no move to stop what it had been doing. Moreover, Simon knew it was far too late for the man in its clutches. His arms hung feebly at his side, no longer struggling against the creature's oversized hands.

With a sharp jerk of its hands, the Golem broke the butcher's neck before tossing the body aside. It turned its small head slowly until it saw the white werewolf standing in the front of their group. A flicker of recognition crossed its face, and it glanced down toward recent stitches across its abdomen.

Turning its frame toward them, it crouched slightly and stared furiously toward Mattie. It growled in a decidedly inhuman manner before charging at them, its long strides quickly covering the space. Simon and Luthor lunged aside from its bull-like charge, hoping its size precluded it from making abrupt turns. Mattie waited for it, her lips peeled back from her elongated canine incisors.

Like the mindless brute it was, the Golem stretched its hands toward her, intent on grabbing her around her neck as it had the butcher moments before. Quicker than it anticipated, Mattie ducked underneath its outstretched arms and slashed the Golem painfully across the belly, reopening the wound that had so recently been closed. The same ochre ooze dripped from the wound as it staggered to a halt beside the wall.

Sensing its disbelief at the new injury, Simon raised his pistol and fired until all six rounds in the revolver had been expended. Time and again, his shots were met with a flash of sparks as the bullets connected with metal components just beneath the skin and sinew. More of the lubricant oozed from the wounds, but the Golem seemed entirely unfazed.

It turned back toward them, ignoring the Inquisitor and apothecary, showing instead a single-minded loathing for the werewolf. It raised its hands, stretching open the gash along its stomach and revealing the spinning gears within.

Blindingly quick, it lashed out at Mattie, who barely avoided the swing. She slashed across its forearm, opening another oozing wound. Before she could move, the Golem brought its other fist to bear, catching her in the chest. Mattie let out a canine's yelp of pain as she was lifted off her feet, flying over the small table bearing one of the two oil lanterns and crashing into the edge of the bed.

Simon finished reloading and raised his pistol again. The Golem turned toward him, a blank expression on its face. The Inquisitor knew it was little more than a mindless killing machine, but the lack of comprehension in the giant's face seemed far more unnerving than if it had worn a look of utter hatred. It advanced on Simon and he fired again, striking the creature in the chest and legs, hoping to slow the beast, but to no avail. It was growing steadily closer, seemingly in no hurry after dispatching Mattie, the biggest threat in the room.

With its back turned, Luthor slashed it across its thighs, to sever the hamstring of the beast. His thin blade had no effect, not even a warranted glower from the Golem as it continued its advance toward the Inquisitor. Feeling helpless, Luthor glanced toward Mattie. He was eager to rush to her side, as she lay crumpled on the ground. His magic could heal her, probably as quickly as his magic could dispatch the Golem, but he dared not use it in front of Simon. Instead, his gaze fell to the oil lantern on the table between him and Mattie. Dropping his sword, the apothecary grabbed the lantern from the table and rushed in between the Golem and Simon. He waved the dancing flame before its face, hoping to distract it from its unwavering path.

The effect on the Golem was as immediate as it was unexpected. The Golem staggered backward, its long arms raised defensively before its face. The normally impassive expression became one of absolute horror. The dark eyes recessed in its head swung from side to side, transfixed upon the movement of the fire within the lantern.

Simon watched the events unfold, as startled as anyone else in the room. "Keep it occupied," he yelled to the apothecary.

Emboldened by the discovery, Simon grabbed the second lantern from its hook on the wall and flung it to the ground between Luthor and the beast. The casing around the lantern shattered on impact, spilling oil across the floor. As the oil struck the burning wick, the ground was suddenly consumed with flames.

The Golem's lips moved as though trying to speak, but all that emerged was a garbled mess of syllables that Simon couldn't understand. It whimpered, shifting first left then right as it sought an escape from the flames.

Luthor dropped his arm, no longer feeling it necessary to wave his covered lantern as a fire slowly consumed the apartment. To his surprise, a hand closed over the lantern's handle. The apothecary turned abruptly as Simon pulled the lantern from his grasp. Before Luthor could ask what Simon intended, the Inquisitor threw the second lantern through the flames.

The lantern struck the Golem's metal breastplate and exploded in a spray of oil and flames. The giant's whimpers quickly became screams of horror as it battered itself in an attempt to brush away the flames. The fire scorched the soft flesh of its abdomen and rolled upward toward its neck and face.

Though the Inquisitor tried to watch the wailing beast, the fire in the apartment was quickly burning out of control. The tall blaze licked the dried timber of the roof. Simon coughed as smoke filled his lungs. His eyes stung, leaving the Golem as little more than an undefined blur on the far side of the brilliant flames.

"Sir, we need to get out of here," Luthor yelled over the crackling of the blaze.

"The Golem..." Simon managed between hoarse coughs.

A loud crash startled the Inquisitor. He glanced sharply to his right and noticed the shattered window. When he looked quickly around the room, he found the Golem was nowhere to be seen. Rushing to the window, Simon arrived in time to see the flaming giant staggering to his feet in the mud below. Screaming, it stumbled unsteadily toward the river's edge, slipping often in the slick, blood-soaked mud.

Though leaning out the window offered a slight reprieve from the blinding smoke, it only infuriated the Inquisitor further. Simon tried to reload, but his mind was muddled with shock and smoke. His fingers refused to cooperate as he fumbled with the bullets. As he watched, the Golem reached the water's edge and dove beneath the eddying current. The air filled with the sizzling of burning flesh striking the cold waters. The Golem disappeared beneath the surface, leaving behind only concentric ripples that slowly faded away. Simon watched as long as he thought safe but never saw the giant reemerge. Cursing, he slammed his fist into the windowsill, slicing his knuckles on shards of the broken glass.

"Sir, we have to leave at once or we'll be trapped," Luthor said, returning to his side.

"Matilda?" Simon asked, his gaze not leaving the river.

"I have her," Luthor replied, a note of hysteria creeping into his voice. "Sir, there's nothing more we can do. We have to leave now."

Furious, Simon turned away and dove back into the smoky room. Mattie had returned to her human form, though Simon wasn't sure if it was of her own volition or by happenstance as a result of her injuries. The Inquisitor pulled off his longer coat and threw it over her, concealing the fact that she was naked. Sharing Mattie's weight between them, they hurried to the shattered door and into the hallway. The hallway offered little reprieve as it had filled with smoke as well. Luthor grabbed Mattie's clothing as he passed and they rushed down the stairs. Though hurt, Mattie was alert and able to walk under her own power, at least enough to hurry down the stairs with a sense of urgency.

They met Doctor Casan halfway down the stairs, the doctor rushing up to assist. "I saw embers falling through the floorboards and heard crashing," he said breathlessly.

"The building is on fire," Simon replied. "We need to leave with all haste."

Casan turned and led them down the stairs. The doctor had been right; embers were raining down on the group as they rushed toward the butcher shop's back door. They burst into the warm midday air, their faces stained with soot and coughing painfully. Mattie wheezed as well, as much from the broken ribs she'd suffered as from the smoke inhalation.

Simon stared angrily at the river, still seeing nothing breaking the otherwise gently lapping waves.

220

CHAPTER

Thirty-two

SIMON LED THE DOCTOR AWAY SO THAT HE WOULDN'T see Mattie hastily dressing behind the smoking shop, changing out of the long coat and into her regular attire. The Inquisitor counted his blessings that the doctor had been preoccupied with the fire and hadn't noticed her state of undress. Flames had yet to tear through the room, but a single glance through the windows showed the smoldering embers and heavy smoke filling the air within. Once she was done, the group hurried along the bank behind a few buildings before daring to turn toward Riverbend Street for fear of appearing culpable in the ensuing blaze.

Throngs of people moved quickly along the street, toward the scene of the fire, some carrying buckets of water that sloshed over the rims and spilled onto the street. Glancing toward Mason and Son Butchers, Simon could see flames licking the broken second story windows that overlooked the street below. Glass and singed wood littered the street beneath the windows, a result of the intensity of the heat shattering the flimsy panes as it sought escape.

People splashed buckets of water into the front of the building but no one dared enter and attempt to extinguish the blaze at its source. They all seemed content to watch the upper building burn while trying their best to keep the fire contained. As such, it didn't take them long to change their tactic. Rather than soaking the butchers, they began pouring water in earnest onto the buildings on either side, going so far as to emerge from sloped windows on the roofs to better soak the thatch.

Embers rose angrily into the air; caught in the breeze they wafted toward buildings nearby. The crowd held its collective breath as they watched the embers fall, each ember holding the potential to start a new uncontained fire.

Simon led the others to the back of the crowd where they stood, soot covered and dour, huddled close to one another. Luthor draped his arm across Mattie's shoulders, though Simon couldn't tell if it was done affectionately or simply to help the injured woman stand upright. They were a terrible-looking group, their eyes rimmed in red and their faces smudged with ash. It clung to their hair in tendrils of white, which only spread further into streaks as they ran their hands across their heads. Doctor Casan was the only one of the group who still resembled himself, the man having not entered the upper floor, faced the Golem, or got caught in the ensuing fire.

Simon laughed unexpectedly, unable to contain the nervous energy within him. He felt that his options had dwindled to laughter or tears, knowing that they faced down the Golem and defeated it; yet they fell far short of destroying the beast. He didn't believe for a second that the creature was capable of drowning in the strong current, though its metal gears would suffer from the soiled water.

The others looked at him incredulously, but they didn't share his mirth. Mattie's gaze drifted back to the upper floor just as a section of roof collapsed. The new fuel fed the blaze and flames shot high into the air.

"It's a shame we couldn't retrieve his body," she sympathetically said.

Casan shook his head. "He deserves to burn with his business. He was the villain in our little tale, need I remind you?"

Simon remained silent, his own doubts rattling through his head. Peter Mason hadn't looked like a villain or a criminal of any sort when he was held aloft by his neck, his face turning purple and his tongue swelling in his mouth. He had looked like a scared child at the mercy of a violent psychopath.

In the distance, they could hear the sound of sirens and the ringing bells of a fire station. Help would be arriving soon, though Simon doubted they'd do more than the townsfolk had already done: wetting the surrounding buildings at the sacrifice of the butcher's shop.

Another siren sounded closer, and the Inquisitor turned as a paddy wagon rounded the corner on the far side of the crowd. The constabulary had arrived far quicker than Simon would have believed. For a second, the Inquisitor felt relieved at the sight, but he quickly remembered both their appearance and the good doctor standing by their side.

"You must go at once," Simon ordered, turning abruptly toward Casan.

"Don't be absurd," Youke replied.

Simon frowned. "The three of us are marked for our part in this debacle, but you're not. Standing by our side isn't a sign of solidarity; it's the quickest way to end your current employment with the constables." He emphasized the last word with a jerk over his shoulder, to where blue uniformed men could be seen climbing from the police cars.

Casan appeared lost in thought, but he eventually nodded his consent. "I'm sorry I have to leave under such circumstances."

"You've been nothing less than instrumental during the investigation," Simon replied to everyone's surprise. "I have no doubt we'll be in touch for future missions."

The unexpected compliment left the doctor smiling as he turned away and hurried around a corner, out of sight of the constables. Simon turned back toward the police and saw more vehicles arriving, a mixture of constables and firefighters. Amidst the crowd, he saw a much more familiar face, that of Detective Sugden.

As though drawn to Simon's presence, the detective caught sight of the trio standing nonchalantly toward the back of the crowd. Despite there now being a number of people who were coated with sweat and ash, he knew instinctively that the Inquisitor had been involved with the fire. The detective pushed his way through the crowd until he stood before the three.

His eyes scanned past the Inquisitor, to the redhead whose smile barely concealed the anguish she felt at standing upright, and finally to the apothecary, who quickly turned his attention away from the prying eyes of the detective.

"Why am I not at all surprised to see the three of you here?" Sugden asked.

"You either suffer from a complete lack of faith in your fellow man or you have incredible insight into the human psyche," Simon replied. "In your case, I actually presume it's a bit of both."

"I won't be swayed by your silver tongue, Inquisitor. What the bloody hell happened here?"

Simon glanced at his friends but immediately knew he'd receive no help from either of them. Instead, he turned toward the detective. "As you well know, we've been investigating the murders of the young women within Solomon's Way."

"An investigation I strictly forbid and, I might add, one that mightily overstepped the authorizations permitted to you by the Grand Inquisitor."

"Semantics," Simon replied with a wave of his hand. "We can argue the nuances of this all night, but the simple fact is that we solved this crime in a far shorter time than it would have taken you and your fellow constables."

Sugden turned red in the face at the backhanded insult. He pointed toward the burning building behind him. "You call this solving the crime?"

For his part, Simon's expression remained impassive. "Of course. Isn't it abundantly clear?" He turned toward Luthor and Mattie as though the question wasn't rhetorical. "It was clear, wasn't it?"

"Abundantly," Mattie grunted, pained by the simple act of taking in a deep breath.

"Crystal," Luthor added, though he still refused to make eye contact with the enraged detective.

"Well, one of you had damned well better explain it to me!"

Simon sighed. "Peter Mason, the recently deceased owner of that very establishment—" Sugden mouthed the word "deceased" but Simon didn't stop his diatribe. "—was your murderer. Using his knowledge of butchering, combined with his rudimentary knowledge of mechanics as seen in the cooler housed on his first floor, he killed and dismembered men and women alike to create part man, part machine abominations."

"Hold it right there," Sugden said, finally interrupting. "These crimes were specifically about butchered women. There was never a mention of deceased men."

"I believe if you examine your files, you'll find cases of men killed in a similar fashion. Having faced his Golem, I can say with some certainty that there are—or were, at the very least—men in Callifax who had been inexplicably murdered and butchered."

Sugden's gaze narrowed. "You say you faced this creation? Is this before or after you killed Peter Mason?"

"During," Simon replied.

"We didn't kill Mister Mason," Luthor quickly added. "We arrived as the creature was concluding with the murder of the butcher."

"At which time..." Sugden left the sentence hanging.

"At which time, we fought against the Golem, destroying it with the same fire you now see burning merrily throughout the upper floor of the Mason and Son Butchers." A crash sounded behind Sugden's shoulder, causing the detective to jump in surprise. "I stand corrected. Burning merrily through *both* floors of the butcher's."

The detective did not seem at all amused, but his expression quickly turned to one of abject concern. "You say you destroyed this Golem, as you call it, in the fire?"

Simon nodded, ignoring the petulant stares of his counterparts. "We did. It seemed impervious to most other attacks, being made up of little more than flesh drawn over gears and other mechanical intricacies, but it seemed quite frightened by the oil lanterns. We set it ablaze before hurrying from the room."

Sugden seemed pale but composed himself before continuing. "It seems I owe you an apology, Inquisitor. I had thought your interference would be nothing short of a detriment to my investigation, but it seems you solved this crime quite well without the assistance of the Solomon's Way constabulary."

"I wouldn't have had it any other way," Simon said, missing the venom in the detective's words. "Will there be anything else? Do you need us to come to the station and file an official report?"

The detective shook his head. "I believe I've heard all that I need to. You're all free to return to your homes."

"Detective," Simon said, "it's been an immense pleasure working with you. I hope we'll have the same honor again in the near future."

Sugden glared daggers at the Inquisitor before turning away and hurrying back toward the constables, barking orders as he passed through the crowd. Simon seemed intent on watching the fire continue, but Luthor pulled him away.

CHAPTER

Thirty-three

WHEN THEY RETURNED TO THE TERRACE IN THE UP-
per Reaches, Simon helped Luthor bring Mattie inside and
up the stairs. They sat her in the tub and retrieved water with
which she could clean before leaving her to her work. Through the closed
bathroom door, they could hear her grimace as she removed her clothing
and exposed the broken ribs.

The two men retreated to the first floor, where Luthor pulled some
washcloths from a pantry. They wetted them and did their best to remove
the soot covering their skin. As the apothecary furiously scrubbed his
muttonchops, trying to remove the unsightly streaks of gray from his
facial hair, he glanced over toward Simon.

"You don't honestly believe what you said to Detective Sugden, do
you, sir?" Luthor asked. "The blatant lie about the Golem dying in the
blaze aside, is there a chance it truly did die even after its escape? Could
it have drowned in the river?"

Simon paused his cleaning and frowned, his stare locked on the nondescript wall before him. "I don't think anything's over, Luthor. I think we
came close to stopping the beast today, but our best wasn't enough. It
escaped to kill again."

"But its master's dead, killed by its own hand," Luthor pleaded, wanting this string of murders to be done.

Simon shook his head and dropped his soiled washcloth into the basin. "Someone went to great lengths to have us believe the butcher was the Golem's master, but I don't believe it for a moment. I saw the frightened look on Peter Mason's face as the monster choked the last vestiges of life from his body. He was a man as startled by the Golem's appearance as we were."

"Is it so hard to believe that the Golem could have turned on its master?"

"A mindless creature doesn't turn on its master; that's a distinct trait of the sentient. Neither was there any indication within the butcher's shop that he had more than a passing knowledge of machinery, especially the type necessary to animate so large a creature. The lie I told the detective was clearly flawed logic. The doctor confirmed that the cooler was of a similar design to the ones used in the morgue. I would venture a guess that with more time to investigate, we would have found a maker's mark on the steel box. The Masons may have purchased the cooler, but they certainly didn't craft it themselves. Moreover, Luthor, did you see a single female's body parts concealed within that cooler?"

"They could have been stored elsewhere within the shop," the apothecary replied, grasping at any hope that the crimes would end with the day's foray.

Simon shook his head. "If you're insinuating that there could have been a hidden basement, let me stop you there. The water level of the river was too high to have dug beneath the foundation of the shop. Any basement, no matter how well crafted, would have eventually flooded, especially with heavy rains like we suffered recently."

Luthor dropped his cloth into the basin as well before drying his face. He stood upright and leaned against the wall as he placed his glasses back on the bridge of his nose. "Then why did you lie, sir? If we stopped nothing tonight, then why tell the detective that the Golem and its master are dead?"

Simon angrily slapped his hand onto the table before him. "Because, Luthor, Detective Sugden has lied to us since this investigation began. He swore he knew nothing of the murders until our evidence revealed otherwise. He provided a convenient story about his involvement due to the loss of his son, yet what did you note about the Golem today? It was decidedly male in every way. Yet you heard Sugden when I brought that to his attention. He knew nothing of what had to have been a previous string of incredibly similar crimes." Simon stood upright, and his eyes narrowed dangerously. "What you may not have noted was the man's lack of expression when I told him the Golem was male. Like the murders before, the detective knows more about the goings on than he revealed to us."

"Are you saying…?" Luthor began to ask.

"I'm saying nothing," Simon said abruptly. "What I will say is that I have a hundred reasons to keep a much closer eye on the goings on within Solomon's Way from this moment forward. Mark my words, we haven't seen the last of the Golem or its mysterious master. I will find it again, only it won't escape me a second time."

Luthor walked into the sitting room and collapsed into a chair, both mentally and physically drained. Simon followed suit, sitting on the couch across from the apothecary. For minutes, they sat as they were, both lost to their thoughts. Eventually, Luthor glanced toward the Inquisitor.

"What shall we do, sir?" he asked. "Shall we get a good night's rest and begin our investigation anew tomorrow?"

Simon glanced toward his friend, noting the weariness in the man's voice. He felt it as well, though for a much different reason. His mouth was dry and his throat parched, though he knew no amount of water would quench the thirst he felt. His eyes flickered to the stocked liquor cabinet but just as quickly returned to the apothecary.

It wasn't just his yearning for a drink that left him taxed. There was something that needed to be done, something Simon had put off for far too long.

With a sigh, Simon shook his head, his eyes shimmering with suppressed tears. "No, Luthor, we won't be searching for the Golem any time soon. It's gone to ground, as has its master, and I don't believe we'll be hearing from either any time soon. Rather, I have something else that must be done, something that will require your assistance, if you feel so inclined."

The grass was damp beneath Simon's feet as he stood in fine livery, his finger's laced before him. He bit his lip until he tasted the satisfying

228

tinge of blood in his mouth. It was a reminder that everything before him was real; yet the pain helped him keep his mind away from the blatant reality before him.

Bishop Hartford glanced up from his reading, his eyes glossing over the coffin before settling on the Inquisitor. The man of the cloth nodded solemnly to Simon before turning to his readings.

"We commend the remains of Veronica Dawn to the earth," Hartford said, his low voice carrying easily to the small crowd attending the funeral. "Her mortal remains will become one with the ground as her eternal soul goes to reside by God forever."

Simon tuned out the bishop's words and glanced around the gathering. He knew all the faces of those present, all dressed as they were in black, many with tears in their eyes or smearing once well-applied makeup. A number of Veronica's coworkers from the Ace of Spades were present. He recognized the bouncer who had, on more than one occasion, allowed Simon to bypass the long waiting line so that the Inquisitor could visit with his fiancée. Beside the burlesque dancers, the crowd was thin. Veronica was well known in her circles, but her circles didn't extend far beyond her work and Simon's friends.

Matilda was present, barely healed from her ordeal. She dabbed her eyes with a handkerchief and glanced cautiously toward the Inquisitor. Luthor had his arm around her waist and looked distraught. The apothecary hated funerals as much as Simon and, had he not had such a close connection with the deceased, he probably wouldn't have come at all.

To Simon's surprise, both Detective Sugden and Doctor Casan were present as well. Casan had become initiated into the folds during the course of the investigation, but he took a great risk being present, especially in the presence of the detective. For his part, Sugden seemed genuinely morose. He looked toward Simon apologetically and nodded toward the Inquisitor.

Everyone looked at him at one time or another. They all expected to see him emotional, crying as they were. Yet Luthor had been far more correct than he would ever believe. Simon was an automaton; a heartless machine as impassive to his emotions as the Golem he had faced. He glanced around the crowd and caught a few eyes. At least, that was the persona he would have them believe.

Within him was a hurricane of roiling emotions, each more painful than the last. He couldn't bring himself to look at the casket, knowing that Veronica was within. Though no one would ever realize, since beginning the funeral arrangements, Simon hadn't slept for longer than a few minutes, and those times were mainly a result of inadvertently falling asleep while performing some task or another.

He had noted that Luthor hated funerals, but his dislike paled beside Simon's. The Inquisitor didn't want to be present. Had he thought himself capable, he would have had Veronica buried without his presence by her side. He would have stayed at home, drinking scotch until he lacked the faculties to stand or form coherent words.

Simon frowned, a gesture that he was sure others would misinterpret as sadness. Drinking was exactly the problem. It had become a crutch throughout his life, especially since becoming an Inquisitor. Finish a mission and drown any pain—physical or mental—with a tumbler of scotch. It had nearly cost him his chance to find Veronica's killer. In hindsight, he realized, it probably had. Had he been sober and his mind clear, he would have interpreted the facts of the case sooner. Perhaps the Golem could have been caught and cornered, unable to escape as it had.

"Ashes to ashes, dust to dust," the bishop concluded, and he slowly closed his book.

People passed by the casket, placing flowers atop the coffin. When it was his turn, Simon strode forward and placed a bouquet, his hands shaking unsteadily as he did so. He stepped back and the attention of the crowd shifted to him. Sugden and Casan approached him first, offering their condolences.

"Forgive our hasty departure," the detective offered, "but crime waits for no man. I'm terribly sorry for you loss. No matter our differences, no one should suffer like you and I have, losing someone we love."

Casan stepped before him and nodded understandingly. "I wish I could have known her better before her death. I'm sorry she was taken from you."

And so it went. People he knew in varying degrees of familiarity shook his hand and offered condolences for his loss. Some hugged him as they cried as though they should share the burden of their loss. Others, like the bouncer, said nothing at all as they shook hands. Finally, it was just Luthor and Mattie, even the bishop having excused himself.

"We can stay if you'd like, sir," Luthor offered.

"If you need someone..." Mattie offered.

Simon shook his head. "Thank you both, but no. I'll be fine. If it's all the same, I'd like to say my final goodbyes alone. I think she deserves nothing less."

Luthor nodded and grasped Simon's shoulder tightly before turning away. Mattie offered a quick hug before hurrying to join Luthor.

When they were both gone and he was alone in the middle of a vast cemetery, Simon laid his hand on the casket. He wanted to say so much to her, but it seemed like his time had passed. She couldn't hear his whispered "I love you" or "I wish you were still here." Knowing that he was alone, Simon did the only thing he thought right.

He fell to his knees on the wet ground and cried until he felt utterly hollow inside.

CHAPTER
Thirty-four

EEP BENEATH CALLIFAX, WITHIN A ROOM CON-
nected only to the complex labyrinth of sewer tunnels, the Golem paced in frustration. Its normally expressionless face was
screwed in a look of fear. Half its face was twisted from the flames, the
skin having melted like wax over the metal plates beneath. The hair was
singed, leaving exposed scalp above a ruined ear. Parts of its left arm and
most of its torso were likewise burned by Simon's well-placed lantern.

It turned sharply on its heel and stalked toward the other end of the
small room. What the room lacked in depth, it made up for in height,
accommodating the towering stature of the Golem. As it passed, it cast its
eyes toward the closed door at the far end of the room, the sole entrance
and exit from the secret chamber.

Footsteps sounded beyond the door, and a jingle of keys could be
heard. The Golem stopped its pacing and turned toward the door, snarl-
ing dangerously. The door swung open slowly, and a man stepped into
the room. The Golem's expression immediately fell, its eyes brimming
with unbridled love for the man.

Detective Sugden walked into the room, closing the door behind
him, and quickly crossed to the Golem. He reached out his hand toward

the creature's face, but it pulled away as his fingertips made contact with the sensitive, ruined flesh.

"It's okay," Sugden cooed. "I'm here now."

The Golem lowered its head and purred as it pressed its face lovingly into his extended hand. Sugden felt the burnt flesh and frowned deeply, his jaw set tightly and his eyes brimming with tears.

"What have they done to you?" he whispered. "Look at what they've done to my boy."

The door opened behind Sugden. The Golem growled, its shoulders taut as it stared at the newcomer. Without turning, the detective told the beast to hush and it slowly relaxed. With the Golem under control once more, Sugden glanced over his shoulder toward the cloaked figure in the doorway. The man's hood was pulled low, revealing nothing of his face beneath.

"Look what they did to my son," Sugden said, his words thick with emotion. "They set him on fire like he was an animal."

"The damage can be repaired," the cloaked man replied.

"Can it?" Sugden asked, disbelievingly. "Can you fix him so that he will be as he was?"

The cloaked figure walked briskly to the Golem's side and examined it as though it were a horse for sale, pulling aside its gums to check the Golem's teeth and lifting its heavy limbs to examine the damage.

"Of course I can," the mysterious man replied. "I built it; of course I can repair it. Then he can go back and finish our work."

END OF BOOK 3

About the Author

Jon Messenger, born 1979 in London, England, serves as a United States Army Major in the Medical Service Corps. Since graduating from the University of Southern California in 2002, writing Science Fiction has remained his passion, a passion that has continued through two deployments to Iraq and a humanitarian relief mission to Haiti. Jon wrote the "Brink of Distinction" trilogy, of which "Burden of Sisyphus" is the first book, while serving a 16-month deployment in Baghdad, Iraq. Visit Jon on his website at www.JonMessengerAuthor.com.

CPSIA information can be obtained at www.ICGtesting.com
Printed in the USA
LVOW06s0711081215

465890LV00008B/15/P